UNTOUCHABLE

Also by Mike Lawson

MIKE LAWSON

A JOE DeMARCO THRILLER

UNTOUCHABLE

Atlantic Monthly Press
New York

FIRST EDITION

Published simultaneously in Canada
Printed in the United States of America

This book was set in 12-pt. Garamond Premier Pro
by Alpha Design & Composition of Pittsfield, NH.

First Grove Atlantic hardcover edition: February 2025

Library of Congress Cataloging-in-Publication data is available for this title.

ISBN 978-0-8021-6445-2
eISBN 978-0-8021-6446-9

Atlantic Monthly Press
an imprint of Grove Atlantic
154 West 14th Street
New York, NY 10011

Distributed by Publishers Group West

groveatlantic.com

25 26 27 28   10 9 8 7 6 5 4 3 2 1

I'm dedicating this book to my friend, James Donohue. Jim is a lawyer who spent the last part of his career as a federal judge, and I've often asked for his advice when I had questions about the law or the way the legal system works, and he's helped me on many of my novels. There was one evening that I'll never forget: my wife and I were hosting a party to celebrate a book that had just been released and Jim was there—but he kept having to leave the room to talk to lawyers on the phone. When I asked him what was going on, the short answer was that while I was drinking wine and signing books, he was engaged in a legal battle with the president of the United States. I remember thinking at the time how glad I was that I had my job instead of his. Thank you, Jim, for your friendship, all your help over the years, and your service to the country.

UNTOUCHABLE

1

The president was engaged in an intense conversation with his national security advisor when four Secret Service agents burst into the Oval Office.

The president, visibly startled by the unannounced intrusion, said, "What the—"

Hawkins, the senior agent, strode toward him, saying, "Mr. President, we need to get you to the bunker. Now." When the president sat there, looking confused, Hawkins grasped his arm and pulled him up from his chair, a breach of protocol unimaginable in any other circumstance. The pen the president was holding fell from his hand, rolled across his desk, and fell to the carpet.

"Put this on, sir," Hawkins said, and handed the president a gas mask.

"What's happened?" the president asked.

"Please put on the mask, sir," Hawkins said. "Right now."

The president noticed that none of the agents were wearing masks, and they hadn't brought one for Eric Doyle, the national security advisor. Maybe there hadn't been time to gather up additional masks. The president put the mask over his face and Hawkins made sure it was sealed properly.

"Let's go," Hawkins said.

The four agents hustled the president out of the Oval Office, surrounding him, forming a human shield, as if their bodies could stop an airborne threat. Doyle followed behind the group. He noticed red lights flashing in the hallways, a sign of an emergency or a lockdown. He saw staffers heading toward the exits, Secret Service personnel hustling them along. Doyle could tell people were frightened—this wasn't a drill—but no one was panicking, and no one appeared to be injured.

Two minutes later the president was in the bunker. The bunker, several floors beneath the main floor of the White House, was a supposedly nuclear blast–proof sanctuary that would serve as a temporary command center if the White House was under attack. A man was already in the bunker wearing a white contamination suit with an air-fed hood. He looked like a spaceman. He was holding an instrument the size and shape of a microphone up to a ventilation outlet while looking down at a box he was holding in his other hand.

Hawkins asked him, "Anything?"

"No. Nothing." Then added, "So far."

The president started to take off the gas mask, but Hawkins said, "Please, sir, leave that on."

"What happened?" the president asked, his voice muffled by the mask.

"The chief of staff's secretary opened an envelope and white powder spilled out of it."

The chief of staff's office was right next to the Oval Office. "We don't know how the envelope got there, how it got through the scanners, who sent it, or anything else at this point. But when the powder spilled out, the secretary started sneezing violently and immediately called to the agent out in the hall. And that's all I know at this time. We're sampling the air and analyzing the powder. You need to leave the mask on until we know more and we're satisfied that the air in this space is good."

The president knew the bunker had its own air supply and a ventilation system designed to keep harmful toxins out of the room. That is, it was designed for *known* toxins, but who knew if a new one had been invented?

"How are you feeling?" he asked the unmasked Doyle.

"Fine," Doyle said.

"Oh, where's the first lady?" the president asked Hawkins.

"Baltimore," Hawkins said.

"Right," the president said. He'd forgotten his wife, Lydia, was visiting an inner-city school, doing a photo op where she'd read a story to a bunch of hyperactive six-year-olds.

After ten minutes the president was told he could remove the gas mask, but he had to stay in the bunker with Doyle for another twenty minutes before the all-clear signal was given. While they were in there, Doyle and the president didn't resume the discussion they'd been having in the Oval Office, not with Secret Service agents in the room. And also, because there was really nothing more to say about the issue they'd been discussing. Doyle knew what he had to do without being told what to do.

They chatted instead about a senator who was currently the hot topic on all the cable channels for being photographed kissing a woman who was not his wife. The reason the media jumped on this minor scandal was that the senator—a self-proclaimed paragon of Christian virtue—was always going on about how the country was going to hell in a handbasket because it was populated by godless unbelievers and sinners. Adultery was one of those sins he frequently and vehemently condemned. In other words, the president and Doyle spent twenty minutes reveling in a political opponent's misfortune and didn't discuss anything of significance.

Hawkins took a call, thanked whoever called, and hung up. He told the president he could return to the Oval Office. He said, "The white power was determined to be talcum powder but mixed into it was a chemical that can induce sneezing."

"So it was a prank?" the president said.

"It's not a prank to the Secret Service," Hawkins said. "We need to find out who sent it and see if we need to change procedures."

The president wasn't concerned. His Secret Service agents were the best bodyguards in the world, and if they couldn't protect him, no one could. But there were also threats the Secret Service couldn't stop, like the one he and Doyle had been discussing before the agents interrupted them.

The president didn't return to his office that day.

Had he, the future might have been different.

Instead, he went to his residence on the second floor of the White House and changed into clothes suitable for golfing. He was playing nine holes with three mega-donors that afternoon. Afterward, he would return to the residence, shower, and change into a tuxedo, and that evening he and his wife would attend a dinner at the White House with the new British prime minister, a woman the president thought was an arrogant bitch.

———————◆◆◆———————

Betty Warner, the president's executive secretary, who had worked for him since he'd been a partner in a Houston law firm, was absent that day. She'd flown home to see her mother, who was dying.

Had Betty been present, the future most likely would have been different.

One of the president's four other secretaries, a young woman named Madeline Bower, was sitting in for Betty, and at the end of the day she went in to tidy up the Oval Office. She was still somewhat shaken by the event that had caused the president to be rushed to the bunker. She cleared away the coffee cups the president and Doyle had used and emptied the wastebasket after making sure there was nothing in it that was classified or official correspondence. The president's desk was orderly, as the president was an orderly man and didn't like a cluttered workspace. There was one thick document in his inbox that Madeline knew was an analysis of an infrastructure bill; she knew this because she'd placed the document in the inbox when the president's chief of staff had told her to do so. She left the document where it was since it wasn't classified and didn't need to go into a safe. Thanks to lessons learned from two of his predecessors, the president was a bear when it came to the handling of classified materials.

In the center of his desk was another document, this one face down. Madeline noticed that the president had doodled on the top page, which was the back of the last page of the document.

The president was notorious for using a Sharpie to doodle when he was in briefings or talking to his staff. He'd doodle on a notepad or whatever document was handy, like a document he was being briefed on. He'd make little spiral-like swirls, hash marks, stars, and geometric figures like boxes or triangles. He'd write down questions related to the briefing. And he'd scrawl comments that were sometimes hilarious, like "This man's an idiot" or "How the hell did this guy get elected?" And sometimes what he wrote didn't have anything to do with the matter being discussed. He would become bored and make a to-do list or jot notes related to a completely different subject. Madeline had seen one list that read: "Call the Speaker about the gun bill." "Tell Lydia to pay a visit to Vetters in the hospital." "Don't forget to send that old bastard Prentiss a birthday card." The list Madeline saw had been written in the margins of a classified document discussing nuclear weapons proliferation.

On the back of the document that was currently on the president's desk were a few short phrases. Betty Warner, the president's regular executive secretary, would have read the phrases and might have saved the document until the next day so the president could decide if the notes were important and related to something he wished to follow up on. Madeline, however, didn't bother to read the notes. She wanted to get going because she had a date that night and needed to get home and change into something slinky. She could hardly wait to tell her date about the poison scare and how she'd never thought that working in the White House could be dangerous.

She flipped the document over and saw it was a speech the president would be giving in two weeks at the United Nations. It wasn't classified.

Scrawled on the top of the speech, in the president's distinctive hand, was "Betty, get this back to Vernon." The president had forgotten that Betty was absent. Vernon was Paul Vernon, one of the speechwriters, a pudgy pipsqueak who was always hitting on Madeline. The note continued: "I've tweaked a couple of things in the front section but other than those changes, this is ready to go." Madeline flipped through the speech and saw the president had made a few comments in the margins of the speech, which she also didn't bother to read, and that he'd crossed out one short paragraph.

She picked up the marked-up copy of the speech, glanced around the Oval Office one last time to make sure everything was in order, and left the room. It was after eight, but she figured the speechwriter would still be in his office. The speechwriters tended to burn the midnight oil as there was always another speech to write. She put on her coat, gathered up her purse, and walked through the West Wing down to the speechwriter's cubicle. He was at his desk, talking to someone on the phone. When he saw her, he placed the phone against his chest and said, "Hey, babe, lookin' good today. What's up?"

Hey, babe. What a pig. Madeline dropped the speech on his cluttered desk and said, "The man's comments on your bullshit," then turned and left before he could say anything.

Vernon glanced at the document, saw it was the U.N. speech, and tossed it into an inbox that was overflowing with other documents. Since the speech wouldn't be given for a couple of weeks, he'd look at it tomorrow. He went back to talking to a colonel at the Pentagon who was feeding him statistics for a different speech.

The next day Vernon picked up the U.N. speech and made the changes the president wanted. He smiled when he saw one comment the president had made: "Don't use the word *ameliorate*. Nobody knows what that means, including me." Vernon suspected the president knew what the word meant, but the president had told him before that he shouldn't use words that the average, beer-drinking American lunkhead couldn't understand.

When Vernon finished making the corrections on the file in his laptop, he printed out a clean copy, then dropped the marked-up speech into a plastic bin filled with other unclassified documents. The bin would be taken in the next day or so to the White House records office. The people there would eventually look at the documents in the bin and then pass them on to the National Archives. Vernon never looked at the back of the last page of the speech; he didn't see the notes the president had made.

The Presidential Records Act of 1978 was established thanks to Tricky Dick Nixon because Congress didn't like the way Nixon had tried to disappear documents and recordings that might have told the full story of the Watergate cover-up. The Presidential Records Act is incredibly complicated and includes provisions designed to separate the president's personal life from his official one, but it basically says that all the president's documents, as well as audio recordings, phone logs, and visitor logs, belong to the American public and not the president and that these documents shall be stored by NARA, the National Archives and Records Administration.

A marked-up speech by the president met the criteria of an item that should be sent on to the National Archives.

And it was.

And the future was altered.

2

The three-story, fully restored antebellum mansion with its white lime-stone Corinthian columns sat in the middle of a five-acre lot, illuminated by a pale full moon. The grounds around the mansion—which featured a pond with a fountain, artfully placed stands of trees, and green squares of carefully tended grass—were enclosed by an eight-foot-high stone wall. A sixteen-foot-wide wrought iron gate barred entry to the long, curving driveway leading to house.

Shaw and Burkhart—dressed in black T-shirts and black cargo pants, and wearing thin black leather gloves, black ski masks, and night vision goggles—jogged from their vehicle to the base of the wall on the west side of the mansion. Shaw was carrying a large, almost empty olive-green duffel bag. Once they reached the wall, they stopped and Shaw pulled out his cell phone.

The house had an ADT security system. The system included motion detectors inside the house and sensors on doors and windows, but Shaw knew it didn't include cameras. It was hard to imagine that the security system for a house this grand wouldn't have cameras, but he'd been assured that there were none.

Shaw brought up the ADT app on his phone and entered the home-owner's username and password into it. He saw that the system was armed in the Stay mode, meaning that the motion detectors in the house weren't activated but door and window alarms were. He pressed a button on the ADT app to disarm the security system. The man who employed Shaw and Burkhart had given them the username and password; they had no idea how he'd gotten that information. They didn't care.

Shaw threw the large duffel bag over the wall, then made a cup out of his hands and Burkhart stepped into it and climbed on top of the wall, then reached down and extended a hand and helped Shaw up. They dropped to the other side of the wall, Shaw picked up the duffel bag, and they jogged toward the front door of the house, almost invisible in the darkness.

They stopped near the front door, a massive oak slab, and Shaw reached into the duffel bag and took out a small explosive charge. He used duct tape to attach the explosive to the front door near the doorknob. Shaw had done this many times before and knew what he was doing. He and his partner stepped back a few paces and Shaw pressed a button on a detonating device and the explosives blew the door open. They weren't concerned about anyone hearing the explosion as the closest neighbor was more than three miles away. And because they'd disarmed the security system, a signal wouldn't be sent to the security company indicating that the door had been breached.

They drew semiautomatic pistols equipped with silencers from thigh holsters and entered the house. The house was enormous, more than ten thousand square feet, but they knew that the master bedroom was on the second floor at the end of a long hallway. They'd been given a schematic that gave them the layout of the house. Shaw dropped the duffel bag by the front door and he and Burkhart rushed up the wide staircase to the second floor and ran toward the master bedroom, Shaw leading the way.

Before they reached the bedroom door, a man stepped through the door and into the unlit hallway. The man was naked and was holding a brass candlestick holder in his hand that was about a foot long. The sound of the door being blown open had obviously woken him and he'd reached for the nearest object that would serve as a weapon.

Shaw could see the man was young and had long hair—he wasn't the primary target—and without hesitating, he fired two shots into the man's chest. Burkhart surged ahead of Shaw, moving toward the bedroom door. As Shaw stepped over the body of the man he'd shot, he fired a third bullet into the man's forehead. Better safe than sorry.

Burkhart rushed into the bedroom and saw another naked man. He was holding a pistol and he fired it as soon as he saw Burkhart. The shot went high and to Burkhart's left, hitting the wall near the door. Burkhart responded automatically—he responded the way he'd been trained—and fired two shots, both bullets hitting the man in the chest.

"Motherfucker!" Burkhart said. "I wasn't expecting that."

"Aw, shit," he heard Shaw say.

Shaw found a light switch, turned on an overhead light, and he and Burkhart took off the night vision goggles. They walked over to the man Burkhart had shot. Burkhart's bullets had hit him in the heart, the two bullet holes spaced only an inch apart. The man was in his fifties, pot-bellied, with thinning dark hair. In his right hand was a chrome plated .357 Magnum. A hand cannon. It was obvious the man was dead, but Shaw put a bullet into his forehead, mainly because he was pissed that Burkhart had killed the guy.

Shaw said, "Goddamnit. We wanted him alive."

"Well, what the fuck would you have done?" Burkhart said. Pointing at the gun in the dead man's hand, he added, "He would have blown my head off with that thing."

Shaw took a breath and said, "Okay. I'll go deal with the safe. You can start collecting the shit up here."

The safe was in a library on the first floor. Shaw picked up the duffel bag by the front door and went to the library and turned on the lights. In the room was an ornate wooden desk that Shaw guessed was a pricey antique, a huge globe of the world in a stand, paintings in gilded frames on the walls, and shelves filled with hardcover books. There had to be five hundred books in the room, but Shaw suspected they were more for decoration than for reading.

As Shaw had been told, the safe was behind a painting of a medieval castle perched on a cliff above a stormy sea. The painting had been done by an eighteenth-century Scottish artist named Alexander Nasmyth and was worth several hundred thousand dollars. Shaw pulled on one side of the painting, which was on hinges; it swung away from the wall to expose the safe.

The plan had been to get the man Burkhart had killed to tell them the combination to the safe and the location of what they'd been sent to find. They would have tortured the shit out of him until he did. Burkhart had some experience interrogating subjects, and he was a sadistic son of a bitch to boot. Shaw figured it would have taken them about five minutes to get the combination. But now, goddamnit, because Burkhart had killed the guy, he was going to have to blow the safe.

They'd planned on this contingency—the unlikely possibility that the man wouldn't give up the combination—so Shaw had what he needed to deal with the safe. He placed a thick bead of plastic explosive along the edges of the safe's door and inserted a detonator. He stepped outside the library and pressed a button on the detonating device. The safe door blew open, destroying the Alexander Nasmyth painting in the process.

Shaw placed the duffel bag on the desk. Inside the safe were a bunch of red file folders containing paper. There were also a few manila envelopes, four stacks of currency bound with rubber bands, an American passport, and two flat boxes that might contain jewelry of some kind. Shaw didn't bother to look in the boxes. He dumped everything in the safe into the duffel bag, then turned his attention to the desk.

There were no papers on the desk but there was a laptop computer. Shaw tossed the computer into the duffel bag. He opened all the drawers in the desk. In the middle drawer, he saw a small leather-bound notebook. Into the duffel bag it went. One of the drawers was a deep file drawer. He glanced at the labels on the files—they appeared to be ordinary household bills, insurance policies, tax statements, that sort of thing—but that didn't matter. He took all the files out of the drawer and dumped them into the duffel bag. Burkhart stepped into the room at that moment. He was holding two cell phones, a laptop, and two iPads. He placed them in the duffel bag.

Shaw looked at his watch. It was almost one thirty. He said, "We got three and a half hours until it gets light outside. You take the second and third floors. I'll take this floor, the garage, and the cabana. We want paperwork, files, notebooks, diaries, photo albums. We want any kind of recording device. If there're DVD or DVR players hooked up to the TVs, get those. Look for flash drives, cameras, CDs—"

Burkhart said, "Hey, this ain't my first fuckin' rodeo, buddy. I know what to look for."

A few minutes before the sun came over the horizon, the two men left the house, Shaw lugging the duffel bag, which was now heavy. He heaved the bag over the wall with a grunt, then he and Burkhart scaled the wall again and walked to their car, a black four-wheel-drive Jeep they'd driven into a stand of trees so it wouldn't be visible from the road. They took off the thigh holsters containing their weapons, the ski masks, and the gloves, and put them into the duffel bag and placed the bag in the rear compartment of the Jeep.

As Shaw backed the Jeep out of the trees, he said, "Let's find someplace that's open in Manassas and get something to eat. I'm starving."

"Roger that," Burkhart said.

"Then we'll call the boss and tell him how you fucked up."

"Hey, I didn't fuck up. I didn't have a choice."

"Yeah, I know," Shaw said. "I'm just givin' you some shit. I just hope we got what he wanted."

"By the way," Shaw said, "there was some cash in the safe. A lot of cash. Should we tell him about it?"

"Hell yes," Burkhart said. "I don't have a death wish."

3

———◆———

Maria Alvarez had been Brandon Cartwright's cook for five years. When Mr. Cartwright was staying at his Virginia estate, she'd arrive at seven every morning to make his breakfast— except for those days when she was told not to come. The yardman and his helper would get there around nine. The housekeeper also about nine. On a typical day, Maria would also make Mr. Cartwright's lunch, a snack in the afternoon, serve drinks and appetizers around five, and his dinner at seven. She usually left about nine after cleaning up the kitchen and preparing for the next day's meals. And if Mr. Cartwright was hosting a party, she might not leave until midnight. But she didn't complain or ever miss a day because the job paid so well.

She used the remote in her car to open the driveway gate and parked her car in one of the five parking spots on the side of the big garage where Mr. Cartwright's guests wouldn't be able to see her Toyota or the old pickup truck the yardman drove.

She walked slowly to the front door; she was a heavyset woman and rarely moved quickly. She had a key to let herself in and knew the code for the security system, but when she saw that the front door was open and the damage to the doorframe near the lock, she stopped. She listened to see if she could hear anyone inside, and when she didn't, she cautiously entered the house. If someone had broken in—and it looked as if some-one had—she doubted they'd still be inside the house after the sun came up. She called out, "Mr. Cartwright? Mr. Margate? Are you here?" No one answered. Mr. Cartwright didn't usually get up until nine, but Mr. Margate was an early riser. He was almost always up when she arrived, usually drinking coffee in the kitchen, reading the news on his iPad.

She walked to the kitchen to see if Mr. Margate was there. He wasn't. After hesitating for more than a minute, she walked slowly up the big staircase, calling, "Mr. Cartwright, are you here?" No one answered. As soon as she entered the hallway leading to the master bedroom, she saw Mr. Margate lying naked on his back on the floor. She clamped her hands over her mouth to keep from crying out, then crept forward until she was close enough to see the bullet holes in Mr. Margate's chest and forehead. Maria had been raised in a rough neighborhood in Richmond; she'd seen dead bodies punctured with bullets before. She had no doubt Mr. Margate was dead.

She didn't bother to look for Mr. Cartwright. She wanted to get out of the house. She hurried down the staircase and went outside and called 911.

A young, skinny white cop in a Prince William County patrol car arrived ten minutes later. Maria had waited in her locked car with the engine running until he arrived. Maria told him what she'd seen, and the cop, looking scared, took out his gun and entered the house. He came back five minutes later and made a call on the radio in his patrol car, and ten minutes after that there were three more patrol cars in the driveway. The four cops, their guns drawn, went into the house to see if whoever shot Mr. Margate was still there, which Maria thought was pretty unlikely. The house was so big that it was twenty minutes later before they all came back outside, and just as they did, an unmarked sedan pulled into the driveway. A tall white man wearing a suit and a pretty, young Black woman, also wearing a suit, stepped out of the sedan. Maria knew these were the murder police.

Darcy Adams stood next to her partner and looked down at the dead body in the hallway. It was that of a handsome, well-built man in his thirties with a smooth, hairless chest and blond hair that reached his shoulders. The guy was so good-looking—except for the hole in his forehead—that, with his long hair, Darcy thought he was prettier than most women she knew.

Her partner, Jim Stratton, pointed at the three shell casings on the hallway carpet and said, "Watch you don't step on those."

They walked into the bedroom and over to the dead man on the floor next to the bed. The man there wasn't pretty. He looked as if he was over fifty, he had a paunch, and his dark hair was thinning. Darcy suspected his hair was dyed and also noticed the tight skin around his eyes, making her think he'd had some work done.

The dead man had a gun in his right hand. Jim knelt down, careful where he placed his knees, and sniffed at the gun but didn't touch it; he'd let the CSIs deal with the gun once they got there. He stood up and looked slowly around the room, pointed wordlessly to the shell casings on the floor, then walked over and pointed to what looked like a bullet hole in the wall near the door.

He stared for a moment at the shell casings to the right of the bedroom door, then went into the hallway and looked at the three casings there. He said, "Looks like two guys, unless it was one guy using two different guns. The shell casings are different. And I'll bet you we don't get a single print off them."

Darcy wanted to ask why he thought that but didn't. Darcy Adams was only twenty-six years old and had been a detective for less than a year. Although she'd worked her ass off as a patrol officer and had performed well on all the written exams and oral boards, she'd heard people thought she only got the job to improve the department's statistics when it came to female and minority promotions. And she was both: a female and a minority.

Fortunately, her partner didn't seem to have a problem with her. Jim Stratton was a lanky, soft-spoken man in his forties. His short, dark hair was just starting to turn gray, and he had smile crinkles near his eyes. He always treated Darcy with respect and took the time to explain things to her to help her become a better cop. And he did this in a manner that wasn't condescending. Jim had only been with the department for ten years but before that he'd spent fifteen years with the Army's Criminal Investigations Division where he'd handled thousands of cases, including several murders. He quit the Army because his wife was tired of having to relocate every three years or so. Jim also had two daughters, and maybe it was because he had daughters, that he looked out for Darcy.

After looking at the bodies, Jim walked slowly through the house as Darcy tagged along behind him. It took them twenty minutes to see all of it. Darcy had never seen a house like this except on TV when they showed the homes of movie stars. There was a wide *Gone with the Wind* staircase going up to the second floor; gleaming hardwood floors covered by large Persian rugs; elaborate chandeliers in the ceilings. A sunken living room had so many couches and chairs and potted plants that it reminded Darcy of a hotel lobby. The table in the dining room would seat twenty people and the kitchen looked suitable for a restaurant with a ten-burner gas stove, a walk-in freezer, two regular refrigerators, and enough pots and pans to prepare a meal for a battalion. She counted ten large bedrooms and at least fifteen bathrooms. A couple of the bathrooms, like the one off the master bedroom, had tubs that were big enough to hold four people comfortably. Outside the house was a four-car garage, a swimming pool with a fancy tile bottom, and a poolside cabana that was about as big as Darcy's house.

When she saw the pool and the cabana, Darcy finally asked: "Who was this guy?"

Jim said, "You don't know?"

"No," Darcy said.

"Geez, Darcy, don't you ever watch the news? They've been talking about Cartwright nonstop the last couple of weeks."

"I guess I missed it," Darcy said. Darcy was a single mother with a three-year-old daughter and was too busy to watch the news—and frankly not all that interested in watching because the news was mostly depressing.

"So who was he?" she asked again.

Jim, preoccupied with his own thoughts, still didn't answer the question. He said, "Let's go look at the safe again."

They returned to Cartwright's library and Jim closely examined the damaged safe, put his face close to it, and sniffed a couple of times to maybe get an idea of what sort of explosives had been used. The painting that had hidden the safe had a scorched hole in the center and was hanging by one hinge.

He said to Darcy, "You know what this whole scene reminds me of?"

"No," Darcy said.

"When I was In Iraq, Special Forces cowboys would raid the houses of Al Qaeda big shots and the houses would look just like this place afterward. They'd blow open the door, rush in and kill everyone in the house, then empty the place of anything that could provide intelligence. And it looks like that's what happened here. Not only is the safe empty but I haven't seen a single computer or a cell phone." He pointed at the desk. "That one file drawer is empty of paper. Why would a thief take paper? And the safe could have contained cash or gold coins or jewelry, but I'll bet you there was also paper in the safe, things like passports and birth certificates, and there's no paper in there now. If these guys had been after money, they would have taken things that were valuable, like that sterling silverware set we saw in the dining room. There was a Rolex sitting on a dresser in the bedroom that probably cost over ten grand, but they didn't bother to take it either. So I don't think they were after money—unless the safe held so damn much that it wasn't worth going after the small stuff." He paused before saying, "I think this was an intelligence raid and I'll bet you the guys who did it were ex-military, the way they took out the front door."

Darcy said, "Okay, but now are you going to tell me who Cartwright was, or do I have to ask Mr. Google?"

Jim said, "Brandon Cartwright was a rich guy worth a couple billion bucks, most of which he inherited from his daddy. In addition to this place, they said on TV that he has a place in Wyoming near Jackson Hole and a villa in Italy. He's also got a yacht that's about a hundred feet long with a crew that took him from one tropical island to another. And as far as I know, he never worked a day in his life. What he did was play. He was a regular at the film festival at Cannes. He gambled at Monte Carlo. Went skiing in the Alps. He's what they used to call a jet-setter, traveling all over the world, from one party to another, when he wasn't giving parties himself. And the people he partied with are all rich and famous. Politicians and movie stars and British royalty and Russian oligarchs. And I'm guessing that one of those famous, rich people had him killed."

"What?" Darcy said.

"If you watched the news like a normal person, Darcy, you'd know that a month ago Cartwright was indicted for sex trafficking a minor. Rumors have been swirling around for years that some of his parties were more than parties. They were *orgies*, and he'd supply handsome men and beautiful women for his famous friends to have sex with. It was also rumored that some of the men and women he supplied were actually girls and boys, some as young as fourteen or fifteen years old. Anyway, about a year ago, one of these girls, for whatever reason, came forward. She's now nineteen or twenty, and she went on TV and said she'd been recruited for one of Cartwright's sex parties when she was fifteen. She was apparently sufficiently credible that the FBI launched an investigation, which took them about a year, and a month ago they indicted Cartwright. Cartwright, of course, threw an entire law firm at the problem to keep from going to jail. And the press has been going bonkers ever since he was indicted, speculating on which of his famous friends attended his sex parties. And what I'm guessing is that one of them was worried that if Cartwright thought he might be convicted, he'd start naming names to get himself a better deal and that's why he was killed."

"Jesus," Darcy said. "So what do we do?"

"I'll tell you what we do. We get the FBI to take this case away from us. We don't even want to try to interview the kind of people Cartwright partied with. Those people will never talk to us, they'll surround themselves with lawyers, and they'll do everything they can with all their money and their connections to squash an investigation. They'll grind us into the ground like a couple of bugs. So I don't want to investigate these murders. I want the big boys in the Hoover Building to take this case away from us and take all the heat."

By the time they were ready to leave, a four-person CSI team had arrived, and they were doing what they did: dusting for fingerprints, photographing the blood splatter, bagging the shell casings, and taking samples of the explosives used to blow open the front door and the safe. The bodies were still lying where they'd been shot but would eventually be hauled off to the morgue for autopsies.

As they were walking over to talk to the cook who'd found the bodies, Darcy said, "Did you see any surveillance cameras? I didn't. You'd think a place like this would have cameras. I wonder if they could be hidden."

Stratton laughed. "There aren't any cameras, Darcy, because the people who visited Cartwright didn't want to have their pictures taken. And I think the guys who killed him took everything that could have provided a list of *who* visited him."

4

Mildred Washington loved her job.

Mildred had been with the National Archives for over thirty years. She started at the bottom, right out of high school, and worked her way up. And on the way up, she went to school at night and got a degree in library science. Her job title was *archivist*, but she was basically a librarian—a librarian who got to see the contents of the history books before the books were ever written.

She had a top secret security clearance, worked in the section that dealt with the president's and vice president's records, and was often privy to correspondence that some people would give their teeth to see. Rough drafts of speeches that ended up being significantly revised when the political winds shifted. Memos from the president to his underlings that had the potential to embarrass both the sender and the receiver. It had been impressed upon Mildred that it was vital that she not discuss the things she saw with outsiders, meaning journalists and political operatives and other nosy pikers. She was told she couldn't even share what she saw with her own family. And she didn't. One of these days, the current president's records would be placed in a library and future historians—and those nosy pikers—could paw through them to their hearts' content when the rules deemed them available to the public. But until then, no one would learn what the records contained—at least, not from Mildred Washington.

Mostly what Mildred did, as librarians tend to do, was catalogue the records, organizing them in an orderly fashion. Paper documents had to be digitized. Copies had to be made. Then everything had to be boxed up and sent to the right place for storage. What she did might sound boring to some, but she found the work fascinating because she often saw history in the making. She saw how a random thought streaking through a president's brain got batted around by his staff, memos flying like bullets, until the random thought became actual policy. She saw, reading between the lines of the correspondence, the infighting, the backstabbing, the wheeling and dealing of the inhabitants of the West Wing. Yes, it was fascinating, and she loved her job.

She reached into the latest box sent over from the White House records section. The first thing she saw was a speech the president had made at the United Nations a while ago. (The White House records people were always a month or two behind—not that she blamed them, considering the number of records they dealt with.) She flipped through the speech and saw the president's notes scrawled in the margin. She smiled when she saw the comment about the word *ameliorate*. That was exactly the kind of thing the historians liked to see. As she flipped over the last page, she saw the president had scrawled some notes on the back of the speech. This president was a doodler and a notetaker, so seeing handwritten notes on his papers wasn't unusual.

Had another archivist seen the notes, they might not have made any sense, but Mildred was a woman who paid attention to the news. She was a news junkie. She watched the cable programs every evening from six until nine, when she went to bed. She read the *Washington Post* on the Metro on her way into work in the morning. The news put the documents she looked at every day in context and allowed her to better understand their significance.

At first, she was puzzled by the notes, then the implication of what she was seeing came to her. She sat back in shock and then had to take the asthma inhaler out of her purse and use it to help her breathe.

She knew she had to do something. She had to. The notes weren't politics as usual. No, this went way beyond politics. And she knew if she kept the information to herself, she could be covering up a crime. A serious crime. Yes, she had to do something, but what could she do? She was just a librarian.

She spent a sleepless night tossing in her bed, trying to decide. The next morning she knocked timidly on the office door of the archivist of the United States. She'd let him deal with it. This was *way* above her pay grade. And if he didn't do anything, so be it. At least her conscience would be clear.

Porter Hendricks, archivist of the United States, sat between the wife of a senator and the wife of a lobbyist.

There were eighteen people at the dinner party, eighteen being the number of seats at Mrs. Osborne's long, polished dining room table. The table was covered with a lace tablecloth made a century ago in Scotland and on it sat plates of Delft Blue earthenware, Waterford crystal wineglasses, and Faneuil sterling silver flatware. Bottles of expensive wine were within arm's reach of the diners. Mrs. Osborne sat at the head of the table. She was a small, thin, woman in her sixties, and she'd reminded Porter of a hummingbird as she'd flitted from one guest to another during the pre-dinner cocktail hour.

Mrs. Osborne had inherited a fortune, was unmarried and childless, and as best Porter could tell her only occupation was hosting dinner and cocktail parties. Her gatherings made Porter think of the great salons of Paris in the 1920s where a hostess would bring together the literary giants of the time like Ernest Hemingway and F. Scott Fitzgerald and Sinclair Lewis. As for Mrs. Osborne's guests, they would usually be an eclectic mix of politicians, political power brokers, tycoons, journalists, and people of a certain class who'd recently made the headlines.

Among tonight's guests were a senator who'd gone into space on one of Jeff Bezos's rockets and come back transformed, claiming to have seen the face of God; the current White House press secretary, who'd recently appeared to be higher than a kite at a press conference; a journalist who'd published a book that dished dirt on a former first lady; a cabinet secretary who'd just come out of the closet; and the lead performer at a Kennedy Center play who'd just come out of a rehab facility. (He was drinking water, not wine.) Also present was John Mahoney, former Speaker of the House, who'd almost literally come to blows on a Sunday talk show when he'd appeared with the man who was currently the Speaker.

Porter had been the nation's archivist for nine years. He was a presidential appointee, one who'd had to get the approval of the United States Senate to get the job. He'd served under two presidents. His position was considered apolitical, the incumbent rarely made the news, and hardly anyone outside of the Beltway—or for that matter, *inside* the Beltway—knew his name.

When most folks think of the National Archives, they think of the grand building on Constitution Avenue with its seventy-two Corinthian columns that houses the original copies of the Declaration of Independence, the Constitution, and the Bill of Rights. What most people don't realize is that the National Archives and Records Administration employs almost three thousand people and manages more than thirty facilities across the United States, including presidential libraries and museums and document storage centers. It preserves an estimated thirteen *billion* pages of documents. It preserves the records of the executive,

legislative, and judicial branches of the U.S. government. The National
Archives and Records Administration is also involved in transmitting
and authenticating the votes of the Electoral College, a function that,
until recently, hadn't been particularly controversial.

So the nation's chief archivist had a big job and Porter was an accomplished and erudite man. Prior to being appointed to his current position, he'd been the director of the New York Public Library system, the
New York Public Library being the second largest in the United States,
the largest being the Library of Congress. And before that, he'd been
director of the library at the Massachusetts Institute of Technology. But
Porter, as accomplished as he was, was not the type of individual usually
invited to Mrs. Osborne's dinner parties. He was, after all, a librarian,
and how interesting could a librarian possibly be?

What changed when it came to Porter was a couple of years ago
the man who'd been president had decided to take boxes of classified
records that belonged in the National Archives to one of his homes—
and then refused to return them and FBI agents had to be sent to
retrieve them. And that's when Porter started getting invited to dinner
parties, people hoping that he'd spill what he knew about the scandal,
but of course he never did. And he hadn't wanted to come to the party
tonight, but his wife had insisted. She loved meeting the kind of people
who attended Mrs. Osborne's soirees. She was currently talking to the
White House press secretary, consoling her for the way the media had
pounced on her last incoherent performance, which the press secretary claimed was due to an allergic reaction to a medication she'd just
started taking.

The woman on Porter's right, the space-traveling senator's wife, was
going on and on about her daughter, who was apparently married to
Attila the Hun, and Porter was nodding sympathetically, trying to pre-
tend he cared. What he was really thinking about was what to do about
the bombshell that Mildred Washington had dropped on his desk that

morning. He knew he had to do something—but, like Mildred, he didn't know what to do.

At the end of the table, John Mahoney laughed, probably louder than he'd intended. Mahoney was drunk. During the pre-dinner cocktail session, Porter had had half a gin and tonic. Mahoney had downed three bourbons in the same amount of time. He was sitting next to the youngest and prettiest woman at the table, the journalist who'd written the tell-all about the former first lady. And even though the journalist was young enough to be Mahoney's granddaughter, he was flirting with her. Mahoney was a legendary womanizer. If the press was to be believed, he'd had countless affairs, and even though his wife was present this evening, it appeared as if he was trying to begin another one.

It occurred to Porter then that maybe he could relieve himself of the burden he was carrying by transferring it to Mahoney. And although Mahoney might not do anything, at least Porter's conscience would be clear.

He knew Mahoney slightly. The congressman represented a good part of Boston, and Porter had met him a couple of times when he'd been MIT's librarian. Mahoney had given a speech to a graduating class—Porter had actually been surprised and impressed by Mahoney's eloquence—and another time at a ground-breaking ceremony for a new science building that Mahoney had falsely taken credit for providing the funds for constructing the building. Porter also knew that Mahoney detested Eric Doyle, the president's national security advisor. The reason he knew this was that Mahoney hadn't been at all bashful about criticizing Doyle both on the floor of Congress and while appearing on various cable shows. Mahoney's low opinion of Doyle, more than anything else, might motivate Mahoney to act.

When the dinner finally ended—Porter about to go insane listening to the senator's wife, who never stopped talking—Mrs. Osborne invited her guests to adjourn to the parlor for coffee or brandy if they preferred.

Porter followed Mahoney out of the dining room and saw him make a beeline for the bar, where he was served cognac in a snifter the size of a goldfish bowl.

Porter caught him before he could head back to chat up the pretty young journalist. He said, "Mr. Speaker, I need to speak to you about something rather important."

Porter knew that Mahoney liked to be called "Mr. Speaker" even though he was no longer the Speaker. He certainly didn't like to be called "Mr. Minority Leader."

"Oh?" Mahoney said.

He was looking over Porter's head at the journalist. Mahoney was less than six feet tall, but he had a broad chest that made him seem bigger than he actually was. He had pure white hair—it was the only thing pure about him—and bright blue eyes. Those eyes were now focused intently on the journalist.

Porter said, "This isn't the appropriate time and place—"

Because you're drunk and ridiculously trying to get into that young woman's pants.

"—but it concerns Eric Doyle."

Now Mahoney looked at him. "Doyle?"

"Yes."

"What did he do?"

"Sir, like I said, this isn't the right place to have this particular discussion. Could I meet with you tomorrow?"

"Yeah, I guess," Mahoney said. "Have your girl call my secretary, Mavis, and we'll set something up."

Porter didn't have a "girl." His executive assistant was a man, but if his assistant had been a woman, he never would have referred to her as his "girl."

Thinking the conversation was over, Mahoney tried to maneuver past Porter to get back to the journalist.

Porter said, "Mr. Speaker, considering the nature of what I have to tell you, it would be best that we not meet at your office or mine."

Mahoney stopped and looked at him again, and even though he was drunk, he now seemed to grasp that what Porter had to tell him was something out of the ordinary.

"Okay," Mahoney said. "I'll see you tomorrow."

5

The next morning, Porter called Mahoney's office personally—he didn't want anyone in his office to know about his meeting with the former House Speaker—and spoke to Mavis, Mahoney's executive assistant who'd been with Mahoney since his first campaign more than forty years ago. He said, "The congressman and I spoke last night at a dinner party and he agreed to meet with me today."

Mavis said, "Yeah, he told me."

"He did?" Porter was surprised that Mahoney, as drunk as he'd been, had remembered their conversation. The fact that he'd mentioned Doyle must have penetrated Mahoney's booze-soaked brain.

Mavis said, "There's an Italian restaurant in Georgetown called Fredo's. It has a private dining room and Mahoney has a relationship with the owner. He'll be there at eleven. The restaurant doesn't open until twelve. If you don't want to be seen, use the kitchen entrance in the back. They'll be expecting you, although they won't know your name."

Porter could tell that this wasn't the first time that Mavis had set up a clandestine rendezvous for her boss.

Porter arrived at a quarter to eleven and stood on the street across from the restaurant in the doorway of a store that had gone out of business. He was wearing the trench coat he'd worn to work that day over his suit, and although it wasn't raining, on his head was a bucket-shaped rain hat he kept in his office for those days when it did rain. He was hoping the rain hat would somewhat hide his features, but with the trench coat and the hat he felt foolish, like an actor portraying a Cold War spy.

He watched as a black Chevy Suburban double parked in front of the restaurant and saw Mahoney get out of the rear seat and walk into the restaurant. His security detail didn't accompany him. Porter waited until exactly eleven, to give Mahoney time to get settled and, knowing him, most likely order a drink. He walked around to the rear of the restaurant where there was an alley with overflowing dumpsters and saw the back entrance to the kitchen. The inner door was open, the way barred only by a screen door. He stepped into the kitchen. There were three cooks, all wearing hairnets, white jackets, and black and white checkered pants. One might have expected them to be Italian, but they were all African American. One of them looked over at him and Porter said, "I'm here to see someone in your private dining room."

The cook nodded, motioned for him to come forward, and led him through the kitchen—which smelled the way heaven must smell—and into the dining room. Porter didn't like the fact that the cooks had seen him, but he doubted they knew who he was. The only one in the dining room was a small man in his seventies with oily dark hair and a thick mustache standing behind the bar. Fredo? The man was looking down at papers on the bar. He glanced up when Porter entered the room but then looked back down at the papers. The cook pointed and said, "Up those stairs."

Mahoney was in a windowless room containing a table that would seat six people. Above the table hung a Tiffany-style leaded glass lamp. On the walls were travel posters showing the canals of Venice, the Leaning Tower of Pisa, and Castel Sant'Angelo in Rome, its bridge guarded by two stone angels. Mahoney had taken his suit jacket off. He was wearing a white shirt and broad red suspenders. On the table was a carafe filled with water, a bottle of wine, two glasses—one empty and the other filled to the brim with red wine—and an antipasto platter containing salami, prosciutto, various cheeses, olives, and roasted vegetables.

Porter sat across from Mahoney. He removed his hat but didn't take off his coat. He didn't plan on being there for very long.

Mahoney said, "Help yourself to the wine and the food."

"Thank you," Porter said, but didn't reach for anything. He was too nervous to feel like eating, and eleven in the morning was certainly too early for alcohol.

"So," Mahoney said. "What's going on? Why the cloak-and-dagger?"

Porter said, "Two months ago, a man named Brandon Cartwright was killed. Also, his assistant, a man named Benjamin Margate. Were you aware of that?"

"Yeah, sure."

"If you don't mind me asking, what do you know about Brandon Cartwright?"

Mahoney shrugged. "I only know what they said on the news. I never met the man. From what I read, he was a pimp to the rich and famous, and he supposedly organized orgies for his pals. And I know he was indicted for peddling the ass of a fifteen-year-old girl, and everyone guessed he was killed to keep him from spilling his guts about whoever he'd peddled her ass to. But what does this have to do with Doyle?"

Porter pulled a folded eight-and-a-half-by-eleven sheet of paper from his back pocket, unfolded it, and placed it on the table.

Mahoney looked down at the paper and saw:

ceoee

☆ CARTWRIGHT A-HOLE !!!
☆ PARDON ? NO F-ING WAY
☆ PAY ?? TOO, RICH $$$
☆ DOYLE'S WAY ?? ONLY WAY

/ / / / /

Mahoney asked, "What the hell is this?"

Porter said, "That's the president's handwriting. And that's a copy of notes he made on the back of a rough draft of a speech he gave at the United Nations." He paused before continuing: "You see, the president is a habitual notetaker and he's always doodling and making notes on whatever he has at hand when he's in meetings. I suspect he often does it unconsciously and might not even be aware he's doing it."

"How do you know that?"

"Because the National Archives gets almost all of the president's papers," Porter said in response to what he thought was a rather stupid question. "And the president is also a former lawyer and, like a lot of lawyers, he was trained to take contemporaneous notes during important conversations so he could later write up an accurate account of the conversation."

"And you're sure the president wrote this?" Mahoney said, tapping the paper.

"Without a doubt. His handwriting, the way he prints, is distinctive, and archives has hundreds of examples of his handwriting. And the way he abbreviates words, like 'a-hole' and 'f-ing.' But there's more than those notes. They were made on a day the president met with Eric Doyle. I know that because the draft of the speech is dated and from the president's calendar and the president's daily diary, which the National

Archives also has access to and retains. And because I made a couple of phone calls."

Mahoney asked, "Did Cartwright ever visit the president at the White House?"

"No. Or at least there's no record of him having done so. And there's no record of the president ever calling him or receiving a call from him. I checked. Very discreetly."

"And what do you think these notes mean?"

"I think the meaning is clear. But I'm not going to tell you what I think. I want to hear what you think."

Mahoney stared down at the paper again, took a sip of wine, then stared some more. Porter knew that John Mahoney was a flawed individual. He was an alcoholic. An adulterer. A liar. He was corrupt. He was dishonest. But he was also an intelligent man.

After a moment, Mahoney said, "I think this means that Cartwright thought he might go to jail and he wanted a presidential pardon if he was convicted. But there was no way the president would ever give a child sex trafficker a pardon. So I think Cartwright had something on the president and the president had to figure out a way to make him keep his mouth shut. But he couldn't pay him to do the time because Cartwright was too rich to be bought off. As for the expression 'Doyle's way,' we both know what that means."

"Yes," Porter said.

The term *Doyle's way* was used frequently by politicians and pundits because, since Doyle had become the national security advisor, it had become common—too common, some said—to use Navy SEALs or drones armed with missiles to kill people considered threats to the country. These people were always identified by the administration as terrorists, but that didn't mean it was always wise for the United States to act unilaterally to rid the world of them. Mahoney thought that Doyle had too much influence over the president, and Doyle's way of dealing with problems was dangerous for the country. But the term *Doyle's way* was clear: if there was no other way to solve a problem, you killed the problem.

"Why are you showing me this?" Mahoney said.

"Because I couldn't think of who else to show it to. I can't take those notes to the FBI or the attorney general. Those notes aren't proof of anything. But more important, if I were to share those notes with law enforcement or the media, it would destroy the National Archives. If people, such as future presidents and members of Congress, believed that archives would use the president's private correspondence to cause him a legal problem or even embarrass him, I believe the National Archives could be dismantled. It would certainly never be trusted again, and new rules would be imposed, and people would be assigned to oversee us to make sure we didn't betray our trust again."

"Yeah, I can see that," Mahoney said. "But what do you expect me to do?"

"Frankly, I don't know," Porter said.

Mahoney said, "Well, fuck me. So your plan was to dump this turd on me and hope I'd do something because you don't have the balls to do something yourself?"

"It's not a matter of courage, Mr. Speaker. Like I said, I can't do anything because it would destroy the organization I lead—an organization whose mission when it comes to the Presidential Records Act is important."

Porter stood up, and before Mahoney could stop him, he picked up the copy of the president's notes, crumpled the paper into a ball, and shoved the ball into a pocket.

"Hey, what are you doing?" Mahoney said.

"I had no intention of leaving that copy with you. I'm not allowed by law to share the president's correspondence with others. But the original is in the National Archives, and it will remain with the president's other papers. It won't be destroyed. And one of these days, those notes might be seen by some historian and maybe that historian will come to the same conclusion you and I have. But that probably won't happen until many years in the future."

Porter stood up and put on his rain hat. "Thank you for meeting with me, Mr. Speaker." And he walked out the door.

"Well, fuck me," Mahoney said again, speaking to an empty room.

He sat a moment sipping wine, refilled his glass, and sipped some more. He finally took out his phone and punched a button. "Mavis," he said, "track down DeMarco. I think he might be in Boston, but if he's in town, tell him to get his ass down to Fredo's."

6

Joe DeMarco shoveled concrete from a wheelbarrow into the hole around a four-by-four eight-foot post, tamped the concrete down, checked again to make sure the post was level, shoveled in some more concrete, and repeated the tamping/leveling procedure.

DeMarco lived in Georgetown in a narrow two-story town house made of white painted brick. A cedar fence separated his backyard from the neighbor behind him and he was rebuilding the fence, a project that he'd started a few days ago and wanted to finish. The posts in the old fence had mostly rotted away after years in the ground, and he was worried that the next windstorm would take the fence down. So he'd decided to replace the fence. And he'd decided to do it himself.

It was a good day for building a fence. It was early March but surprisingly warm. It felt as if spring had truly arrived. DeMarco was wearing a wash-faded, red Nationals T-shirt, jeans splattered with concrete, and work boots. He was supposed to be in Boston, but he hadn't felt like spending hours in airports and on airplanes and dealing with Boston's nightmarish traffic, then spending two hours drinking tea with Bitty. And if Mahoney asked why he hadn't gone to see Bitty—and that was assuming that Mahoney's bourbon-pickled brain even remembered that he was supposed to go see Bitty—he'd lie and say that Bitty was vacationing in the Bahamas. There was no rush when it came to Bitty.

Bitty—her full name was Elizabeth Hancock Montrose—was a wealthy Bostonian who contributed generously to Mahoney. She was a descendant of the Hancock who'd scrawled his name larger than anyone else on the Declaration of Independence. Bitty contributed to Mahoney in part because she agreed with his purported political views—views that could swing like a weather vane in a hurricane—and in part because Mahoney had charmed the pants off her, something he did very well when it came to women her age. But Bitty wouldn't simply mail Mahoney a check. She insisted on giving him cash, like a campaign contribution was a transaction between a junkie and a drug dealer. The reason for this was that her late husband had been a Republican and all her friends and relatives were Republicans, and Bitty wanted no record whatsoever that she supported the demon libs. And after the first time DeMarco—Mahoney's bagman— collected a brick of cash from her to pass on to his boss, she'd insisted that he collect all future contributions because Bitty liked DeMarco's looks. Bitty, although in her eighties, flirted like an eighteen-year-old coed.

But DeMarco wasn't thinking about Bitty. He was thinking about his father. Gino DeMarco had possessed the knowledge and the skills to tackle almost any project around Joe DeMarco's boyhood home. He replaced the roof, remodeled the kitchen, replaced windows, rebuilt staircases, rehung doors. And when DeMarco was a kid, he'd been his father's helper, and his dad had tried his best to pass on his knowledge to his son. The truth was that Joe would never be the craftsman his father had been because he didn't have the patience or, for that matter, the interest. He preferred to spend his free time playing golf. But occasionally he'd taken on some simple job that didn't require much in the way of precision or talent—like building a fence—and every time he did, he thought about his father.

Fixing things around his home wasn't something that Gino did just to avoid the expense of paying someone else to do the job. Doing things with his hands, immersing himself completely in some home improve-ment project, allowed him to forget, at least for a while, what he did for a living. Gino DeMarco had been an enforcer for a mob boss in Queens named Carmine Taliaferro. Gino DeMarco killed people.

While Joe was growing up, his mother used to say that his father was a property manager, meaning that he maintained the rental houses and apartment buildings his boss owned. And his father actually did main-tenance work for Taliaferro when Taliaferro didn't have more impor-tant things for him to do. But the neighborhood that Joe grew up in in Queens was a village—and the village knew that Taliaferro was Mafia and they knew what Gino did for him. Gino's exploits spread through the village in whispers, in low conversations in neighborhood bars, about the witness who'd been about to testify against Taliaferro who had disap-peared, about the fool trying to muscle in on Taliaferro's territory who couldn't be found. Until he was killed himself, Gino DeMarco had been one of the most feared men in Queens.

Joe's mother, however, maintained the fiction that his father, who everyone knew was handy at fixing things, was just a simple property manager, refusing to acknowledge even to herself what her husband really did. And in his grade school years, Joe believed the fiction his mother had created. But by the time he was in high school he knew the truth. He couldn't avoid the truth. He knew what Carmine Taliaferro did and what the men he employed did and he'd heard the rumors about his father from the sons of other men Taliaferro employed.

But Joe never learned anything from his father, who refused to talk about what he did or how he felt about what he did or how he became the person who did what he did. And the Gino DeMarco that people feared and whispered about wasn't the man his son knew. Joe saw a gentle, seem-ingly humble man who rarely spoke but who was always patient and kind to him. He was never the least bit violent; he never hit Joe and rarely raised his voice when his son misbehaved. As far as Joe was concerned, he couldn't have had a more loving father. Gino had taught him how to throw a baseball and ride a bike. He'd taught him how to use a hammer and a saw. He took him to ball games and came to his son's games when Joe was in school. It was Gino who insisted that he go to college, and, most important, he did everything he could to steer Joe away from the criminals he worked with.

As Joe aged—he was now about the age his father had been when he died—he'd come to look more and more like his dad. Sometimes he'd catch his reflection as he walked past a window and noticed he even walked like his late father. Gino had been a handsome, broad shouldered, muscular man with a prominent nose and a cleft in his chin. And other than the fact that Joe's eyes were blue and his father's had been brown, Joe had the same face. When he went home to see his mother, who still lived in the same house in Queens that his father had maintained, he'd encounter people who'd known his dad and they'd often react as if they were seeing a ghost. The ghost of a killer.

DeMarco's phone rang, interrupting his reverie. *Aw, shit.* It was Mavis, Mahoney's secretary. After speaking to Mavis, he took a three-minute shower and put on a suit and white shirt but didn't bother to don a tie.

DeMarco found Mahoney in the private dining room at Fredo's, sitting at a table with a plate of antipasto that was more than half gone and a bottle of wine that was three-quarters gone. He took a seat and Mahoney said, "The guy who runs the National Archives dropped a turd in my lap today."

And DeMarco knew immediately that the turd was about to be transferred from Mahoney's lap to his.

Mahoney, in between sips of wine and while nibbling from the antipasto plate and licking the oil off his fingers, went on to explain that the National Archives had gotten a copy of a speech and on the back of the speech were notes in the president's handwriting indicating that he may have conspired with Eric Doyle to have Brandon Cartwright killed.

"You really believe he'd do that?" DeMarco said.

"Yeah, I do. If I didn't, I wouldn't be wasting my time talking to you."

"Where's the speech?" DeMarco asked.

"The original is at the archives. Hendricks only had a copy of the page with the notes and he took it with him."

Before DeMarco could respond, Mahoney said, "What do you know about Doyle?"

DeMarco shrugged. "Only what I've read in the papers. He went to West Point, rose through the ranks like a rocket, was made a general in his early forties, resigned and started his own private security company, where he made a fortune, and then he became the president's national security advisor."

"That's the gist of it," Mahoney said, "but what you don't know is that he used his contacts in the Pentagon to get contracts that his company wouldn't have gotten otherwise."

DeMarco shrugged again, thinking: *So what else is new?* That happened all the time: some high-ranking guy retires from the military and then starts milking the system.

Mahoney said, "Doyle's mercenaries have augmented the U.S. military in Afghanistan, Iraq, Somalia, and a bunch of other places. His guys would be used to guard supply convoys, protect facilities, guard prisoners, the sort of stuff the military didn't always have the manpower for or didn't want to waste its manpower doing. But Doyle's outfit, because it was Doyle's outfit, would also do other stuff, like spying on bad guys and tracking them down. They'd be sent into places like Pakistan where the military wasn't allowed to go to acquire intelligence and snatch terrorists because if they got caught doing something shady the U.S. government could deny having sent them there."

DeMarco imagined that Mahoney knew all this not only because of his connections but also because he was a member of the Gang of

Eight, the group of Senate and House leaders that was briefed by the intelligence agencies.

Mahoney said, "I hate these fuckin' private security firms. The money spent on them should be spent on the military itself, and they get paid outrageous amounts. And Doyle's outfit is the worst of the bunch. His guys were arrested twice for killing civilians in Afghanistan and both times they got off because the U.S. government helped them get off and because Doyle bribed the right Afghans. Doyle's firm also hires itself out to scumbag dictators who don't trust their own people to protect them. His company is currently helping out a thug in Libya who's trying to become the next Ghaddafi. And Doyle gets away with shit because he's protected by his old pals in the Pentagon, who I'm sure are getting kickbacks from him. And then, of course, he's the president's best buddy."

"What does this have to do with Cartwright?" DeMarco asked.

"Shut up. I'm just giving you the background so you'll know who you're dealing with. But the worst thing about Doyle, like I said, is he's the president's best buddy and the president goes and makes him his national security advisor. And that scares the hell out of me, because Doyle's a super-hawk who thinks bombing people is the best solution to every problem. Since he's been in the White House the number of drone strikes has tripled. The guy is just looking for an excuse to start another war, even though the last two were complete disasters."

"Where does he know the president from? The president never served in the military."

"Harvard. The military sends its superstars—the ones who appear to have the potential to become admirals and generals—to postgraduate schools. And that's where he met the president and they've been pals for thirty years. They took vacations together when the president was still a lawyer and after he became a senator. When I say he's the president's best buddy, I mean that literally."

"But what does this have to do with Cartwright?"

"Are you just pretending to be extra thick today, or what? Cartwright was blackmailing the president. That's the only thing that makes sense. Cartwright thought he might be convicted and the only way to keep from going to jail was to get a pardon, but there was no way the president would give a guy procuring teenage girls for sex a pardon. So what options did he have? Well, I can think of one. If your best friend has a company filled with a bunch of military-trained killers, who'd be a better person to deal with the problem?"

"Is Doyle still running his firm now that he's the national security advisor?"

"Supposedly not. When he was appointed, he turned the company over to a vice president and he claims he's no longer acting in it in any capacity. But that, of course, is bullshit. It's still his company."

"What could Cartwright have been blackmailing the president with?"

"I don't know, but considering Cartwright's reputation, I'm guessing it would have to do with sex. That's the only thing I can think of that makes sense."

"You seriously think the president would have attended one of Cartwright's orgies?"

"No. He'd never be that stupid. But it has to be something along those lines. Cartwright was a pimp. He provided sex partners, including underage kids, for his friends. Or at least, that's what everyone says he did. So I don't know exactly what he had on the president, but it has to be connected to what Cartwright was arrested for."

"But what do you expect me to do? Prove that the president of the United States conspired with his national security advisor to kill Cartwright? I mean, get real. The FBI probably couldn't prove that, and if they could, they wouldn't be able to do anything to a sitting president."

"All I want you to do is poke around. See if there's something out there, something more than this note that Hendricks dropped on me. Just, hell, I don't know. Poke around."

"Well, fuck me," DeMarco said.

7

As DeMarco hadn't eaten lunch, and as his self-centered boss hadn't offered him any of the antipasto sitting on the table in front of him, he left Fredo's, walked down M Street, and found a place that made a decent Reuben and ordered one.

While eating, he used his phone to see what was happening when it came to Brandon Cartwright's murder. Cartwright had been killed two months ago. A month before he was killed, he was indicted for sex-trafficking a minor named Tracy Woods. Woods, now an adult, claimed that when she was fifteen, she'd been paid to have sex with two middle-aged men. She wasn't able to identify the two men, however, because they wore masks when they had sex with her. But her accusations had apparently been credible and the FBI launched an investigation, which dragged on for months, and Cartwright was eventually indicted.

The media, of course, went ballistic, dredging up stories with unnamed sources about how Cartwright would organize orgies for his famous friends. One tabloid called him the "Pimp to the Stars." Cartwright immediately sued for defamation. Photos of Cartwright posing with some of his pals—an heir to the British monarchy, CEOs of various companies, the owner of an NFL team, half a dozen movie stars, a couple of senators, and even one ex-president—were shown on the cable channels.

Cartwright naturally denied that he'd ever hosted orgies; he said all he'd ever done was organize dinner parties and trips on his yacht. His famous friends admitted that they'd socialized with Cartwright occasionally but also denied that they'd ever participated in any sort of debauchery—and said they'd sue the ass off anyone who claimed they did.

A month after he was indicted—one week after the president scrawled his notes on the back of a speech—Cartwright was killed. According to the cops, someone had broken into his home and shot him and his assistant, Benjamin Margate. The cops said that Cartwright had apparently tried to defend himself, as he was found with a gun in his hand and the gun had been fired. The media went nuts again, speculating that one of the two men that Tracy Woods said she'd been paid to have sex with had killed Cartwright. Or, the media speculated, if he wasn't killed by those two men, he could have been killed by some famous person he'd invited to one of his orgies because that person didn't want Cartwright blabbing during his trial.

The murder was investigated by the Prince William County Police Department, making DeMarco wonder why the FBI hadn't taken charge of the investigation. The chief of the department said he believed Cartwright was killed in a home invasion because Cartwright's house had been ransacked and a safe had been blown open. The chief said there was no evidence that Cartwright had been killed by one of his famous pals and he thought it irresponsible for the media to make those accusations. The media heat died down a couple of weeks after Cartwright's murder when nothing came out of the investigation and because the media, which has a microsecond attention span, had moved on to other scandals. And two months after Cartwright was killed, as best DeMarco could tell, the cops had made no headway in finding out who'd killed him.

DeMarco also googled Cartwright, Eric Doyle, and the president and didn't see a single article that connected Cartwright to Doyle or the president. And according to Porter Hendricks, Cartwright had never visited the White House and no one in the White House had ever called him. But that assumed that someone hadn't diddled with the White House logs.

DeMarco finished his Reuben thinking that the assignment Mahoney had given him was absurd. There was no way he was going to be able to show the president had conspired with Doyle to kill Brandon Cartwright. About all he could do was poke around as Mahoney had demanded, report back to Mahoney where he'd poked, and hope that Mahoney—who obviously had a major hard-on when it came to Doyle—would allow him to stop poking.

He decided the first place he'd poke was the FBI. The whole Cartwright saga began with the FBI arresting the man, so that was as good a place as any to start. And it was something he could tell Mahoney he'd done.

But that could wait until tomorrow.

He was going to spend the rest of the afternoon on his fence.

8

It took DeMarco half a dozen phone calls to track down the FBI agent who had the lead on the Cartwright sex-trafficking investigation, and when DeMarco told him that the Congress of the United States had a few questions for him, the agent reluctantly agreed to meet with him.

The agent's name was Al Burton. He worked out of the bureau's Washington, D.C., field office located on 4th Street NW, and DeMarco asked Burton to meet him at a nearby coffee shop. DeMarco didn't want to meet Burton in his office, where he would have been given a visitor's badge and escorted to Burton's office and his visit would have been recorded. DeMarco preferred to minimize the number of records and witnesses when it came to what he was doing.

The FBI has a mandatory agent retirement age of fifty-seven, and DeMarco figured Burton had to be near that age. He was gray-haired, double-chinned, red-faced, and overweight. His gut slopped over his belt. He was dressed in a wrinkled white shirt, a clip-on tie, and a rumpled blue suit sprinkled with dandruff on the shoulders. The man would not be appearing soon on any G-man recruiting posters.

Burton started off by saying, "Can you explain to me why Congress is interested in the Tracy Woods case?"

DeMarco said, "Agent, I'm just an errand boy. I'm an independent lawyer who works for the House—I'm not on any legislator's staff—and sometimes, when the lawmakers don't want to use their own people to do something, they'll use me."

All that was mostly bullshit, but not entirely.

DeMarco said, "This time a couple of congresswomen were sitting around gabbing one day and they started wondering why the FBI hadn't yet arrested the men who took advantage of that poor girl. So they sent me to find out. And I was hoping we could keep this informal, just between you and me. You know, as opposed to these congresswomen dragging you and your boss up to Capitol Hill by your nuts and asking you questions in a televised hearing. All I want is the background on the case, which I don't have, and an idea of where things stand now. And hopefully I'll be able to go back and tell these women that the Bureau is doing everything it can and that'll be enough to make 'em happy."

Burton, obviously feeling put upon, shook his head. He said, "The only reason the FBI got involved was that Tracy went on TV and told the whole world that when she was fifteen she was driven to Cartwright's mansion one night where she was paid to have sex with two men. But she couldn't identify the two men. They wore masks when they had sex with her and didn't have any distinguishing marks, like scars or tattoos or birthmarks."

"Yeah, I read that," DeMarco said. "What kind of masks?" DeMarco was visualizing the masks worn by the weirdos in that creepy Kubrick movie *Eyes Wide Shut*, the one with Tom Cruise and Nicole Kidman when they were still married to each other.

"Plain black masks," Burton said. "Tracy called them Lone Ranger masks. Anyway, a limo took Tracy from an Applebee's in Manassas to Cartwright's house. When she got there, she was met outside by a woman who Tracy said was about forty and who never introduced herself. The woman took Tracy in through a back door and up a flight of stairs and Tracy never saw Cartwright or anyone else in the house, but she could hear music and people talking like there was a party going on. The woman took her to a powder room where she had Tracy fix her makeup—the woman said she had on too much eye shadow—then gave her a drink to relax her and a thousand bucks in cash, after which she took her to a bedroom. A little while later, the two men came in and spent a couple of hours with her, having sex with her in every way they could think of, and then left her in the room. The woman who met her when she arrived at the house eventually came back to the bedroom, told her she was done for the night and to get dressed, then led her out of the house to where the limo was waiting. The woman told Tracy that maybe she'd contact her again but never did. The woman also told Tracy that if she talked about that night, not only wouldn't she get another gig, but someone would do something very bad to her, but she didn't say what. Tracy said that the woman, who up until then had been really nice to her, turned into a 'scary fucking bitch.' Tracy's words."

"How was Tracy recruited for this thing? Did they find her standing on a corner like a hooker?"

"No. According to Tracy, she was sitting on a bench in a courthouse one day—she'd been arrested for trying to steal a thousand-dollar cell phone out of the Best Buy in Manassas—and while she's sitting there, another woman, who Tracy said was in her twenties and really good-looking, asked if she'd be willing to party for money. When Tracy asks how much, the woman says a thousand bucks and Tracy says hell yes. I figured the woman worked for an escort service and she liked Tracy's looks, Tracy being a hot-looking young fifteen-year-old at the time, but a fifteen-year-old who'd ended up on the wrong side of the law."

"Why do you think the woman worked for an escort service?"

"If all the stories about Cartwright hosting sex parties are true, he had to find attractive people to screw his buddies. What better place to go than to an escort service, a high-end one, that employed people who could keep their mouths shut? But an escort service most likely wouldn't have underage kids on their payroll, so if Cartwright's friends wanted minors to play with, Cartwright had to find them someplace, and what I think he did was arrange for some of these escorts to be talent scouts. Anyway, what happened next is the gal Tracy met at the courthouse took her photo and said if the people she knew liked her looks, someone would get in touch with her. A day later Tracy gets a call from a woman—I'm guessing it was the woman who met her at Cartwright's house—who asks for her full name, birth date, and Social Security number."

"Why would she do that? Ask for a Social Security number?"

"So she could check Tracy out. And what she would have found is that Tracy was a kid who'd been picked up by the cops for shoplifting, underage drinking, assaulting a couple of other girls, doing drugs, and so on. She barely attended school, had been abandoned by her father, and was raised by an alcoholic mother who'd been arrested a dozen times for prostitution. In other words, she would have found out that Tracy was exactly the kind of fifteen-year-old who might be willing to sell her young ass for sex. One of the things I did was make Tracy look at about a million photos of escorts in D.C. and Northern Virginia to see if she could spot the woman who approached her at the courthouse, and of course she couldn't."

Burton sighed. "Tracy Woods is about the worst witness imaginable. She admitted the only reason she came forward, three years after the crime took place, was that she was broke and Fox paid her ten thousand bucks to tell her story. She has an IQ that I suspect is lower than room temperature. And like her mom, she's an alcoholic who's gotten two DUIs in the last two years. She's also gained about fifty pounds since she was fifteen and it's almost impossible to imagine that when she was fifteen she could have been attractive enough to interest Cartwright's friends. I mean, I believe her, but if Cartwright's case had gone to trial, what a jury would have seen is money-grubbing, trailer park white trash.

"The main thing that got the whole investigation rolling after Tracy appeared on TV was a female senator who demanded that DOJ do something about a fifteen-year-old who'd been raped. So I spent six months trying to track down the two men and the woman who met Tracy at Cartwright's house. Like I already said, Tracy couldn't tell us anything we could use to identify the men. As for the woman, all Tracy could remember about her is that she had short, dark hair cut in a 'super-cute' style—Tracy's words—and wore red Jimmy Choos. I also couldn't find the limo driver who took her to Cartwright's house because Tracy couldn't remember a damn thing about him other than he was Black and drove a big black car. And there was no camera near the Applebee's that videoed the limo. It took three months before I was able to interview Cartwright because he and a battalion of lawyers stonewalled me. Then it took another couple of months to prove that Cartwright lied to me during the interview. He claimed not to be home when Tracy went to his house, and it took me two months to prove he was actually there. And none of the famous rich people who hung around with Cartwright would talk to me and I couldn't force them to talk because I had no evidence that they were there that night."

"How were you able to indict him?" DeMarco asked.

"We found a sympathetic judge, a woman, and got the indictment solely based on Tracy Woods's statement that she was at Cartwright's and the fact that Cartwright lied to us. I think we would have been creamed if we'd taken the case to court, but we were hoping that the indictment might scare Cartwright into giving us the names of whoever had sex with Tracy. In other words, we were willing to cut Cartwright a deal. We'd have given him a reduced sentence—or no sentence—if he gave up the two guys. But Cartwright wouldn't cooperate. He was confident that, with all his money and all his influential pals, nothing would happen to him. And then someone goes and kills him."

"Is the case still open?"

"Yeah, technically. But we're never going to be able to identify the two men who had sex with Tracy unless someone comes forward and names them. And face it: we're not talking about the Boston Marathon bombing here. But the Bureau, meaning me, has put in a lot of man-hours trying to ID these guys and I haven't had any luck. There were no cameras at Cartwright's place. Cartwright's staff—his housekeeper, his cook, and the yard guy—weren't there the night Tracy had sex with these guys. Cartwright's assistant, who probably could have told us something, was killed along with Cartwright. And like I already said, all of Cartwright's rich buddies—and a lot of them don't even live in the United States—all told me to go fuck myself when I tried to question them."

"I see," DeMarco said. "But can I ask you something? Why didn't the Bureau take over the investigation of Cartwright's murder?"

"Because murder doesn't fall under the FBI's jurisdiction except in special circumstances, like serial killers or the killing of a politician or a killing on tribal land."

"Yeah, but the two guys you were looking for had to be considered likely suspects."

"I suppose," Burton said, which DeMarco thought was an odd answer. "But the chief of the Prince William County Police Department said it looked to him like a straight-up home invasion. Cartwright was a wealthy guy who lived in a mansion in an isolated area, and a couple of pros decided to rip him off."

"Yeah, but—"

"And Prince William County never asked the Bureau to take over the investigation, and if the county *had* asked, my bosses most likely would have refused. Like I said, murder isn't a federal crime, like sex trafficking, and, well . . ." Burton shook his head.

When Burton didn't continue, DeMarco said, "Well, what?"

"DeMarco, Brandon Cartwright was a tar baby. He hung around with powerful, rich people, including some who work on Capitol Hill, and those people just want Cartwright to go away. They want the world to forget he ever existed and that they ever knew the man. And I'm pretty sure my bosses weren't all that anxious to start questioning these powerful people and riling them up, not when the victim was a guy who was basically a pimp. The Bureau's job was to find out who had sex with Tracy, and like I told you, I did my best."

"Yeah, okay," DeMarco said.

"So what are you going to tell the congresswomen who sent you?"

"I'm going to tell them the Bureau did everything it could do to track those guys down and is still digging, but don't get your hopes up. I think all they really want is to know that the case is still being worked and I'll tell them that it is."

He didn't want Burton to think he was going to say anything negative about him because he might want to talk to the man again.

"Well, I appreciate that," Burton said.

———— ◆◆◆ ————

After Burton left the coffee shop to return to the field office, DeMarco had another cup of coffee and an apple fritter and thought about what Burton had told him. If the case against Cartwright was as weak as Burton had said, why would Cartwright ask the president for a pardon? He supposed the answer to that question was that maybe Cartwright wanted an insurance policy. Or maybe Cartwright thought the case was stronger than it actually was because Burton had lied to him. It was a crime to lie to the FBI, but it wasn't a crime for the FBI to lie to suspects. So Cartwright had wanted to be sure that he wouldn't go to jail if he was convicted for any crime, including lying to the FBI, so he squeezed the president.

DeMarco also found it interesting, yet understandable, that the decision-makers in the FBI and DOJ would not want to get involved in the murder investigation. Like Burton had said, there were a lot of rich, powerful people who didn't want to get dragged into any investigation that tied them to Cartwright's sex parties. And maybe one of those people was the president.

The last thought he had was about Burton himself. Burton may have been the FBI's own Columbo, a plodding, shabbily dressed genius, but DeMarco doubted that. It took Burton forever to build the case against Cartwright, and it sounded as if he'd been working mostly on his own. The case obviously hadn't been a high priority for the FBI, and it didn't seem to him as if the Bureau had assigned a superstar to the investigation. And he wondered if that was intentional.

9

The next morning, DeMarco put on a dark suit, a white shirt, and a tie, figuring he needed to look like a lawyer, and drove to Woodbridge, Virginia, about forty minutes south of D.C. The headquarters for the Prince William County Police Department was located in Woodbridge.

Upon his arrival, he stopped at the front desk, where a young, attractive Black woman in a uniform was seated. Her name tag said "D. Adams."

DeMarco said, "I need to speak to the chief of the department about the Brandon Cartwright investigation."

Adams said, "Are you a reporter? If you are, you need to talk to the people in media relations."

"I'm not a reporter." DeMarco took out his congressional ID and showed it to Adams. He said, "I'm a lawyer who works in the House of Representatives and some of those representatives want to know about the status of the investigation."

Adams studied DeMarco's ID badge for longer than seemed necessary, then studied his face. He thought the look she gave him was odd. She pointed to a plastic chair near her desk and said, "Take a seat and I'll let the chief know you're here."

The chief of the Prince William County Police Department was a man named Brian Harmon. He was a burly man in his forties with a cowlick in his thick brown hair. He was sitting behind his desk and wearing a black tie and white uniform shirt stretched tight over his gut. On the wall behind him were a dozen photos of him posing with various people, including the current governor of Virginia and the House majority whip, who was also from Virginia.

He smiled when DeMarco entered his office and came around his desk and shook hands with DeMarco, saying, "What the heck does Congress have to do with Brandon Cartwright?" He had a noticeable Southern accent and was wearing cowboy boots.

DeMarco's first impression of Harmon was affable, beer-drinking, barbecue-loving good old country boy—but DeMarco had googled him before coming to see him. Harmon was well educated. He had a bachelor's degree in criminal justice and a law degree from a second-tier Virginia law school. Four years ago, he'd run for Congress and lost.

Answering Harmon's question, DeMarco said, "To tell you the truth, I don't really know why Congress cares."

"You don't?" Harmon said, naturally surprised. "Then why—"

Repeating the lie he told the FBI agent, DeMarco said, "I'm an errand boy, a lawyer who does odd jobs for the legislators when the job isn't important enough to use their own staffs. I was just told to see what was happening with the investigation because it appears to have gone cold."

"Well, it really hasn't," Harmon said. "But—"

DeMarco interrupted him. "You see Congress is kind of like high school. You got over four hundred people, and they form up into little mean girl cliques and fight with each other. You know: the ultra-progressives in one corner, the hard-core righties in another, and they go around starting rumors and bad-mouthing people they don't like in the press. Well, one rumor is that a few congressmen had been invited to Cartwright's parties and some of their so-called colleagues are hoping they'll be named and get creamed in the press. In fact, one rumor is that the two men who had sex with Tracy Woods were congressmen, although there's nothing to support that. So, anyway, all I was told to do was see what's happening with the investigation and if you're any closer to catching whoever killed the man."

Harmon said, "First of all, and like I've told the media repeatedly, I don't have any evidence to show that Cartwright's murder had anything to do with Tracy Woods or Cartwright's sex parties or anything like that. Cartwright was a rich guy who lived out in the woods and a couple of pros decided to rob him."

"Why do you say they were pros?"

"Because they knew how to use explosives to blow open his safe and his front door. Your average junkie home invader doesn't have those kinds of skills. And also because they didn't leave any useful evidence behind."

"So what have you done to catch them?"

Harmon said, "Everything you'd expect. We did ballistics tests, so we'll be able to identify the guns they used if we find them. We tested the explosives, and they were military-grade, so we've contacted every military base within five hundred miles of here to see if any of them are missing plastic explosives and detonators. We interviewed all of Cartwright's staff to see what they might know, but none of them were there the night he was killed and didn't know anything. We've contacted pawnshops and known fences to see if any of his stuff was sold to them. Cartwright didn't have any security cameras at his place, so we looked at cameras his neighbors had and cameras in stores on the roads going to Cartwright's house, to see if we could spot anybody who looked suspicious. The other thing you gotta understand—and I'm not apologizing for this at all—is that at the time Cartwright was killed, he wasn't our top priority."

"What was?" DeMarco said.

"Little Amy Lee."

"Who's—"

"You must have heard about Little Amy. She was this beautiful nine-year-old child who disappeared a few days before Cartwright was killed, and then the poor girl's body was found. Well, the people in Prince William County cared a whole lot more about Little Amy than they did about some rich pervert, and I had about ninety percent of my force focused on finding out what happened to her. That doesn't mean we didn't investigate Cartwright's murder, but like I said, it wasn't my top priority."

"Did you ever find out who killed Amy?" DeMarco said.

"Yeah. It turned out to be some semi-retarded kid who lived a few miles from Amy's house. The kid's parents knew he did it, but they covered for him as best they could, but we eventually got him. And his parents. Breaks my heart every time I think about that poor child."

"So where do things stand with the Cartwright investigation?"

"The case is still open, but right now mostly what we're doing is staying in touch with other law enforcement agencies to see if any similar home invasions have happened. You know, guys breaking into some super-rich guy's place using explosives, killing the homeowners, but so far have struck out. I mean, there've been a bunch of other home invasions all over the country since Cartwright was killed, but most of those were done by addicts breaking into places near where they live, and the cops caught almost all of them. But that's what we're focused on now, hoping these guys will act again, and when they do, leave some evidence behind."

"Did you ask the FBI for help?"

"Well, yeah. I mean, I didn't ask them to take over the case, but I asked if their investigation into Cartwright for the sex-trafficking thing pointed to anyone who might have killed him, and they said no. To tell you the truth, I got the impression the FBI wasn't all that interested in who killed Cartwright. They were just glad that he was dead so they wouldn't have to follow through with trying to prosecute him for the Woods girl."

DeMarco said, "I'm just curious, Chief, but has anyone with serious political clout, like any of the big shots rumored to have attended Cartwright's parties, shown any interest in the murder investigation?"

What DeMarco wanted to ask was if Eric Doyle had shown any interest in the case but couldn't figure out a way to bring Doyle's name into the discussion.

Harmon said, "No. I personally don't think that anyone important cares that Cartwright is dead, and I suspect that the people who socialized with him would like to see the media forget the man ever existed."

Which was exactly the same thing that Agent Burton had said.

DeMarco thanked Harmon for his time, said he'd pass on what he'd learned to the legislators who'd sent him, and left his office thinking that meeting with the man had been a waste of time.

———◦◦◦———

As DeMarco was about to exit the police station, a voice called out, "Hold on, Mr. DeMarco."

He turned to see the young uniformed officer, Adams, who'd been sitting at the front desk when he entered the station. She was walking toward him. When she reached him, she smiled and said, "You forgot this," and handed him a thin magazine with a uniformed police officer on the cover. Without thinking about it, he took it from her, and she whispered, "You need to look inside that."

10

Harmon snatched up the phone on his desk and made a call.

"This is the chief. Where are you at right now?"

"Sittin' in my office. I was just about to—"

"Shut up. There's a guy who just left my office. He's wearing a dark suit, slicked-back hair, cleft in his chin. Get your ass down to the lobby, run down the stairs, and follow him when he leaves the building. And make damn sure he doesn't spot you."

"Yes, sir."

Bobby Cooper worked narcotics. He spent most of his time these days trying to track down dealers killing the local addicts with fentanyl-laced opioids. He had no idea why the chief wanted him to follow this guy. Nor did he know why the chief had picked him, other than the fact that he'd been a detective for ten years and the chief had seen him a few minutes ago and knew he was in the building.

Cooper got to the lobby just in time to see a man with dark hair, wearing a dark suit, go out the door. He looked around and didn't see anyone else wearing a suit. He followed him out the door and watched him walk to a car parked on the street about halfway down the block and toss his suit jacket onto the back seat.

Cooper hustled across the street to the lot where his car was parked, started the engine, then just sat there waiting for the guy, whoever he was, to take off. It was a good thing he'd filled up the tank on his way to work that morning.

After talking to Cooper, Harmon made another call, which, not surprisingly, went to voicemail. He left a message saying, "Mr. Doyle, this is Chief Harmon. Give me a call when you can. A lawyer named DeMarco, who works for Congress, just came to see me. He was asking questions about the Cartwright investigation, and I thought that maybe you'd like to know."

When Brandon Cartwright was murdered, Harmon had been surprised to get a call from the president's national security advisor. Well, *surprised* wasn't the right word. The right word was *shocked*.

Doyle had started off by saying, "Chief, I know this is going to seem a little strange to you, but I'd like to be kept abreast of the Cartwright investigation. As I'm sure you know, there's been a lot of talk in the media about Cartwright having sex parties with important people and I suspect that those rumors are true. The thing is, some of the people who socialized with Cartwright do things that have an impact on national security. Like one guy, he's a member of the Saudi royal family and he's involved in oil production over there. Another guy, he's on the board of directors of the World Bank, which has a significant role in global economic policy.

"Now, I don't know about you, Chief, but I don't really give a damn if these people were having sex with each other or with hookers or with whoever else Cartwright invited to his parties. They were consenting adults. Well, not the Woods girl, but all the rest of them. So I don't care who these people had sex with, but if your investigation points to anyone specific, I'd like to know right away so I can decide if the administration needs to take any sort of action. You get me, Chief?"

"Uh, yes, sir."

"And the other thing is, I don't want to see people get smeared in the press just because they knew Cartwright as that could also cause the administration problems. You see what I'm saying here, Chief? I'd like to see your investigation closed as quickly and quietly as possible without dragging a lot of important, innocent people into it for no good reason and only ask that you keep me informed so I can take action on the president's behalf if necessary."

"Yes, sir, I can do that," Harmon said.

"Now don't misunderstand me, Chief. If you identify whoever killed Cartwright, no matter who it is, then of course you should arrest that person. I just want a heads-up first. Okay?"

"Yes, sir," Harmon had said. But he knew that Doyle was asking for more than a heads-up. He was saying that he didn't give a damn who killed Cartwright and to make the case go away without impugning people the president or Doyle cared about.

"Good," Doyle said. "By the way, Chief, I know that you ran for Congress a couple years ago. Well, sir, I also know that you're the type of man the president would like to see up there on the Hill. The man currently representing your district is, well, let's say not impressive."

Doyle was saying: *You play ball, and you might get invited to the big dance.*

"Sir, if you don't mind me asking, is the president aware of this phone call?"

"Of course not," Doyle said. "The president doesn't get involved in things like this. He has no idea I'm talking to you. But, Chief, if you do decide to run for Congress again, I know my boss will be there for you."

Doyle called Harmon back an hour after DeMarco left his office. Without saying *Hello* or *How you doin', Chief?* or anything else, he asked: "So what did this lawyer want?"

"He said he wanted to know about the status of the investigation. Said a few folks in Congress were wondering where things stood. But there was something off about the guy. I mean, if some congressman wanted to know something, why wouldn't he just call me and ask? Anyway, I told one of my detectives to follow DeMarco after he left. I wanted to see where he was going next and see if I could figure out what he was up to."

There was a brief pause before Doyle said, "I really appreciate you taking that sort of initiative, Chief. I knew I could count on you. I'm going to do some research into Mr. DeMarco, and while I'm doing that, I want you to keep me informed of what he's doing."

"Yes, sir."

11

DeMarco tossed his suit jacket onto the back seat of his car and then got behind the wheel. The magazine that Adams had handed him was a brochure that was similar to what was on the Prince William County Police Department's website, which he'd already looked at. It contained information about the force, how it was organized, the number of cops, the wide area the department patrolled, and recent crime-busting accomplishments. Inside the magazine was a folded sheet of plain copy paper. DeMarco unfolded it and read:

If you really want to know what's going on with the Cartwright investigation, you need to talk to me. Call me after six today, followed by a phone number.

DeMarco glanced at his watch. It was only noon, and he had six hours to kill before he could call Adams. He decided that after he had lunch, he'd go see the woman who had started everything: Tracy Woods. She lived in Manassas, thirty minutes away from Woodbridge.

He figured he probably wouldn't spend more than an hour talking to Woods and then he didn't know what he'd do for the rest of the afternoon. He could go home and work on his fence for a while, then drive back, but that seemed like too much of a hassle. He normally kept his golf clubs in the trunk of his car, and if they'd been there, he would have killed some time at a driving range. Unfortunately, he'd taken his clubs out of the trunk the other day when he went to buy the bags of cement he needed for his fence and forgot to put them back in the trunk before driving to Woodbridge. Anyway, he'd have a long, slow lunch, go talk to Woods, find some way to kill a few hours afterward, then call Adams. He really was curious about what the woman had to say.

Agent Burton had called Tracy Woods "trailer park white trash" and she actually did live in a trailer park. He'd found her address using one of those online people search engines where you could invade a person's privacy for only $9.95.

Tracy's trailer was about thirty feet long and had dirty white aluminum siding and a moss-covered roof. It sat on cinder blocks and the steps leading to the door were also made of cinder blocks. In front of the trailer was a weed patch that served as Tracy's front yard. On it were two folding plastic lawn chairs, a coffee can filled with cigarette butts, and half a dozen empty beer cans lying on the ground. Off to one side was a red Ford Focus with a dented rear fender and gray duct tape over a broken taillight.

He knocked on the door of the trailer. He could hear a television inside. A moment later, Tracy opened the door. Frowning, she said, "Who are you? If you're from that collection agency that called about—"

Tracy was short and broad. She had a pug nose and small eyes set a bit too close together. She was wearing shorts that revealed two thick thighs and a yellow tank top containing heavy breasts and exposing a roll of fat where the tank top met the waistband of her shorts. Her hair was dyed blond with dark roots showing. DeMarco could see that she'd probably been pretty when she was younger, when her face had been thinner and she'd weighed less, but now no one would call her pretty and she looked older than her nineteen years. If he'd been asked to guess her age, he would have said she was in her mid-twenties.

"I'm not from a collection agency. My name is DeMarco. I'm an investigator for Congress." He showed Tracy his congressional ID.

"Congress?" Tracy said. "What the hell do you want with me?"

"There are some members of Congress who are still interested in the Brandon Cartwright sex-trafficking case because it involved sex with a minor, which, of course, is despicable. But the case appears to have reached a dead end when Mr. Cartwright was killed."

"No shit," Tracy said, sounding bitter.

"Anyway, these members of Congress asked me to review what happened to you to see if anything else can be done. So can I talk to you?"

"Yeah, you bet," Tracy said.

It occurred to DeMarco that Tracy had had her fifteen minutes of fame when she was interviewed on Fox and talked about having attended one of Brandon Cartwright's orgies when she was fifteen. And if Cartwright had lived and his case had gone to trial, Tracy would have appeared as a witness—and would again be in the spotlight and maybe be able to leverage her courtroom appearance into another paid interview or two. But with Cartwright dead, there would be no trial and no one cared about Tracy. On the other hand, if Tracy could somehow be useful in solving Cartwright's murder or could come up with additional information about the two men who'd had sex with her, then maybe someone would take an interest in her again. So DeMarco wasn't surprised that Tracy was willing to talk to him.

The interior of the trailer was what DeMarco had expected after seeing the exterior: a small sitting area with a stained beige couch pointed at a TV with a twenty-five-inch screen, the couch covered with clothes Tracy had tossed there. There were dirty dishes on the coffee table in front of the couch and more dirty dishes in the kitchen sink. On the floor near the refrigerator was a cat's litter box that DeMarco could smell from ten feet away, but he didn't see a cat. At the rear of the trailer was an unmade bed. Tracy turned off the television that had been tuned to a talk show and pointed DeMarco to one of two chairs near a small dining table. She didn't bother to clear the plates and beer cans off the table.

She lit a cigarette and said, "So. What do you wanna know?"

DeMarco said, "According to the police, Cartwright was most likely killed during a home invasion. Whoever killed him knew he was rich and broke into a safe and took whatever was in it and probably anything else of value they could find. But another possibility is that someone killed him to keep him from talking about the people who had sex with you when you were fifteen."

"Yeah, I thought about that," Tracy said, tapping the ash from her cigarette into one of the empty beer cans.

"What I'm hoping is that you might have some information that might point to one of those people. Now, I realize that the FBI has already questioned you extensively—"

"That's for damn sure," Tracy said.

"—but I was hoping that maybe since then you've been able to recall something new."

"Like what?"

"You told the FBI the two men who had sex with you were older. About how old?"

"I'd guess around fifty or so."

The president and Eric Doyle were both *around fifty or so.*

"You also told the FBI there wasn't anything distinctive about the two men, like tattoos or scars, but did either of them have an accent?"

The president had been raised in Texas and had a bit of a Texas twang, which became more noticeable if he was speaking to a crowd from his home state or trying to make folks believe that he hadn't come from a privileged background and gone to Harvard.

"The FBI guy already asked me that," Tracy said. "They just sounded like ordinary Americans. Didn't have a Southern accent or a New York accent or a foreign accent or any other kind of accent. They were just a couple of old, flabby white guys who I suspect had to use Viagra to get it up. One guy was bald, the other wasn't. He had this sort of wiry red hair. One guy was heavier than the other, one guy was taller than the other. They had ordinary-sized dicks and they were circumcised. There just wasn't anything about them that stuck out." Tracy laughed. "Well, except for their dicks."

DeMarco was thinking that pretty much eliminated Eric Doyle and the president, neither of whom was bald or flabby, nor did either of them have red hair.

"The FBI told me that you were"—he didn't want to use the word *recruited*—"that you were initially approached by a woman at the court-house here in Manassas. Is that true?"

"Yeah, I got caught trying to steal a cell phone out of the Best Buy and they made a big fuckin' deal out of it. So I had to go to court, where some bitch judge wagged her finger at me. She couldn't do much else since I was a juvenile. Anyway, while I'm sittin' there, waiting, some girl walks up to me. She was older than me, maybe twenty-five. And good-looking. I mean, *really* good-looking, like a model. I figured out later she might be some kind of call girl but she sure as shit didn't look like the hos hanging around the truck stop, I can tell you that. Anyway, she flat out asks me if I'd be interested in partying for money. I said, 'Maybe. How much we talkin' about?' and she says, 'Like, a thousand bucks,' and I said, 'You gotta be shittin' me.' She asks if she can take my picture and I said, 'Sure.' For a grand, I'd been willing to strip naked right there in the courthouse. So she takes my picture and asks for my phone number and says if the people she works with are interested, someone will give me a call.

"A couple days later, a woman calls. She said she was an *associate* of the woman who talked to me at the courthouse. She asks again if I'd be willing to party for a grand and I said, 'Hell yeah.' The woman said she liked my looks but first she needed to check me out. She asked for my Social Security number and my birth date and my parents' names and where I went to school. I was still going to school then. I'm thinking, 'Maybe it's a scam to steal my identity,' then decided, 'Fuck it, who cares if it is?' So I told her what she wanted to know."

Burton had already told DeMarco all this, but he wanted to hear Tracy's version of the story to see if he could learn anything new and didn't interrupt her.

Tracy said, "A day or so later, the same woman calls me back. And before you ask, she never gave me a name. She tells me, if I'm still interested, to dress up in something simple, something that makes me look young, not sexy. Like, not a low-cut blouse or real short skirt, just a normal dress or a skirt and a plain white blouse and not too much makeup. I said okay and she tells me to be waiting out in front of the Applebee's at nine and a guy driving a limo would pick me up."

DeMarco said, "Weren't you worried about someone abducting you?"

"A little, but we're talking a thousand bucks. Anyway, the limo driver takes me to this mansion. There's a woman there, she's maybe forty, and she had this really cute short haircut that she probably paid a couple hundred for at some salon. I could tell by her voice she was the one who'd talked to me on the phone. She looks me over and tells me I got on too much eye shadow and takes me to a bathroom to scrub it off. Then she tells me I'll have to wait a little while, gives me a drink, tells me to help myself if I want another, and leaves me alone. She comes back a bit later, takes me to a bedroom, and a little while after that these two guys in masks show up. Do you want to hear what they did to me?"

"No, that's okay," DeMarco said.

"Well, that old FBI guy wanted every fuckin' detail, and he recorded it all. I think he kinda got off on hearin' about it. Anyway, after they finished with me, they left, and the woman comes back and takes me down to the limo. She tells me she might give me a call again, but then she never did. She also told me to keep my mouth shut about what happened or I'd regret it. This woman, she was, you know, sophisticated, sounded educated, like she came from money, but when she said that, I gotta tell you, she scared me."

DeMarco asked, "How did you know you were at Cartwright's house? You told the FBI you never saw Cartwright that night."

"I didn't. But have you seen his house?"

"No, not yet."

One of the things he'd do to kill some time before calling Adams was drive by Cartwright's place.

Tracy said, "Well, I'd never seen anything like it in my life. But I didn't know it was his house at the time. The limo driver took me there in the dark and we drove all over the countryside and I didn't even know where I was. But when we got to the house, we went through this big black iron gate that opened automatically and then drove up this long, curvy driveway and I could see the outside of the house because it was all lit up. It was fuckin' enormous and had these white columns in front and this big chandelier hanging over the front door and off to one side there was this fountain shootin' water into the air. Well, about three years later, I'm at the nail place one day, having my nails done—"

DeMarco noticed then that Tracy's bright red fingernails extended about an inch beyond the end of her fingers and he wondered how she could button a shirt with nails that long.

"—and on the TV, they showed Cartwright, although I didn't know it was him, walking some woman through his house, pointing out all these paintings he had. I wasn't really paying all that much attention, but then they showed the outside of the house, and I recognized it. The same big gate and the white columns and the chandelier over the door and the fountain off to one side. Like I said, this was, like, three years after what, you know, happened to me. And a couple of weeks later there was this story on TV about some shitbag congressman, Matt somebody down in Florida, being in trouble for having sex with a seventeen-year-old. And that's when I thought about telling what happened to me." She stopped and said, "I am a victim, you know. What those people did wasn't right, taking advantage of me when I was so young."

"So that's when you got ahold of Fox and told them about being taken to Cartwright's mansion?"

"Yeah."

DeMarco knew he should be feeling some compassion toward her. She really was a victim, but she'd become one long before she was fifteen. According to Burton, she'd been raised without a father and by an alcoholic who'd been a prostitute. She'd most likely been ignored and neglected as a child, and it was no wonder she became her mother and started selling herself for sex as a teenager. Her life story was a tragedy. *She* was a tragedy.

Tracy was still talking. She said, "And after I went on Fox, then the FBI got involved and I was interviewed a bunch of times and they eventually arrested Cartwright but then someone goes and kills the son of a bitch before they could hold a trial."

"One last thing," DeMarco said. He took out his phone and showed her a photo of Eric Doyle that he'd found online. "Do you recognize this man?"

"No. Who is he?"

DeMarco didn't answer the question. He said, "Try to imagine him wearing a mask."

"He's not one of the guys who fucked me, if that's what you're asking. I told you one was bald and the other had this wiry sort of red hair and it was thin. So who's the guy?"

"If you don't recognize him, it doesn't matter."

"So what's going to happen with me?"

DeMarco shrugged. "Because Cartwright's dead, probably nothing is going to happen when it comes to you. If you could identify anyone who worked for him, like the woman who recruited you, then maybe there'd be a case of some kind. But because you can't, well—"

"So I just go on livin' in this dump? The only reason I'm not homeless is I inherited this shithole trailer from my mother. I need money."

DeMarco thought for a second about saying, 'Well, you could stop drinking, get your high school degree, and get a job'—but didn't. He wasn't a social worker, and he was sure nothing he could say would change the vector of Tracy Woods's life.

12

Cooper called Harmon. He said, "Chief, that guy's at a trailer park on Wellington Road, south of Manassas. He's talking to some chubby blonde. He knocked on her door and she let him in and I saw her. But I don't know who the woman is. I'm going to see if I can get a phone number for whoever manages this park and find out."

"No, don't bother doing that," Harmon said. "I know who she is."

DeMarco was visiting Tracy Woods.

Harmon said, "Just stick with him and call me when you have something new to report."

"Yes, sir," Cooper said.

Harmon sent a text to Doyle saying: *DeMarco is talking to Tracy Woods right now. I've told my guy to stick with him after he leaves her place.*

Doyle texted back: *Good.*

Doyle had never heard of DeMarco, so he told his deputy to find out who he was, but to do so discreetly.

His deputy was a woman named Kristin Albright. She was six foot four—she'd played basketball in college—and Doyle didn't like looking up at her. She was three inches taller than he was. But he'd hired her because she was bright and ambitious, would work until she dropped, and was very good at her job. She was also ex-Army, like Doyle, and had the same attitude that he did when it came to dealing with the country's enemies. She'd spent most of her twenty-year career at the Pentagon, the last ten years with the Defense Intelligence Agency, and had been a lieutenant colonel when she retired.

Albright was back in his office half an hour later. She said, "This guy, DeMarco, is interesting. He's a GS-13 lawyer who works for Congress. According to his position description on file with the OPM, he provides services to legislators on an ad hoc basis, meaning, I guess, if some congressman needs a free in-house lawyer, he can call on DeMarco. And DeMarco has a law degree, although he's never practiced law. He's single. He was married but has been divorced for a number of years. He has no criminal record. He never served in the military. He's paying the mortgage on a town house in Georgetown and his finances are about what you'd expect for a GS-13. He's not rich. Where it gets interesting is that a few years ago the Republican minority whip at the time, a guy named Lyle Canton, was killed by a U.S. Capitol cop. Do you remember that?"

"Yeah, I remember but I didn't follow the case. I think I was in Afghanistan when it happened."

"Well, DeMarco was arrested for killing Canton. It turned out he was framed and, like I said, a Capitol cop killed Canton but because of all the interest in the case, the media learned that DeMarco is really John Mahoney's guy. He's Mahoney's fixer."

"Mahoney?"

"Yeah. But Mahoney and DeMarco have always denied that they had any connection whatsoever, and DeMarco's not a member of Mahoney's staff, so make of that what you will."

"Mahoney," Doyle said again. *Son of a bitch.*

"One final thing," Albright said. "DeMarco's father was a guy named Gino and he worked for the Mafia up in New York."

"The Mafia?"

"Yes, sir. Gino DeMarco was an honest-to-God Mafia button man. He's dead now. He was killed. But I didn't find anything to show that DeMarco has anything to do with organized crime, and his father was killed when he was in college. So that's about it. You want me to dig deeper?"

"No."

"You want to tell me why you're interested in this guy?"

"No."

—◆—

Doyle looked out a window and noticed there was a protest going on in Lafayette Square, the park directly across the street from the White House. There was always a protest taking place in the square, citizens exercising their First Amendment rights, expressing their displeasure with whatever the president was doing that displeased them. Today about twenty people had gathered, holding signs over their heads, some clown yelling into a bullhorn, a few bored cops looking on. Doyle couldn't hear what the speaker was saying through the bulletproof glass of his windows, and he couldn't read the lettering on the signs, but if he had his way, the cops would fire hose the bastards to drive them off.

What the hell was going on? Why would Mahoney's fixer be running around and talking to people like Tracy Woods and asking the cops in

Woodbridge about Cartwright's murder? That goddamn Mahoney had been a thorn in his side ever since he was appointed as the national security advisor. And if Mahoney found out he had had anything to do with Cartwright's death, that could be a problem—but how would Mahoney even know there was a connection between him and Cartwright? Goddamnit, this didn't make sense. He needed to find out what was going on here.

He stood a moment longer, glaring at the protesters, then took out one of the three burner phones he carried in his briefcase and dialed a number.

He said, "I want you and Burkhart to head toward Manassas right away. There's a man named DeMarco who works for Congress that's interested in the Cartwright case. Right now, he's being tailed by a cop. I want you to take over following him. When I know where he's at, I'll text you a location and whatever other information you'll need. Do you understand?"

"Yes, sir," Shaw said.

———◆◆◆———

Doyle had met Shaw and Burkhart in the Army. They'd been members of a Special Forces team assigned to his command. And like all the Special Forces guys, they were superbly trained, gung-ho killers, and if you pointed them at an enemy, God help the enemy. When Doyle had been in the Army, he'd been a good commanding officer and had gone into the field with his troops numerous times before he got his general's stars. To Shaw and Burkhart, a couple kids raised in foster homes, he became a father figure.

When he started the security company that made him rich, Shaw and Burkhart mustered out of the military and applied for jobs. He hired them immediately. He knew they were men he could count on. The first time he'd used them for something out of the ordinary was when his company was being investigated in Afghanistan for killing a

couple of civilians. Kids actually. Doyle's mercenaries had been guarding
a convoy that was attacked by the Taliban, and—in addition to killing the attackers—they killed two teenage boys who'd been innocent
bystanders. The boys were shot because they were standing nearby, and
Doyle's men were in a killing frenzy and the boys looked like the guys
who'd attacked the convoy. Their deaths should have been dismissed as
unfortunate collateral damage, but a tenacious Afghan prosecutor got it
into his head that Doyle's company should be held accountable and the
men who'd killed the boys should be prosecuted for murder. And when
the prosecutor wouldn't be reasonable and accept the bribe he'd been
offered, Doyle told Shaw and Burkhart that the prosecutor had to go.
Yes, sir, they said. If Doyle said the prosecutor was an enemy, that was
all they needed to know. It probably helped that the prosecutor was an
Afghan. To Shaw and Burkhart, after their experience in the country as
soldiers, there was no such thing as a good Afghan.

The second time he used them, however, didn't involve a foreigner. It
was an accountant at the Pentagon digging into a contract that Doyle's
company had been awarded, and he'd been about to blow the whistle
on bribes that had been paid and some "irregularities" when it came to
billing. Doyle himself could have gone to jail. So he went to Shaw and
Burkhart, explained the situation and the jeopardy he faced. They were
loyal to him and wanted to please him. They also sincerely believed that
if something was bad for him, it was bad for the country.

Shaw and Burkhart were patriots—and they did as he asked. Doyle, to
show his appreciation, rewarded them with bonuses and pay raises and
perks not given to their coworkers. Years passed, his company thrived,
and he had to use Shaw and Burkhart a couple of other times when he
had problems that couldn't be solved by money and lawyers, and when
he became the president's national security advisor, they remained with
his company but were available when he needed them.

He'd needed them for Cartwright.

And now he needed them again.

———— ❖ ————

DeMarco drove past Cartwright's mansion and saw the big wrought iron gate, but that was about all he could see because of the stone wall surrounding the place. Now, what the hell was he going to do until it was time to call Adams?

———— ❖ ————

Cooper fell in behind the guy after he left the trailer park and watched as he drove slowly past Brandon Cartwright's mansion. Then he headed north and half an hour later pulled into the Manassas National Battlefield Park and parked in the lot by the visitors' center.

He wished he knew who the man was and why Harmon wanted him followed.

Half an hour after he entered the visitors' center, he came out and started walking around, looking at the plaques posted around the park, the ones giving the history of the two battles that had been fought there.

Cooper decided he should call the chief again. He said, "Boss, he's at the Manassas Battlefield."

"What's he doing there?"

"As best I can tell, just being a tourist. He went in the visitor center and now he's just walking around."

"Is he by himself?"

"Yes, sir."

"Stay with him. I'll get back to you."

Cooper hoped the guy was going to be there for a while because he was hungry and needed to piss so bad, his bladder was about to burst. He went inside the visitors' center, used the restroom, then grabbed a hot dog and walked back outside, eating the hot dog. The guy he'd been following was standing a couple hundred yards away, near an old cannon.

— ❈ —

Doyle received a text. It was from Harmon. It said: *He's at the Manassas Civil War Battlefield. He appears to be sightseeing, acting like a tourist. My guy's still on him.*

Doyle looked at his watch. Shaw and Burkhart must be close to Manassas by now.

He texted Shaw. *Head to the Manassas Battlefield Park. Text me when you get there.*

He called Albright and told his deputy, "Find me a photo of DeMarco ASAP and text it to me. Get one from the DMV or whoever makes the badges for Congress."

"Yes, sir."

Fifteen minutes later he had DeMarco's photo. Five minutes after that, Shaw texted him. *We're at the battlefield.*

Stand by, Doyle texted back.

Doyle called Harmon. He said, "Call the guy you have following DeMarco and find out where he is right now. Put me on hold while you make the call."

Harmon called Cooper. "Where's the man you're following?"

"Still here at the Battlefield. He's just walkin' around."

Harmon got back on the line with Doyle and said, "He's still at the battlefield."

"Tell your guy to give you the make and model of DeMarco's car and his license plate number. Put me on hold again."

Two minutes later, Harmon was back on with Doyle. "He's driving a black four-door Toyota Camry with D.C. plates. Here's the number."

Doyle wrote down the plate number, then said, "Chief, tell your guy he can stop tailing DeMarco. Tell him to go back to the station or go home or whatever. And, Chief, I really appreciate your help on this. I won't forget it."

"Well, if there's anything else I can do, sir, you just let me know."

Doyle texted Shaw DeMarco's photo and the information on his car. Then he called Shaw and said, "He's at the battlefield. Find his car and follow him when he leaves and then keep me posted."

"Yes, sir," Shaw said.

13

DeMarco had no interest whatsoever in the Civil War. All the years he'd lived in D.C., he'd never taken the time to drive to Gettysburg or Bull Run, a creek flowing near Manassas. As far as he was concerned, the Civil War was a blight on the country's history and there was nothing about it worth celebrating. He didn't think renaming military bases named for Leonidas Polk, John Bell Hood, and Braxton Bragg was worth the expense, as you probably couldn't find a hundred people in the country who knew they were Confederate generals a hundred and sixty years ago, but he was bewildered by those who acted as if the Confederacy and those who fought for it were somehow noble. It pissed him off every time he saw a Confederate flag in the back window of some redneck's pickup.

That day he learned that two battles had been fought at Manassas in the early stages of the war, and as best he could tell, about twenty thousand men were killed and maimed. The number of casualties was relatively low compared to later battles, as both armies were just learning how to become really proficient at killing each other. During the first battle, spectators, including mothers and their children, had picnicked nearby and watched the battle as if it had been a sporting event. He learned that Thomas Jackson, famously nicknamed Stonewall for fending off a Union attack, was later killed when he was accidentally shot by his own soldiers. Mostly he was amazed by the historians who'd taken the time to research and document every detail related to the two battles.

As he stood next to an old cannon, looking out at a grassy field, he tried to imagine young men running across it, being cut down by musket balls and cannonballs, screaming as they lay there dying—and wished he'd remembered to put his golf clubs in the trunk of his car so he could be doing something he enjoyed.

He left the battlefield, stopped for an early dinner at a place called Logan's Roadhouse, where he had shrimp and steak for dinner, and where he couldn't believe he watched a cornhole match on a television in the bar. Cornhole is a game where beanbags are tossed at a board with a hole in it, the winner being the team who gets the most beanbags in the hole. DeMarco had thought it was a game only played by kids and other amateurs at backyard parties, and he'd had no idea that there were professional cornhole players and leagues and a national championship and that some events were televised. The guys he was watching on TV didn't look like world-class athletes to him, but then, how athletic do you have to be to toss a beanbag? They looked like guys who probably spent a good deal of time sitting on barstools, drinking beer, talking cornhole strategy, which sounded to him like a training program he could handle and much better than one involving running laps and lifting weights.

At six, he called Darcy Adams.

He said, "It's Joe DeMarco. I'd like to hear what you have to say, but I don't want to do it over the phone."

He didn't want the woman hanging up on him in case he started asking questions she didn't want to answer.

She said, "That's fine. But I don't want to meet anyplace in Wood-bridge. I live here and a lot of people know me."

"So where would you like to meet? And pick someplace in the direction of D.C., because I'm planning to head back there after we talk."

The phone went silent for a moment.

"There's a bar called the Hideout on Pohick Road near Fort Belvoir. It's about twenty minutes from Woodbridge and mostly guys from the military base go there and not folks I know. And it's in Fairfax County, so it's out of the department's jurisdiction. I'll be there at seven."

DeMarco arrived at the Hideout a little before seven, looked around for Adams, and didn't see her. He got a beer from the bar and took a seat at a table that didn't have anyone sitting near it.

The bar was a typical bar: small dance floor, a couple of pool tables, muted television sets over the bar tuned to sporting events, country western music coming out of invisible speakers, mismatched tables and chairs around the dance floor. It would probably hold a hundred and fifty people on a crowded Saturday night. At seven on a weeknight, there were maybe twenty people in the place, seventy-five percent of them young, fit-looking young men with short hair that DeMarco suspected were from Fort Belvoir.

Fort Belvoir, by the way, was not your average military base. It employed about twice as many workers as the Pentagon, was the largest employer in Fairfax County, Virginia, and served as the headquarters for a number of military commands including the United States Army Intelligence and Security Command, the United States Army Military Intelligence Readiness Command, the National Geospatial-Intelligence Agency, and the National Reconnaissance Office, the outfit that operated the military's spy satellites. In other words, there were a lot of spooks at Fort Belvoir. There were also several regular military combat units, including the Virginia National Guard's 29th Infantry Division and the 249th Engineer Battalion—folks, DeMarco suspected, who might have access to the kind of explosives that blew open Brandon Cartwright's safe.

By seven fifteen, Adams hadn't arrived, and DeMarco was wondering if she'd changed her mind about meeting him, but then she walked in looking harried, as if she'd rushed there trying not to be late. She looked around the bar and DeMarco waved at her, and she headed his way. When he'd seen her at the police station that morning, she'd been wearing a uniform and her hair had been tied back in a bun. Her curly brown hair was loose now, hanging down to her shoulders, and she was wearing skinny jeans and a sleeveless T-shirt exposing well-toned arms. She was a pretty woman and had a nice figure and most of the guys in the bar turned to look at her as she walked across the dance floor.

She sat down across from him and said, "I'm sorry I'm late. I got a three-year-old daughter and she decided to have a meltdown just as I was trying to get out of the house, and it took me a while to settle her down."

DeMarco noticed she wasn't wearing a wedding ring and wondered who was taking care of her daughter but didn't ask.

He said, "That's okay. You want a drink?"

"I could use one, but I better not. The last thing I need is to get stopped by a cop on the way home with booze on my breath. I'll have a Coke."

DeMarco waved at a passing waitress and ordered a Coke. While waiting for the drink, DeMarco said, "What's your first name? Your badge said 'D. Adams.'"

"Darcy."

"Well, Darcy, the first thing I'd like to know is why you decided to talk to me."

"Because there's something seriously wrong with the Cartwright case and because Harmon screwed me over and I'm really pissed about that."

DeMarco wanted to ask her what she thought someone from Congress could do for her but didn't ask because he wanted to hear her story first.

The server brought Darcy's drink and after she departed, Darcy said, "When Cartwright was killed, the case was assigned to a senior detective named Jim Stratton and I was Jim's partner. Well, the first thing that happens is Harmon pulls Jim off the case and says I'm going to have to handle it on my own. Harmon said that Jim was needed on the Little Amy case. You know about Little Amy?"

"Yeah," DeMarco said.

"What Harmon did was bullshit. Half the department was already working Little Amy and it wasn't like they needed another detective, but if they did need one, Harmon should have assigned me and not Jim. I'd only been a detective for a year when Cartwright was killed and there's no way a first-year detective should have been assigned to handle Cartwright, considering who he was and the fact that the suspects were liable to be people richer than God. It was like Harmon didn't want the case solved.

"The other thing is, Harmon keeps telling people that Cartwright was killed in a home invasion by a couple of guys who broke in to steal Cartwright's shit. Well, this wasn't no ordinary home invasion."

"Why do you say that?" DeMarco asked.

"For one thing, Cartwright's house was filled with expensive stuff. Paintings, sterling silver, Rolex watches, that sort of thing. There was one little statue of a rabbit made by some famous artist in Santa Fe I'd never heard of, but one of the CSI guys said it was worth over twenty grand. Now, I don't know what was in Cartwright's safe. Maybe it contained gold bars or cash or jewelry. But what I do know is that whoever broke in left a lot of valuable stuff. The other thing is, Jim, who's ex-military, said it looked to him like an intelligence raid."

"What do you mean by that?"

"You ever see that movie *Zero Dark Thirty*? Where the SEALs blow the door off bin Laden's house in Pakistan, shoot his ass, and then start packing up every computer and cell phone and piece of paper in sight? Well, that's what happened at Cartwright's place. There wasn't one cell phone, computer, or iPad in the house—and I know Cartwright and Margate both had iPads because Cartwright's cook told me. There weren't any flash drives there, no external hard drives for computers, and, on top of that, there wasn't any paper in the house. There was this one file drawer in a desk, the kind of drawer where you'd keep household bills or tax statements or whatever, and the drawer was empty. The guys who killed Cartwright took every piece of paper they could find. They were after *information*, not money, and Jim and I told Harmon this, but he keeps peddling this bullshit to the press that it was your basic home invasion robbery.

"And I'll tell you something else. Maybe whoever hit the place found what they were looking for, but maybe they didn't. I've investigated home invasions where some junkie knucklehead breaks into a house, but what the junkie doesn't do is shoot the homeowner as soon as he's inside. What he does is point a gun at him and maybe smacks him around to make him tell where his cash is hidden. I think what Cartwright's killers planned on doing was making Cartwright give them the combination to his safe, but then they had to kill him because he took a shot at them when they first broke in."

"How do you know that?"

"Because he was lying right beside his bed, like the noise of them blowing open his front door woke him up. Anyway, I think that's why they had to blow the safe, but it makes me wonder if whatever they were looking for might not have been in the safe. And with Cartwright dead, they had no way to ask him, and that's why they had to take everything from the house that might have contained information."

Now, that was interesting, DeMarco thought.

He said, "What did you do to solve the case?"

"Everything I could—that is, everything I could do on my own. The explosive used to blow open the safe was military C-4 shit, so I contacted military bases all over the place to see if any explosives were missing. I submitted the ballistic tests on the bullets that killed Cartwright and Margate to the FBI to see if they had a match to some other crime. I spent hours looking at surveillance camera footage taken from cameras within a five-mile radius of Cartwright's house hoping to spot someone driving around after midnight that looked suspicious, which of course was futile. I contacted Cartwright's insurance company to see if he'd insured shit in his house, like his paintings, and, if he had, if any of the stuff he'd insured was missing. Well, a couple of paintings were missing, and so I checked out pawnshops and suspected fences, but then I found out later that Cartwright had sold the paintings and hadn't gotten around to telling his insurance company. But I still visited every pawnshop within about fifty miles of Manassas to see if anyone had tried to sell any kind of fancy artwork.

"I also talked to the FBI to see where things stood on the sex-trafficking case. I figured two logical suspects for killing Cartwright were the two guys who had sex with Tracy Woods—you know, thinking they might have wanted to permanently shut him up to keep him from blabbing about them. Well, the FBI, some fat-assed old agent named Burton who I suspect couldn't find his own butt with two hands and a flashlight, told me he didn't have any idea who the two guys were. When I asked if I could look at his files, he said, 'Not on your life, honey,' which made me just want to smack him. And by the way, when Harmon learned I'd driven to D.C. to talk to the FBI, he chewed my ass out because I didn't clear it with him first. He told me there was no connection between Cartwright's so-called home invasion and the Woods case and not to talk to the Bureau again."

DeMarco said, "Were you able to identify anyone other than Tracy Woods who'd actually gone to one of Cartwright's orgies?"

"No. According to Cartwright's cook, Cartwright had two different kinds of parties. The cook said she'd be asked to prepare a meal for twenty people, and she'd bring in extra help to serve and tend the bar and clean up afterwards. She was present for these parties and she recognized some of the guests because they were famous. But there was a second kind of party where Cartwright would tell the cook to set up a big buffet table loaded with food and to set up a bar where people could help themselves and then she'd be told to leave. She'd also be told not to come back until after noon the next day to clean things up. I'm guessing these were the sex parties, and Cartwright didn't want her seeing sleeping, naked people lying around his house."

Darcy shook her head. "The thing about Cartwright is I couldn't identify one person who was close to him who could tell me anything about him. Like someone he might have confided in. The only person close to Cartwright was his buddy Margate, who was lying in bed with him before they were both killed. He doesn't have any brothers or sisters. I looked at all the articles written about him and didn't see one person who was identified as Cartwright's best buddy, some guy he'd gone to school with, or someone he hung around with a lot. He knew a million people and he socialized with them, but, like I said, other than Margate, he didn't have a good friend I could talk with to learn more about him.

"I did call a bunch of people that the media said knew Cartwright— you know, all the folks who admitted going to his dinner parties but denied ever being involved in any kind of sex stuff. I called a couple of movie stars—talked to their agents, not them personally—and half a dozen big-shot businessmen, and I couldn't get through to any of them and none of them returned my calls. I even went to see this one senator. He and his wife were in a photo with Cartwright at some party, so I called his office. He didn't return my call, but I found out he has a place on the Potomac not far from here where he keeps a boat and goes on weekends. So I went to see him on my own time, but he wouldn't talk to me. And when Harmon found out I'd gone to see him, he went ballistic, saying who the fuck did I think I was, calling on a United States senator?"

"How did Harmon know you went to see the senator? Did you tell him?"

"No, but he found out somehow. Maybe the senator called him to complain about me. The last thing I did before Harmon pulled me off the case is I went to see the law firm in D.C. that was representing Cartwright for the Tracy Woods thing. I figured that Cartwright's lawyers must've had some kind of defense strategy to keep him from going to jail and one strategy might be naming the two guys who'd had sex with Tracy. What I'm sayin' is, if Cartwright gave those two guys up, maybe he could have cut a deal to keep from doing any time. So I went to see the law firm representing him. I said, 'Since Cartwright's dead, can you help me out here, can you give me any information on the two guys, since maybe they're the ones who had him killed?' Well, this snooty bitch wearing a two-thousand-dollar suit said, 'What planet do you live on? We're not going to tell you anything about a client of ours, living or dead.' Then she flicked her fingers at me—"

Darcy made a flicking motion with her right hand.

"—and said, 'Go away,' like I was some kind of fly buzzin' around her head."

DeMarco laughed but Darcy said, "It wasn't funny. But me going to see the law firm was the last straw for Harmon. Again, I don't know how he found out about it, but he did, and he told me he was taking me off the case and sticking me behind the desk in the lobby. He said he couldn't trust me and wanted me somewhere he could keep his eye on me. He didn't take away my detective's rank or cut my pay because he knew if he did that I would have gone to the union and made a stink, but my career's effectively over with. I'm trying to find a job with some other law enforcement agency, but I live with my mother and she takes care of my daughter when I'm working, so it's got to be a job within a reasonable commute of Woodbridge."

"So who's working the case now that you've been pulled off it?"

"Nobody."

DeMarco was silent for a moment. "Darcy, what are you expecting from me?"

"I don't know exactly. But you work for Congress, and I figured maybe you could do something. I can't go officially complaining to somebody in the county or state government, like the attorney general, because all that would happen is that I'd get fired. But I was thinking that maybe you could talk to somebody, somebody who might care that the way Harmon is handling the Cartwright investigation stinks and, when I tried to do my job, he retaliated against me."

DeMarco liked Adams. She was bright and committed but also naïve. Time would take care of that. DeMarco walked her to her car, thanked her for talking to him, said he'd pass on what she'd told him to the person who'd sent him, a person he couldn't name. He said that if that person decided to do something, he'd let her know. Which was probably a lie.

He never noticed the two guys sitting in a black jeep in the bar's parking lot and he didn't notice them as they followed him back to D.C.

14

The next morning, DeMarco worked on his fence for a couple of hours and finished installing the remaining posts. Once the posts were installed, the next step would be to get two-by-fours to use for fence rails and some six-foot cedar planks and nail 'em all together. While he was mixing the cement and water to pour into the remaining post holes, his thoughts drifted to his father again.

One time, years ago, not long after DeMarco had graduated from college and had just gone to work for Mahoney, DeMarco had gone home to see his mother and accompanied her to a wedding for a girl in the neighborhood. He was standing near the bar at the reception when a small, flat-nosed man walked up to him and said, "Goddamn, I can't believe how much you look like him." The man introduced himself as Tony Vitale.

"Were you one of my father's friends?"

"I wouldn't say a friend. We worked together, but your dad was a guy who kept to himself."

DeMarco, who was always looking for some insight into how his father became a killer, said, "All those stories I used to hear when I was growing up, about what he did for Taliaferro, I always had a hard time believing them. My dad was a good man."

"Oh, the stories are true," Tony said, "but you're right. Your dad was a good man. He wasn't like most of the goombahs Carmine employed." Tony laughed and said, "Including me. He didn't cheat on your mother, he didn't gamble, he wasn't a boozer. He was pretty much what you'd call a family man."

DeMarco responded with "Yeah, except for the fact that he was a killer. If the stories were true."

"Well," Tony said, "I'll tell you something about that. Your dad never killed a civilian."

"What do you mean by *civilian*?"

"I mean someone who wasn't a criminal. There were times when Carmine, who could be an asshole, wanted some civilian popped just because he'd pissed Carmine off or disrespected him or wouldn't pay for protection, but your dad wouldn't do it. Your dad, I guess you'd say, had a code."

DeMarco said, "You have any idea how he got started doing what he did? My mother won't say."

"Yeah," Tony said. "The economy."

"The economy?"

"Yeah. Your dad couldn't get a straight job, so he went to work for Carmine, and one day, when Carmine wanted someone hit—someone who was going to be really tough to hit because he had protection—Carmine offered a lot of money and your dad raised his hand because your mom was pregnant with you at the time and Gino couldn't pay the mortgage. And the guy Carmine wanted taken care of, he was an evil son of a bitch. He was a bad, bad man. But after that first time—" Tony shrugged. "Well, you know how it is, one thing leads to another, then you're stuck."

When the final post was in place, DeMarco decided it was time to get back to work on the assignment Mahoney had given him. But because he couldn't figure out what to do next when it came to Cartwright, he concluded that what he should do was talk to someone smarter than he was.

He showered and then noticed the weather was cool but sunny, not a raindrop in sight. So he put on a golf shirt, a lightweight sweater, khaki pants, and Top-Siders and tossed his golf clubs and his golf shoes in the trunk of his car in case the person he was going to see couldn't come up with something productive for him to do. On the way to her place, he stopped at a Home Depot and ordered the fence boards and two-by-fours and arranged for them to be delivered to his house.

Half an hour later, he parked in the driveway of a stately brick home in McLean, Virginia. The home was worth a couple million bucks and the landscaping was magnificent because the homeowner was a fanatic about her yard. DeMarco had always felt sorry for her gardeners. He walked up to the door and rang the bell, and the door was answered by a tall, lean woman with silver-blond hair. Her cheery greeting was "What do you want?"

Shaw parked half a block away and saw DeMarco go into the house. He told Burkhart, "I'm going to drive by the house. Get the address."

Five minutes later, Shaw had the homeowner's name and texted it to Doyle.

Doyle looked at the text and thought: *What the hell is this bastard up to?*

Last night DeMarco had met with the detective that had been assigned to the Cartwright murder investigation. Shaw and Burkhart knew who she was because Doyle had them follow her for a while after she'd been assigned to the case to see what she was doing and who she was meeting with. He wasn't worried about the detective telling DeMarco anything that could hurt him because the detective didn't know anything, and he knew this because Harmon had kept him apprised of everything she'd done during her investigation.

What he didn't know was *why* DeMarco would have met with her. He supposed DeMarco could have talked to her because he wanted to hear for himself what the lead investigator had to say, but he knew Harmon wouldn't have allowed her to meet with DeMarco or he would have told Doyle that she was meeting with him. Which meant that the detective had gone behind her boss's back. And that, too, was troublesome.

He needed to decide if he should tell Harmon what the detective had done or just keep that information to himself. If he told Harmon, he might fire her, and he didn't want that happening right now. He didn't want the woman running to the media or the police union or doing anything that would shine a spotlight on the Cartwright murder investigation. Anyway, he'd decide later what to do about the detective. What he needed to do now was find out who this woman in McLean was and see if DeMarco meeting with her could be connected to Cartwright.

He called Albright and told her to come to his office.

He handed his deputy the slip of paper on which he'd written the woman's name and address and said, "I need information on this woman."

Albright looked down at the paper and said, "Jesus. Emma."

"You know her?"

"Yeah. She was at the DIA when I was there. You never encountered her when you were in the Army?"

"No."

"Well, I never worked for her directly, but she was a legend at the DIA. I don't know what she did early in her career, but by the time I got there she was running black ops, the kind of ops where even the code names of the operations were classified top secret. And I was told she ran the kind of ops where the Joint Chiefs were kept completely in the dark so if the shit hit the fan, none of it would splatter on the chiefs. I know she speaks Farsi and that she spent a lot of time in the Middle East. She's a striking-looking woman, and I saw her one day walking around the office and asked this one old-timer who she was. I mean, she just *looked* like someone important. He's the one who told me about her running black ops, but he wouldn't tell me anything specific and whatever she did is documented in files that won't see the light of day for fifty years. I don't think even you, in your current position, would be able to look at those files."

"Does she still work for the DIA?"

"No, she retired not long after I got there. Funny thing was, they didn't hold a retirement party for her because she wouldn't allow them to. One day she was there and the next day she was just gone. You want me to see if I can find out what she's doing now?"

"Yes, but do it carefully. I don't want to advertise the fact that you're researching her."

He thought about asking Albright to see if she could find any connection between Emma and Mahoney but decided not to. He didn't want Albright knowing any more than she already did.

An hour later Albright was back.

"Like I said, she's retired. She didn't get a job after she left the government. She lives with a woman who plays the cello in the National Symphony Orchestra. And she's a lot richer than your typical retired civil servant. She gets a pension but makes most of her income off investments, but I couldn't find out how she got so rich in the first place. She runs in marathons and she volunteers at Walter Reed, helping wounded veterans. One funny thing: her travel history, based on passport data on file with Customs and Border Protection, showed that after she retired, she took trips to Syria, Iran, and Iraq. Those are hardly places you'd go to for a vacation, which makes me wonder if she's totally retired."

Albright paused. "That guy you had me check out yesterday: DeMarco? The only time he ever made the news was when he was arrested for killing Lyle Canton. Well, that's also the only time Emma has ever made the news. Ever. When Canton was killed, she was appointed by the president's chief of staff at the time, a guy who once worked for her, to oversee the FBI's investigation. Think about that. Think about the kind of clout it would have taken to make that happen. Now, I don't know what the link is between her and DeMarco, but there obviously is one. Would you like to tell me what's going on here, boss?"

"No," Doyle said. "But thanks. You did a good job."

Doyle couldn't tell Albright the link between DeMarco and Emma because he had no idea what it could be. All he knew was that some former superspy with political connections was now talking to Mahoney's fixer—and that wasn't good.

15

"What do you want?" Emma said.

DeMarco noticed she was wearing a long-sleeved white shirt that was untucked and an old pair of jeans. Paint was spattered on the shirt: red paint, blue paint, yellow paint, green paint. She was holding a small paint brush, and the hand holding the brush also had paint on it.

DeMarco said, "What are you painting?"

"What do you want?" she said again.

"I want to talk to you about Eric Doyle."

She looked at him for a beat, then said, "Okay. I need to wash my hands. Wait for me on the patio."

DeMarco didn't immediately go to the patio as instructed. He waited for Emma to walk down a hallway and enter a bathroom, then took a quick peek into her office. There was a three-by-three-foot canvas on an easel streaked with the same colors that had been on Emma's shirt and hands. But he couldn't figure out what it was she was painting. It might have been a person's face—that is, if the face was being depicted by Picasso. He wasn't even sure it was a face. He'd always thought that Emma was capable of doing anything and doing it extremely well. It appeared, however, that she wasn't, nor would she ever be, an artist. He also figured that she had to be bored out of her mind if she'd decided to take up a hobby like painting. He scurried out to the patio before she could catch him admiring her artwork.

Sitting on the patio in her backyard, DeMarco was treated to the sight of budding shrubs and delicate flowering trees. Water flowed over the rocks in a man-made stream and into a small pool. The lawn was as lush and green as the fairways at the Masters. Emma couldn't paint but she could garden. Or, to put it differently, she demanded perfection from the gardeners she hired.

She came out of the house holding two glasses of lemonade. She sat down across from DeMarco and handed him a glass. "So, what about Doyle?" she asked. Before DeMarco could answer, she said, "That man poses a significant danger to this country. He's going to get us into a war if the president doesn't quit listening to him."

"Mahoney said exactly the same thing."

"Hmph," Emma said.

Emma despised Mahoney. She thought he was a corrupt, alcoholic, lying womanizer—which he was—and she considered him unfit for any public office. She also disapproved of DeMarco working for him, and disapproved of DeMarco in general, because she thought him to be lazy and unambitious—which he was. But she helped DeMarco out sometimes when he needed help and if she approved of what he was doing. One reason she helped him was the way DeMarco had met her. He happened to be in the wrong place at the right time and he saved her life when two Iranians tried to kill her. Why they'd tried to kill her, she wouldn't say, but because he'd saved her life, she owed him. The second reason was that after doing whatever it was she did at the DIA for so many years, retirement bored her—and he suspected that boredom was a greater motivator than a sense of obligation when it came to helping him.

DeMarco told her about the notes in the president's handwriting that the head of the National Archives had shown Mahoney. He concluded by saying, "Mahoney believes that Cartwright had something that he could use to blackmail the president and when he demanded a pardon, Doyle, acting on the president's behalf, had the man killed."

Emma didn't seem shocked by what he had told her. It was impossible to shock her. She'd seen too much death and destruction—too much deceit, corruption, and treachery—to be shocked by anything. She said, "Is there any evidence to support that accusation other than the notes?"

"Yeah, a little," DeMarco said. "All of it circumstantial."

DeMarco told her about his meetings with FBI agent Burton, the chief of the Prince William County Police Department, Tracy Woods, and Darcy Adams, relaying as much of the conversations as he could remember verbatim, knowing the more he told Emma, the better she'd be able to find a path forward. While he was talking, she closed her eyes and listened without interrupting—and DeMarco felt like Archie Goodwin briefing Nero Wolfe.

DeMarco said, "I think somebody with clout got to Harmon and told him to derail the murder investigation. That could have been Doyle. And the guys that killed Cartwright were most likely military—they had access to military explosives and knew how to use them—and Doyle has a security company that employs those kinds of people. That's the circumstantial evidence. But there's no connection that I've been able to find between Doyle, the president, and Brandon Cartwright. There's no evidence that the president or Doyle even knew Cartwright. Cartwright never visited the White House, no one from the White House ever called him, and no one has ever accused the president of socializing with Cartwright. If the president had ever attended even one of Cartwright's normal dinner parties, much less an orgy, someone would have blabbed that to the media. The only evidence that the president knew Cartwright is this note at the archives.

"Anyway," DeMarco said, "that's where things stand right now, and I don't have a clue what to do next. You got any ideas?"

"Yes," Emma said. "I have two."

When she didn't say anything immediately, he said, "Well, are you going to tell me what they are or am I supposed to guess?"

"Find the woman with the cute haircut and the Jimmy Choos."

Before DeMarco could ask how he was supposed to do that when the FBI couldn't, Emma said, "Someone had to recruit or hire the prostitutes and the young girls and boys Cartwright used for his orgies. Maybe he did it himself, but I doubt it. People like him always have someone else do the work. And it sounds as if this woman who Tracy met at Cartwright's house was the one who recruited people or directed their recruitment. And if she performed that function for Cartwright, she would have been someone close to him, someone he would have trusted completely, and she might be able to tell you if Cartwright had any connection to Doyle or the president."

"But how do I find her?"

"Talk to Cartwright's staff. Burton told you that Cartwright had a cook, a housekeeper, and a gardener, but Burton said he didn't question them because they weren't there the night Tracy Woods was. And Burton wasn't involved in the murder investigation, so he didn't ask the staff any questions related to that. If I'm right about Miss Jimmy Choos, and she was someone close to Cartwright, she might have visited him frequently, like when he was planning his parties, so Cartwright's staff might know who she is."

"Okay," DeMarco said. "What's the second thing?"

"Search Cartwright's house."

"What? Are you out of your mind?"

"I'm intrigued by what the detective said. That the people who killed Cartwright, killed him before they could ask him for the combination to his safe and before they could question him. Now, it's possible that they didn't need to question him and that simply killing him eliminated him as a threat, but I think it's also possible, like that detective suggested, that they didn't find what they were looking for and that's why they took everything from the house that might have contained information. Assuming they got the information they wanted doesn't do you any good. So assume they didn't and search the house."

"And how am I supposed to get into the house to search it?"

"Hell, I don't know, Joe. Figure it out. And after you do, let me know, and if I'm not doing anything more interesting, I might help you search it."

Yeah, Emma was definitely bored.

16

DeMarco called Darcy, waiting until after six, when she wouldn't be at work. When she answered, he could hear a child laughing and another woman saying, "Olivia, you stop that."

Darcy said, "What's going on?"

"I want to talk to Cartwright's staff. I know he had a cook, a house-keeper, and a yardman. Can you text me their names and addresses?"

"Yeah, but why do you want to talk to them?"

DeMarco didn't want to tell her. He said, "It has to do with the Tracy Woods case, not Cartwright's murder. And I can't tell you more than that right now."

"Have you talked to anyone about what Harmon did to me and how he screwed up the investigation?"

"Only my boss," DeMarco said, "but he's not willing to do anything about Harmon until I collect more information."

Darcy didn't say anything.

DeMarco said, "Look, Darcy, I'm on your side, but you're going to have to trust me."

"Okay. I'll text you tomorrow morning. I'll go in early and get the info from the file and you'll have it by seven. But if you learn something pertinent to the murder, you have to tell me."

"I will," DeMarco said.

And maybe he would.

———◆◆◆———

DeMarco decided to start with the cook.

Maria Alvarez lived in a well-maintained Craftsman home in Manassas. The siding appeared to have been painted recently, the lawn was mowed, the bushes were trimmed, and the flower beds were free of weeds. DeMarco had learned online, from Maria's website—he'd been surprised that she had a website—that she had a degree from the Culinary Institute of Virginia in Richmond, that she offered her services as a cook for private dinner parties and catered events like weddings and funerals, and that she provided one-on-one cooking lessons for those in need. She also taught Spanish speakers English and English speakers Spanish. She was quite the entrepreneur, and DeMarco imagined the reason she had these other jobs was that working for Cartwright wouldn't have been a full-time gig, as he'd often been away from his Virginia estate, living and playing elsewhere.

From her Facebook page, he learned that Maria had been born in Puerto Rico but was raised in Richmond, that her husband's name was Raphael, and that he was a diesel engine mechanic. She had three children: a daughter who was a teacher, a daughter who was a nurse, and a son who was an active-duty soldier currently stationed in Germany.

He'd called her before driving down from Washington and lied to her, choosing his words carefully, saying he wanted to ask about her experience catering private dinner parties, implying he was thinking about hosting one. He'd just wanted to make sure she'd be available before driving to Manassas; he hadn't wanted to say that he wanted to talk to her about Cartwright and give her the chance to refuse to meet with him.

He rang her doorbell, and she opened the door saying, "Mr. DeMarco?"

"Yes, ma'am," DeMarco said.

She was a stout woman, one who obviously enjoyed her own cooking. She was in her fifties, had midnight-black hair, thick eyebrows, and a beautiful, welcoming smile. He almost felt bad about lying to her.

She led him to a kitchen, where something that smelled marvelous was bubbling in a pot on the stove. She asked him if he wanted coffee and a pastry, adding that she'd made the pastry herself just that morning. He really did want the pastry but decided he'd better tell her the truth before accepting one.

He said, "Mrs. Alvarez, I—"

"Call me Maria."

"Maria, I may have misled you when I said I wanted to talk about your experience catering dinner parties. You see, I'm from Congress and—"

"Congress?"

"—and I need to talk to you about Brandon Cartwright."

She didn't say anything. She was frowning at him, probably the same frown her children had been treated to when they were growing up and misbehaved. It was an intimidating frown.

"I would have told you that over the phone when I called this morning, but I didn't want to take the chance that you'd refuse to see me. What I need to ask you about is important."

She said, "I don't understand. What's Congress have to do with Mr. Cartwright?"

"I can't get into all the details, but it has to do with Cartwright prostituting that girl Tracy Woods when she was fifteen."

"I'm gonna stop you right there. I never saw any young girls around his house. Never. And I don't believe all that stuff about him having sex parties. Mr. Cartwright was a wonderful man, very generous and kind to me. I would have stopped working for him if I thought any of those stories were true."

DeMarco didn't believe her. She may not have seen teenage girls in Cartwright's house, but Maria had told Darcy about the two types of parties that Cartwright hosted, the ones Maria was present for and the ones where she laid out the food and wasn't present for and told not to come back until noon the next day. She had to have known something fishy was going on, but he suspected she kept working for Cartwright after he was indicted because he paid very well.

DeMarco said, "I believe you. But I still need to ask you a couple of questions."

She was silent for a moment, then said, "You want a cup of coffee?"

"Yes, please." He noticed she didn't offer a pastry. And he suspected she was only offering him coffee to give herself time to think.

She poured them cups of coffee. The coffee was delicious, and he wanted to ask the brand but didn't.

"All I want to know about is a woman you may have encountered while working for Cartwright. This woman has short, dark hair. One witness described her hairstyle as cute and expensive and said that she wore Jimmy Choos, which I guess are also expensive. The witness also said the woman was in her forties, was educated, sophisticated, and well-spoken. The main thing is she would have been a close friend of Cartwright's, someone who visited him at his home on occasions other than the parties you cooked for."

Maria looked downward, sipped her coffee, and didn't say anything.

DeMarco said, "Maria, you're not in any trouble. You didn't break any laws. And right now, I'm the only one asking you questions and I'm not in law enforcement. But if I have to get the FBI involved, then things will get complicated. You might have to hire a lawyer, and lawyers are expensive. And if you lie to the FBI or withhold information, well, then you could be in serious trouble."

She looked at him again. He could tell she was frightened now, and he felt somewhat bad about that.

She finally said, "Her name is Max."

"Max?"

"Her actual name is Maxine, but Mr. Cartwright called her Max."

"What's her last name?"

"Barkley. She was introduced to me as Miss Barkley and that's what I called her."

"Where does she live?"

"I don't know. But not near here. I remember one time she complained about the hotel she was staying at in Washington. I think she lives in New York, but I don't know why I think that. It must have been something I overheard."

"What can you tell me about her?"

Maria shrugged. "Just that she was an old friend of Mr. Cartwright. I remember one time they were laughing about something that happened in school, but I don't know what school, but if she knew him in school, she knew him for a long time. All I know is that when Mr. Cartwright was staying in Virginia, she'd usually show up. Sometimes she stayed at his place; other times she didn't. And like you said, she sounded educated and always wore expensive clothes."

"What did she do when she was visiting Cartwright?"

Maria shrugged again. "She just visited, spent a lot of time talking to him and Mr. Margate. Sometimes she'd sit out by the pool in a bathing suit if the weather was nice. She has a nice figure for a woman her age."

"And what age is that? In her forties, like I was told?"

"She's probably in her fifties, like Mr. Cartwright, but she looks younger. She takes care of herself."

"Did you spend much time talking to her yourself?"

"No. She was never rude to me, but she treated me like the hired help. Mostly when she talked to me it would be about the menu for a dinner: be sure to get this kind of wine, don't put any nuts in anything because one of the guests was allergic. That sort of thing."

He stood up and said, "Thank you for talking to me, Maria."

He figured he'd gotten enough information from her to locate Maxine Barkley. Well, he wouldn't locate her, but he knew a guy who could.

"Will I have to talk to the FBI?" Maria asked.

"No. I'm sure you won't."

He wasn't sure of that at all, but why cause her more anxiety than he'd already caused her.

———

Shaw texted Doyle: *He's visiting Cartwright's cook.*

Roger that, Doyle texted back.

Goddamnit, what was that son of a bitch doing? Doyle thought.

———

An hour later, Shaw texted Doyle again: *He's in an office building in Georgetown. It's a four-story building with a bunch of tenants, real estate agents, a couple of lawyers, a CPA, a website designer, and a PR firm. I don't know who he's seeing.*

———

DeMarco was seeing a man named Neil. Neil owned the building, and his office was on the fourth floor, but his name wasn't listed on the sign in the lobby that identified the building's tenants.

Neil was an overweight white man who tied his thinning blond hair in a short ponytail, and he wore Hawaiian shirts, cargo shorts, and sandals regardless of the season. He was a man who ventured outdoors only when forced to by necessity. Neil was not interested in the world outside his office. He lived in the realm of the Internet where ordinary mortals couldn't travel, and he spent every day and most every night sitting in an ergonomic chair, drinking coffee and Red Bull, his fingers dancing across a keyboard.

DeMarco came to Neil when he wanted information—the kind of information protected by firewalls—because that was what Neil did for a living: he stole information hidden in computers and banks of servers, information supposedly protected by impregnable programs intended to stop people like him, and then he sold what he stole to people willing to pay for it. He should have been residing in a federal prison, the corpulent bride of some muscle-bound, tattooed inmate, but due to luck and skill and the fact that he was a genius, he roamed free. And currently the likelihood of him going to jail was even less than it normally would have been because Homeland Security, in an act of desperation, had recently hired him to stop cyberattacks. DeMarco couldn't think of a better example of irony.

When DeMarco told him he needed his help to identify someone, Neil told him to go away, that he was busy. He said he was engaged in mortal combat, going mano a mano with some guy in Belarus who was trying to sneak into the machines at NASA's Johnson Space Center in Houston.

"Emma sent me," DeMarco said. That was a lie but the best way to motivate Neil.

"Oh," Neil said.

Emma had introduced him to Neil. She had some sort of hold over him, one that they both refused to explain, but whatever it was, Neil was terrified of her.

DeMarco said, "All I need you to do is locate a woman named Maxine Barkley. She's in her late forties or early fifties, went to school with a man named Brandon Cartwright, and—"

"Brandon Cartwright? You mean the guy—"

"Yeah. And she might live in New York. Get me an address and a phone number for her, find out whatever you can about her quickly, and text me the information."

DeMarco knew that it would take Neil five minutes to write a program to find Barkley and then his computers would do all the work.

DeMarco left Neil's office and drove home, unaware that he was being followed. Before he arrived home, Neil texted him Barkley's phone number and address in New York and a brief bio. Tomorrow morning, he'd head up there to talk to her.

17

Shaw called Doyle on the burner and said, "DeMarco's at National Airport. He just went through security. He didn't have a carry-on bag or a suitcase, so he's not taking a long trip, but I have no idea where he's going."

Doyle called Albright and told her, "DeMarco is at National about to catch a flight. I want to know where he's going. Contact the TSA."

"Yes, sir," Albright said.

Ten minutes later, Albright told Doyle, "He's going to New York. LaGuardia. I have his flight number if you want it."

Doyle called Shaw back and gave him DeMarco's flight number. "Get on board that flight."

Fifteen minutes later, Shaw called back and said, "The flight's full. Unless you can pull some strings, I can't get on it and it's leaving in a few minutes."

Doyle didn't have any assets on the ground in New York City. No one from his company was stationed there. He thought about that for a moment, then called Albright. "Get me the name of a top-notch private detective agency in New York. And I want the name of whoever runs the company and a phone number."

Ten minutes later, Doyle was on the phone with a man named Louis Halbrook. He told Halbrook, "This is Eric Doyle. The president's national security advisor."

Telling people who he was and what his job was tended to make things happen.

"Yes, sir," Halbrook said, and Doyle could visualize Halbrook sitting up straighter in his chair, like he was standing at attention.

"I want a man who's on his way to New York followed when he gets off a plane at LaGuardia. I'm not going to tell you the man's name because that's classified, but I'll text you his photo and the flight he's on. I can't tell you why, because the reason is also classified, but I can't use federal law enforcement to tail him and that's why I'm hiring you."

"You won't regret it, sir," Halbrook said.

"I want whoever you assign to call me directly—I'll text you a phone number—and report to me what the man does and who he sees while he's in New York. I don't expect him to stay overnight. Text me the amount I'll owe you and you'll be paid, but I don't want any record of this assignment. That's also for national security reasons. Do you understand?"

"Yes, sir. No records. I'll assign two of my best operatives."

Tina Wooten checked the photo on her phone and compared it to the man walking toward her, headed for one of the airport's exits. Yep, it was him. He was wearing a dark suit, a blue shirt, no tie. He was a good-looking guy but also a hard-looking one, making her wonder what he did and if he might be dangerous. She wasn't too worried about that, however: he probably didn't have a gun as he'd just gotten off an airplane, and she had a .357 revolver in her purse that would blow a hole through him the size of a navel orange.

She followed him outside the terminal and, as she'd expected, he went to stand in a line to catch a cab. She walked over to her car. It was parked at the curb in a no-parking zone. Her partner, Jackie Machinski, was behind the wheel. Jackie had given the airport cop who was supposed to hand out tickets and have cars towed away a hundred bucks to leave her be. The client, of course, would be billed for the hundred.

Tina and Jackie had both spent twenty years with the NYPD, Jackie mostly in narcotics, Tina on the anti-terrorism team. They never met while they were employed by the city, which was understandable in a force that employed over thirty thousand people, but now they worked together frequently and were best friends.

The assignment was a weird one. Halbrook had told her they were to follow this guy and report directly to the client, but they weren't given the client's name or the name of the subject, only a phone number. Nor were they told anything about the man they were following or why they were following him. Whatever. As long as they didn't have to break too many laws, it didn't matter to her and Jackie.

Ten minutes later, the man was in a cab and she and Jackie were behind the cab.

Forty minutes after that, the cab dropped him off in front of a building in Hudson Heights.

Maxine Barkley lived in a fifteen-story apartment building in the Hudson Heights neighborhood of New York. According to Neil, she lived in P1, the *P* standing for *Penthouse*. DeMarco figured that from her apartment she'd have a pricey view of the Hudson River and the George Washington Bridge. He went over to a bank of labeled doorbells near the main entrance and saw there were two penthouse apartments: P1 and

P2. P1 was identified as belonging to M. Barkley. He pressed the buzzer. No one answered. He waited a moment and pressed it again.

———◆◆◆———

When Tina saw the man walk up to the building and press a doorbell, she said to Jackie, "Shit. Unless the building has a doorman—and it doesn't look like it does—how in the hell will we be able to find out who he's visiting?" But then they saw him walk away from the building after he'd pressed the doorbell a couple of times. It looked as if whoever he'd come to see wasn't home.

He started walking west, toward the river, at a leisurely pace. Jackie parked the car, then they both got out and followed him, Jackie on one side of the street, Tina on the other.

———◆◆◆———

Well, shit, DeMarco thought. He'd stick around for a while and if she didn't come back soon, he'd have Neil track her down using her cell phone. But he wanted to talk to her in person and not over the phone.

He walked up the street and found a coffee shop, ordered a cup of coffee to go and a bagel with cream cheese, walked back to Barkley's place, and took a seat on a bench across the street from the building. The bench was shaded by a small tree that was somehow thriving in an atmosphere polluted with exhaust fumes.

As he sat there, he watched the people walking by: an Asian couple with a Saint Bernard the size of a Shetland pony, speaking in what DeMarco thought was Chinese. An elegant woman in her sixties wearing a red beret, talking to someone on her phone in French. Two long-legged women holding hands, wearing leggings and baggy sweatshirts, who moved like Broadway dancers and chatted in Spanish. A bald man with a neatly trimmed gray goatee talking on his phone in what DeMarco thought might be Russian. He'd read somewhere that only sixty-five percent of the twenty million people in the greater New York City area were English speakers and that there were over two hundred different languages spoken there. Finally, an English speaker walked by the bench and DeMarco heard him say into this phone: "Well, you tell that motherfucker if he don't pay me, I'm gonna break his fuckin' face." New York, New York. It was so nice they named it twice.

A cab stopped in front of Barkley's building and a woman with short, dark hair who appeared to be in her forties, wearing a short leather jacket over a white T-shirt, formfitting jeans, and knee-high leather boots that matched the jacket, stepped from the cab. She entered the building with a key and DeMarco could see her through the glass in the front door waiting for the elevator. DeMarco waited five minutes, then crossed the street and pushed the buzzer for P1.

Tina and Jackie returned to their car and watched the subject sitting on a bench, munching on his bagel, Tina wishing she had one, as she'd skipped breakfast that morning. As they sat there, Jackie spent most of the time bitching about her eighteen-year-old daughter, who'd decided she didn't want to go to college and wanted to spend a year bumming around Europe.

"She calls it a 'gap year,'" Jackie said. "And I said, who do you think is gonna pay for your fuckin' gap year, because it sure as hell ain't gonna be me."

A cab pulled up in front of the building and a woman with short dark hair emerged from the cab. Tina suspected that the jacket and boots the woman was wearing would retail for about a grand. Five minutes later, the subject got off the bench and walked across the street toward the apartment building.

"I wonder if the lady who got out of the cab is the one he's here to see," Jackie said.

"Could be," Tina said.

Tina left the car, walked across the street, and watched the subject press on a doorbell again. His back was to her and he didn't notice her standing fifty feet away on the sidewalk, pretending to talk on her cell phone.

The thing that made Jackie and Tina so effective when it came to tailing people was that they were practically invisible. They were average-looking forty-year-old women. They weren't pretty. They were both a bit overweight. They dressed in drab clothing. They blended into the urban landscape like soldiers in Iraq dressed in desert camo.

Tina could hear DeMarco talking to someone on the building inter-com after he pressed the doorbell, but she couldn't make out what he was saying because of the traffic going by on the street.

———◆———

A woman answered after DeMarco pressed the doorbell for P1. She said, "Yes? Who is it?"

DeMarco said, "Miss Barkley, my name's Joe DeMarco. I work for Congress and I need to speak with you."

"Congress?"

"Yes."

"Why do you want to talk to me?"

"If you can let me in, I'll tell you."

"No. Not until I know why you're here."

"I want to talk to you about Brandon Cartwright."

"I don't know a Brandon Cartwright."

Fuck this, DeMarco thought. "Ms. Barkley, if you don't let me in, I'm going to call the FBI and tell them you're the woman who pimped Tracy Woods when she was fifteen."

After a brief silence, the latch holding the door clicked open.

Tina saw the subject reach for the door handle, and she rushed toward him and called out, "Hey, can you hold the door, please?" He did and she said thanks as she entered the building ahead of him.

He pressed the button for the elevator and the door opened immediately. A gentleman, he let Tina enter the elevator first. Instead of pressing a button, she pretended to fumble in her purse, mumbling, "Where in the hell are my damn keys?"

He pressed a button labeled *P*, which she guessed stood for *Penthouse.* He asked her, "Which floor?"

Tina said, "Ten. Thanks."

When the elevator reached the tenth floor, Tina nodded to him and got off, then walked down a hallway until the elevator door closed. She hustled back to the elevator and pressed the down button. Back outside the building, she looked at the names on the panel next to the doorbells. M. Barkley lived in P1. J. Conway lived in P2.

Back in the car, she told Jackie, "We need to figure out who an M. Barkley and a J. Conway are. They both live on the penthouse floor of the building, Barkley in P1, Conway in P2. I'll take Barkley; you take Conway."

They both started tapping on their phones.

As DeMarco had suspected, Maxine Barkley had a lovely view of the Hudson River, the GW Bridge, and Hudson Park on the Jersey side of the river. Her living room was decorated in blacks and whites: a white couch with matching white armchairs; a white rug; black end tables and a black coffee table. On the walls were black-and-white landscape photographs he found depressing. The only thing that wasn't black or white was a single bloodred artificial rose in a slender glass vase on her dining room table.

When Barkley let DeMarco into her apartment, the first thing she said was "Show me some ID." She looked tense, wound up tighter than a jack-in-the-box spring.

DeMarco showed her his congressional ID and she pointed him to one of the white armchairs, then sat down on the couch across from him, her arms crossed over her chest.

"What do you want?"

In the time it had taken DeMarco to ascend from the ground floor to the penthouse, Barkley had figured out that if he'd wanted to turn her over to the FBI, he would have already done so, so he must have some other agenda.

But before DeMarco could answer her question, she said, "And I don't know anything about Brandon Cartwright and Tracy Woods."

"Yeah, you do. Tracy told the FBI that a woman matching your description paid her to have sex with the two men. Well, the FBI didn't identify you because the guy they assigned to the case isn't that bright and he didn't question Cartwright's staff or didn't ask them the right questions. But I did. I got your name from Cartwright's cook after I described you to her."

"Brandon's cook might know who I am, but that doesn't prove I had anything to do with Woods. And if that little tramp accuses me of something, it'll be her word against mine."

DeMarco laughed. "Maxine, the FBI proved Cartwright was in his home the same night Tracy Woods was, and when he lied to them about being there, he was arrested. And the same thing will happen to you. They'll show your photo to Tracy, and she'll say that you were the woman who paid her to have sex with the two men. And then the Bureau will prove you were there that night, and you'll be arrested and spend the next ten or twenty years in a federal prison for prostituting a fifteen-year-old."

DeMarco could see Barkley's brain spinning, looking for a way out, but before she could say anything, he said, "But I'm not here about Tracy Woods. I think what you did to her was despicable, but she's not my main concern. And if you don't tell me what I want to know, I will give you up to the Bureau."

"What do you want to know?"

"I want to know about the relationship between Cartwright and the president of the United States."

"The president! I don't know what you're talking about."

"Yeah, you do. I know that Cartwright was blackmailing the president. And I know he asked the president to give him a pardon if he was convicted for trafficking Tracy."

DeMarco didn't know either of those things for sure, but those were the only facts that explained the note in the archives.

Barkley said, "A pardon?"

When she said this, DeMarco got the impression she was telling the truth. Maybe she didn't know about the pardon. Maybe Cartwright hadn't told her that he'd asked for one. But he kept going.

He said, "I think your pal Brandon arranged for the president to have sex with someone, and after he was arrested for Woods, he told the president that if he didn't get a pardon, he was going to tell the world what happened. And I think you know that."

Again, DeMarco didn't know for sure that Cartwright had obtained a sex partner for the president, but as Mahoney had said, only something along those lines explained why Cartwright thought he could get a pardon.

"I don't know what you're talking about," Barkley said.

"Yes you do. And the reason I know is that you're the one who pimped women for Cartwright's pals, just like you lined up Tracy Woods for the two guys who had her."

"I did no such thing."

But before she spoke, her eyes flicked to the left and away from DeMarco—a little tell that she was lying. And DeMarco knew he was right. She was the one who'd arranged a woman—or at least he thought it was a woman—for the president.

DeMarco said, "Quit stonewalling me. I want details. I want to know who the woman was, if it happened more than once, and where and when it happened."

DeMarco figured if he could confirm that Cartwright had gotten a sex partner for the president, then that fact, combined with the note in the archives, would establish a motive for the president having Cartwright killed.

Barkley started to say something, then she stopped and got up off the couch.

DeMarco said, "Where are you going?"

She ignored him and walked over to a small ebony cabinet behind the couch, opened it, took out a bottle of Scotch and a glass, and poured a shot, which she drank in one swallow. Then she poured a second drink and turned to face DeMarco. DeMarco figured she may have needed the booze because of what he'd said, but he suspected her real reason for getting a drink was to give herself time to think.

When she finally spoke, she said, "I don't know what you're talking about. I've never met the president."

"I didn't say you met him. I said you helped Cartwright arrange someone for him."

"I didn't."

"How 'bout Eric Doyle? Have you ever met him?"

"I don't know who that is."

"He's the president's national security advisor."

"Oh, right. But I never met him either."

DeMarco got the impression she was telling the truth about Doyle—but lying about everything else.

"Maxine," he said, "I'm not fucking around here. If you don't tell me what you know about Cartwright blackmailing the president, I'm going to turn you over to the Bureau. And you're going to get arrested just like your pal Cartwright."

"I'm through talking to you. Get out of here."

"Okay," DeMarco said, and stood up. He took a business card from his wallet, one that had only his name and cell phone number on it, and placed it on the coffee table. "I'm going to give you a day to think this over before I call the FBI, so if you change your mind, call me. If you don't call, I'm giving you up to the Bureau. That's a promise."

As DeMarco was descending in the elevator, he thought: *I blew it.* While Barkley was pouring her drink, she'd figured out that as bad as going to jail might be, if she talked about the president, she could end up as dead as Cartwright. And she might have figured something else out: that if she was arrested, she could cut a deal by naming the men who'd had sex with Woods. Whatever the case, she hadn't confirmed a damn thing that he needed confirmed. Maybe she'd call after she'd had some time to think it over.

Then he thought: *No, she won't.*

―――――◆◆◆――――――

Jackie and Tina watched the subject come out of the building. He took out his phone, made a brief call, then stood on the curb.

"He's waiting for a cab," Jackie said.

Ten minutes later, a yellow cab glided to a stop in front of him, he got in, and Jackie followed the cab.

"It's time to call the client," Tina said.

She dialed the number she'd been given, and a man answered, saying only "Yes."

Tina said, "This is Tina Wooten from the Halbrook Agency. The subject went from LaGuardia to an apartment building in Hudson Heights. He spent about fifteen minutes in the building. The person he visited lives on the penthouse floor of the apartment building and there're only two tenants on that floor. One is a Maxine Barkley. The other is a Jason Conway."

"How do you know he visited someone on the penthouse floor?"

"Because I followed him into the building and saw him press the elevator button. And like I said, there're only two tenants on that floor."

When the client didn't interrupt, Tina continued. "Barkley is a fifty-two-year-old woman who's single, never been married, and whose state tax returns list her as self-employed, but no occupation is provided. Conway is an eighty-four-year-old widower. He's been retired for twenty years, and prior to retiring he worked for a number of Wall Street firms as a broker. I have their DMV photos if you'd like to see them. "

"How did you get the DMV photos and the tax return information?"

"I'm an ex–NYPD cop and I have connections. And I didn't tell anyone why I wanted the information."

"Good."

"I suspect, although I don't know for sure, that the person the subject visited was Barkley. When he first got to the building, he rang one of the doorbells and no one answered. So he waited around, and an hour later Barkley came home—I saw her get out of a cab—and after she went into the building, he rang the doorbell again and someone let him in. So, like I said, I'm not positive, but if I had to guess, I'd say he met with Barkley."

"Text me the photos and the address of the building. Where's the subject now?"

"In a cab. I'm following him."

"Report back when you have something new to tell me."

"Yes, sir," she said. Whoever the client was, he sounded like a guy used to giving orders.

An hour later, Tina called the client again. "He's back at LaGuardia, just went through security. I'm guessing he's heading back to wherever he came from. He didn't meet or talk to anyone after he left the apartment building in Hudson Heights."

18

Doyle looked at the photo of Maxine Barkley. He'd never seen the woman before. He had no idea who she was and why DeMarco would be meeting with her.

He hated to do it—Albright already knew more than he wanted her to know—but he needed to see if Barkley had any connection to Cartwright. He called Albright and told her to start digging, again not telling her why.

Half an hour later Albright reported back. When you worked for the president's national security advisor and have at your beck and call every intelligence and law enforcement agency in the federal government, it doesn't take long to acquire information, even if some of that information requires a warrant to see.

Albright said, "Maxine Barkley is fifty-two years old. She inherited about five million from her father when he passed away—her father worked for Goldman Sachs—and as near as I can tell, she hasn't had a job in the last twenty years. Most of her net worth is tied up in her condo in New York, which is valued at about two million, and she's got another million or so in liquid assets. So she's rich, but not superrich. Her income tax return for last year showed she made a little over thirty thousand off investments, stock dividends, treasury bonds, that sort of thing. Which brings me to the only interesting thing I found out about her. Five years ago, she was indicted for insider trading along with a man named Brandon Cartwright. I assume you've heard of the late Brandon Cartwright."

"Yes," Doyle said, his face showing no reaction to Cartwright's name.

"The case was settled after she and Cartwright paid a fine. But Cartwright actually paid her fine. I found out that she and Cartwright both went to the same university at the same time, so they were friends since college, and she was apparently a good enough friend that he didn't mind paying her hundred-and-twenty-five-thousand-dollar fine."

Doyle knew about the insider trading indictment. Before he'd contacted Cartwright on the president's behalf, he'd personally researched the man. Albright hadn't been involved. One of the things he'd learned was that Cartwright mingled with the sort of people who often had the inside track on moneymaking ventures, and they shared information with Cartwright, and Cartwright used what he learned to make himself even richer. He'd invested in start-ups and real estate developments and bought stocks based on things his wealthy, influential friends told him. What Doyle hadn't known was that Barkley had been indicted at the same time as Cartwright. But it appeared, like Albright had said, that Cartwright had shared information with his good friend Maxine Barkley, which landed them both in a spot of trouble with the SEC.

And there was one other connection to Cartwright that Albright hadn't uncovered because Albright didn't have the inside track on the Tracy Woods investigation, whereas Doyle did. Doyle knew that the FBI had been looking for the woman who paid Tracy Woods to have sex with Cartwright's twisted pals. Now, after seeing Barkley's photo and learning that Barkley had been involved in an insider trading scheme with Cartwright, he wondered if she could be the woman the FBI had been looking for.

Albright was still talking. She said, "The other thing about Barkley, which I can't prove yet, is that I think she lives above her income. Based on passport and credit card information, she travels extensively, and she travels first-class."

As did Cartwright, Doyle thought. He wondered, if he compared Barkley's travel history to Cartwright's, if he'd find that they'd traveled to the same places at the same time. But he wasn't going to ask Albright to do that.

Albright said, "She dines out in very pricey restaurants, and she spends a lot of money on spas and expensive clothes, but she doesn't have any significant credit card debt. What I'm saying is that after she spent two million on her condo, and since she hasn't worked in twenty years, at the rate she spends money, she should have gone completely through her inheritance, but she hasn't. I think she's got some source of income she doesn't report on her taxes."

Yeah, Doyle thought. *Money Cartwright gave her to recruit underage whores like Tracy Woods.*

"Anyway," Albright said, "that's about all I was able to learn about her. She's a lady who travels a lot and has a nice lifestyle and appears to live above her means. Do you want me to go deeper? Look at her phone and text records to see who she's been talking to? Dig harder into her income?"

"No," Doyle said. He'd heard enough. Now what he had to do was confirm what he suspected. And he could think of only one way to do that.

He thanked Albright, dismissed her, and called Shaw.

"Where are you?"

"At National. We're waiting for DeMarco to get back from New York so we can keep following him like you wanted."

He thought for a moment about splitting Shaw and Burkhart up, having one go to New York and the other stay on DeMarco, but decided not to. The New York job might need more than one man. He also thought about having someone else tail DeMarco but didn't want to do that either. He had to minimize the number of people involved in this whole mess.

He said, "Forget about DeMarco for now. I want you and Burkhart in New York City tonight. Here's what I need you to do."

19

DeMarco drove to Emma's house after the shuttle landed at National.

He told her how, with the help of Neil and Cartwright's cook, he'd identified Maxine Barkley and about his meeting with her.

He said, "The damn woman said she didn't know about Cartwright blackmailing the president and asking for a pardon. And I believe her. But I know she's the one who lined up a woman—or women—for the president. I know it. But even after I threatened to tell the FBI about her pimping Woods, she refused to admit it. She's not an idiot, and she figured out if she told me anything, she could get killed, and getting killed is worse than going to jail."

"So what are you going to do?"

"I'm going to talk to Mahoney unless you have a better idea. I'm going to tell him that he needs to get DOJ and the FBI involved in this mess. And DOJ needs to assign a special prosecutor because it involves Doyle and the president. I'm not the guy who should be pursuing this."

"DOJ isn't going to do anything," Emma said. "For one thing, the attorney general works for the president and the president appointed him because he's a spineless wimp he can control."

"Which is why a special prosecutor needs to be assigned."

"The other thing is, the only evidence you have is a cryptic note in Archives that the guy in Archives refuses to show anyone."

"So the special prosecutor gives him a subpoena."

"Based on what? Mahoney *saying* that he saw the note? I don't think Mahoney would do that. He wouldn't go on the record saying he's convinced the president or Doyle had Cartwright killed based on that note alone. And the note isn't proof of murder."

"But it provides a motive for a murder."

"You *think* it provides a motive, and you may be right, but all you have are the words *Cartwright, pardon*, and *Doyle's way* on a piece of paper. There's no evidence that Cartwright asked for a pardon. There's no evidence that the president did anything that Cartwright could use to blackmail him with. And there's no evidence that Doyle had Cartwright killed. You need to find some evidence."

"Wait a damn minute. How in the hell did all this become my problem?"

"It's your problem because Mahoney made it your problem. And because you know a crime has been committed, you have a moral obligation to do something. More than you've already done."

Moral obligation, my ass, DeMarco thought.

But before DeMarco could give voice to that sentiment, Emma said, "Let's say, just for the sake of argument, that Barkley admitted she procured a woman for the president. And let's say she names the woman, and the woman is willing to come forward. You know what would happen next? The president would deny it ever happened and say: *Prove it. Prove I had sex with anyone.* And the president wouldn't be dumb enough to have a money trail leading to a sex worker. So all you'd end up with is the word of the president of the United States against the word of a money-grubbing, publicity-seeking hooker and a pimp. And if the woman wasn't underage at the time, there isn't even a crime."

"The crime was having Cartwright killed."

"Exactly. But there's no evidence they had him killed."

"But if the FBI took the Cartwright murder case away from Prince William County, then maybe they'd find some evidence."

Emma countered with "But the FBI has already said they're not going to take over the case. It's on you."

DeMarco threw up his hands in frustration. There was no talking to her.

Emma glared at him. "This can't stand the way it is. I won't let it stand."

DeMarco stood up.

"I'm going to go see Mahoney tomorrow. And I'm going to tell him that I'm turning Barkley over to the Bureau. Once the FBI has her in custody and she knows she's going to jail, then maybe she'll talk. And that's the best I can do."

Emma shook her head, her disappointment in him palpable.

Well, screw her and her disappointment.

20

Maxine watched an ugly, rust-streaked cargo ship on the Hudson moving downstream toward the bay, and as absurd as the idea was, she wished she was on it.

She'd thought that her life couldn't get any worse, but she'd been wrong. If that bastard DeMarco told the FBI about her, her life was going to get infinitely worse than it already was, and she had no idea what to do to keep that from happening.

When Brandon was alive, he'd supplemented her income, paying her in cash or stock tips for being his party planner. He'd also paid when she traveled with him and put her up in the finest places. She'd mingled with movie stars and world-class athletes and the richest, smartest people in the world. She'd skied in the Alps, gambled in Monte Carlo, sunbathed on the deck of Brandon's yacht in the Caribbean, attended fashion shows in Paris and Berlin. She'd gone to the film festivals at Cannes and Sundance and Toronto every year because Brandon loved film festivals. She'd basically had the same lifestyle as Brandon but was actually paid to enjoy it.

But when he was killed, all that went away. Her apartment was paid for, and she had some money in the bank, but less than a million—and a million wasn't all that much these days. She was only fifty-two, and if she lived another thirty years, which was certainly possible, she'd have to get by on roughly thirty grand a year. And half of that would go to property taxes and utilities. She wouldn't be able to dine out, unless you considered eating at McDonald's dining out. She wouldn't be able to afford new clothes; she'd be shopping in consignment shops. Her lifestyle would become roughly the same as that of a welfare queen without the welfare.

She'd known ever since Brandon was killed that she was going to have to sell the apartment, which would net her at least two million, but she'd been putting that off. She didn't want to move. She loved her apartment. Nonetheless, if she sold the apartment, that would triple the amount of cash she had, but then she'd have to find someplace else to live and it would have to be someplace where the cost of living wasn't as high as it was in New York. She could just see having to move to New Jersey. *My God.*

And she'd have to get a job, but what kind of job could she get? She had a degree in English literature, which was worth about as much as the paper the degree was printed on. Twenty years ago—before she started working for Brandon—she'd worked briefly as an assistant to an editor at HarperCollins, meaning she'd basically been a secretary. But she doubted that anyone in publishing would hire a fifty-two-year-old woman with that single job on her résumé, and she didn't know anyone else like Brandon who would employ her to do what she did for him. So what could she do? Get a job as a clerk at Neiman Marcus selling the kind of clothes she used to buy?

But as bad as her situation was, if DeMarco told the FBI about her, she had no doubt she'd be arrested. Just as Brandon had been arrested. Then she'd spend what little money she had on a lawyer to minimize the time she spent in jail; she sure as hell wasn't going to rely on a public defender. She might be able to cut a deal with the FBI by naming the two men who'd had sex with that little slut—but that was dangerous, and she'd most likely have to plead guilty and would have a record as a felon. She could end up on a sex offender registry like some perverted child molester. She supposed she could run to some country that didn't have an extradition treaty with the United States, but there wouldn't be time to sell her apartment before she ran. Which made her wonder if the government could freeze her assets, in which case she'd be living in some hellhole overseas without a penny to her name.

She felt like killing herself.

She met Brandon in college, and they hit it off instantly. She became his best friend. He confided in her about everything. She was the first one he came to when he needed a shoulder to cry on—and he cried a lot. They had sex once—this was when Brandon was still trying to come to terms with his sexuality—and it had been awful, but it drew them even closer together. She became the sister he never had and a substitute for a mother who had wanted nothing to do with him.

Although they went their separate ways after college, they always stayed in touch. She used some of her inheritance to travel and to buy her apartment. She never married but had several affairs, all of them regrettable or forgettable. She took the job at HarperCollins because she thought she'd enjoy becoming part of the literary world, discovering brilliant new talents while hobnobbing with famous, witty authors. The only contact she had with the famous authors was bringing them coffee when they came to see her boss.

As for Brandon, after college, and after his parents passed away, he began doing what he did for the rest of his life: he partied. But whenever he was in New York, they'd always get together for drinks and dinner, and usually at the latest must-go-to, impossible-to-get-into restaurant in Manhattan. On one of those occasions when he was in New York, he told her he wanted to host a dinner party for some friends in the city—and then began whining about what a hassle it was to host a party. He didn't have a home in New York—he stayed in a suite at the Plaza—and would have to come up with a suitable private venue. He'd have to coordinate with some of the more important people he wanted to invite to determine a date when they'd all be available. He'd have to find a decent chef or caterer. He'd have to create a menu, including the right kind of wines to serve, and then arrange for everything to be delivered. And that's when she said, "If you invite me to the party, I'll do all that for you." And she did—and she did a superb job. A month later he called her and told her he was planning another dinner party at his estate in Virginia, this time with a gaggle of important politicians, and would she mind flying south and planning the party for him?

That's how it all began.

She became his party planner, and her role expanded into something more than that. She planned his trips; she shopped for his clothes; she hired and fired cooks, maids, and gardeners. Brandon used to introduce Ben Margate, the other man killed the same night Brandon was murdered, as his executive assistant, but Margate was just his latest boy toy. She was Brandon's real executive assistant.

It wasn't long, however, before he asked her to plan a different sort of party for him. He told her that four of his friends from Dubai would be coming to D.C. but that these four men expected to be entertained in a way they couldn't be entertained back home.

She asked, "What does that mean?"

"It means," he said, "that they expect to have sex with companions that I arrange for them."

"Oh," she said.

"What you need to do," he said, "in addition to planning the dinner party, is contact an escort service and arrange for four of their most stunning employees to attend the party."

That's when she became Brandon's party planning pimp.

Brandon became famous within a small circle of very wealthy people for the orgies she helped him arrange. And she was sometimes a participant, taking advantage of the attractive young men—and occasionally young women—who attended. And several times the people Brandon invited to his parties wanted to have sex with very young people. Not children, but not adults, either: people like Tracy Woods who were experienced beyond their years.

Then one day Brandon told her she needed to find a woman for a special friend. He said the woman had to be extraordinarily beautiful and had to come from some country other than the United States. Her job would be to locate the woman and arrange for her transportation. She would pay the woman and also make sure she understood that if she divulged who she had sex with, terrible things would happen to her. Brandon never told her who the special friend was, but she arranged three liaisons for him, and as best she could tell, everyone was happy with her arrangements. But now, after talking to DeMarco, she knew who the special friend was.

Brandon had never told her about asking the president for a pardon or blackmailing him, but when she thought back on the way he'd acted after he was arrested, she believed DeMarco was telling the truth. When Brandon was indicted, she called him, of course, to see how he was doing. She thought he'd be terrified of going to prison, but he hadn't been. He told her, sounding all sly at the time, that he wasn't worried at all. Oh, he'd spend a lot of money on lawyers, of course, but he had plenty of money and in the end he'd be okay. She wondered at the time why he'd been so confident—and now she knew. Yes, she knew who his special friend was and now she couldn't help but wonder if his special friend had had him killed.

When Brandon was killed, she never bought the story that he'd been the victim of robbers during a home invasion. She thought, just as everyone else thought, that one of Brandon's friends had him killed because they were afraid he might talk about them. The most likely suspects in her mind were the two men who had had sex with Tracy Woods. They were both extraordinarily wealthy—they were partners in a California venture capital firm—and they were a couple of sociopaths who had the resources to hire a killer. But now there was another possibility for who'd killed Brandon.

She started crying. Right now, she was looking at abject poverty and time in prison, but poverty and prison were better than putting herself in the crosshairs of the most powerful man in the world.

She really did feel like killing herself—but knew she wouldn't.

21

Shaw and Burkhart waited until one in the morning.

They'd parked near Barkley's building earlier that evening and watched the lights on the top floor. They couldn't tell from the street which of the two penthouse units was Barkley's, but when the lights went out in both apartments, they drove around to the side of the building where there was a loading dock.

They were wearing gloves and had put on black ski masks in case there were security cameras nearby—although they hadn't seen any cameras—and approached the loading dock doors. They'd taped over the license plate numbers on the rental car they were driving. There were two doors, a roll-up metal door like a garage door secured with a padlock at the bottom and a normal door. Burkhart took a rake lockpick out of one of his cargo pants pockets and used it to open the regular door. They got into the elevator, keeping the ski masks on, and took it to the penthouse floor. Luckily, no one got on the elevator as it was ascending; if someone had gotten on, they would have killed whoever it was.

They walked down the hallway to apartment P1 and listened at the door. They didn't hear anything. Barkley had gone to bed. Burkhart knelt and, using regular lockpicks—not the rake lockpick—picked open

Barkley's door. The rake would have been quicker, but it sounded like an eggbeater beating glass and might have woken Barkley up.

Burkhart was proud of his newly acquired skill to unlock doors. During the pandemic, when he didn't have anything better to do, he found a class on YouTube where an ex-burglar taught how to pick locks. The shit you could find on YouTube was unbelievable. He went on Amazon and bought the lockpick set, the rake pick, and a bunch of doorknobs, which he mounted on a piece of plywood, and watched the burglar's videos and practiced on the locks. He wasn't an expert at it, however, and because he didn't do it very often, it took him over five minutes to pick Barkley's lock while Shaw stood behind him, muttering, "Hurry the fuck up."

They entered the apartment, let their eyes adjust to the darkness, then walked through the apartment and found the master bedroom. The bedroom door was open, and they could see Barkley lying under the covers. Burkhart flipped on the bedroom overhead light, and Shaw walked over to the bed and threw back the covers and grabbed the front of Barkley's nightgown. She was wearing a white cotton nightgown that reached her knees.

Shaw was six foot two and weighed one ninety; he could bench press two hundred and fifty pounds. Barkley was five two and weighed one ten. He yanked her out of the bed as if she were no heavier than the pillow her head was on. When her eyes popped open and she started shrieking, Shaw shook her like a rag doll, her head snapping back and forth as he did. He said, "Shut up or I'll break your fuckin' neck."

Shaw pushed her into the living room and shoved her onto the couch.

Barkley, looking up at the two masked men, said, "Please, don't hurt me. I've got money and I'll—"

Shaw pointed at her and said, "Shut up."

He took out his phone and called Doyle. "Okay, we're with her," he said.

"Give her the phone," Doyle said.

Shaw handed the phone to Barkley and said, "Talk to the man."

Barkley took the phone from him and said, "Who is this?"

Doyle said, "The two men in your apartment work for me and they'll force you to talk if you don't answer my questions quickly and honestly. They'll torture you."

"Who are you?"

Doyle said, "You met today with a man named DeMarco. I want to know what you and he talked about. And before you answer, I know he was interested in Brandon Cartwright and a woman named Tracy Woods." He didn't know for sure that DeMarco had talked to Barkley about Cartwright and Woods, but since he'd talked to the FBI and the chief of the Prince William County Police Department and the detective who'd investigated Cartwright's murder, Doyle figured he was right. Plus, it was important for Barkley to think he knew more than he actually did.

Barkley hesitated then said, "DeMarco accused me of recruiting Woods when she was fifteen to have sex with two men at Brandon's place. He said he was going to tell the FBI what I'd done. But I told him that I didn't have anything to do with Woods."

"How did he tie you to Woods?"

"He talked to Brandon's cook, and she identified me as one of Brandon's friends. But like I said, I didn't have anything to do with Tracy Woods."

"Is that true?"

A pause. "Yes."

Doyle said, "Give the phone back to the man who gave it to you."

Barkley handed the phone back to Shaw and said, "He wants to talk to you."

Shaw said, "Yes, boss."

"Show her it's a mistake to lie to me."

"Yes, sir," Shaw said.

Shaw put the phone down and nodded to Burkhart. Burkhart walked around the couch, behind Barkley. He took a clear plastic bag out of a pocket, put it over Barkley's head, and twisted the bag to seal it around her throat. Shaw went to the couch and held Barkley's hands so she couldn't reach the bag.

In a few seconds, the bag was sucked up against Barkley's face and she was thrashing because she couldn't breathe. Shaw let her suffocate for over a minute. He'd heard that a person could survive without oxygen for at least three minutes; he hoped that was true. Finally, he nodded to Burkhart and Burkhart removed the bag and Barkley began gasping and wheezing as she sucked in air.

Shaw picked up his phone and said to Doyle, "I think she got message."

"Give her the phone."

Shaw handed the phone back to Barkley and said, "Talk to the man. And this time, tell the truth."

Barkley took the phone and said, "Please don't hurt me. I'll tell you whatever you want to know."

"Were you the woman who recruited Tracy Woods?"

"Yes."

"And what did you say to DeMarco?"

"I lied to him. I told him I didn't have anything to do with Woods. When he told me he was going to tell the FBI about me, I told him to go ahead, that it would just be that slut's word against mine."

"Did you routinely recruit women for Cartwright's sex parties?"

Barkley hesitated.

Doyle said, "Give the phone back to the man."

"No, wait. Yes. He had me hire people from escort services to have sex with some of his friends."

Doyle said, "What else did DeMarco want to know?"

"He didn't want to know anything else. He was just trying to get me to admit that I recruited Woods for Brandon's friends. And when I wouldn't admit to anything, he left, saying he was going to talk to the FBI. Who are you?"

"I think you're lying to me again. You spent more than fifteen minutes with DeMarco. You talked about more than that. Give the phone back to the man who gave it to you."

"I'm not lying. I'm telling you the truth."

"Give the phone back to the man or I'll call the other man and they'll take the phone from you."

Barkley held out the phone to Shaw. "He wants to talk to you. Tell him I've told him the truth."

Shaw took the phone and said, "Yes, boss."

"She's still lying to me."

"Okay," Shaw said, and nodded to Burkhart.

They repeated the procedure with the plastic bag. Shaw thought her eyes were going to explode; they looked the size of hard-boiled eggs beneath the plastic compressed against her face, and Shaw was afraid she might have a heart attack. He gestured for Burkhart to remove the bag when he thought she was about to pass out.

He said to Doyle, "I think maybe now she'll cooperate. You want me to give her the phone again?"

"Yes."

Shaw handed Barkley the phone and said, "Quit fuckin' lying."

Barkley took the phone back. Doyle could hear her taking ragged breaths.

He said, "What else did DeMarco talk to you about?"

She said, "Okay, okay, and this is going to sound crazy, but I swear it's the truth. DeMarco wanted to know about the relationship between Brandon and the president. The president of the United States."

Oh, fuck, Doyle thought.

"And what did you tell him?" Doyle asked.

"I told him that I wasn't aware of any relationship between Brandon and the president. And that's the truth."

"What else? What else did DeMarco say? Tell me everything."

"He said he knew Brandon was blackmailing the president and that Brandon had asked the president to give him a pardon if he was convicted for the Woods thing."

Doyle was so stunned, he couldn't speak for a moment. *How in the hell did DeMarco know that?*

"And what did you tell him?" Doyle asked.

"I told him I wasn't aware of Brandon blackmailing anyone or asking for a pardon. And that's the truth. Brandon never told me anything about that. I swear."

"What else did DeMarco say?"

"He accused me of providing a woman for the president. I told him I didn't."

"Did you tell him the truth?"

A slight hesitation. "I've never met the president."

"You didn't answer my question. Give the phone back to the man."

"Wait, wait. I may have provided women for him, but I don't know for sure if I did."

"What does *that* mean?"

"Brandon asked me to get women for a special friend—that's how he referred to him, as a 'special friend'—but I didn't know who the friend was. The arrangements were complicated. Elaborate. So maybe the special friend was the president, and Brandon asked him for a pardon, but I don't know that for a fact. Like I said, I've never met the president and I didn't know anything about Brandon blackmailing him. You have to believe me. I'm telling the truth. I told DeMarco I didn't have anything to do with providing women for the president. And that's the truth too. Who are you?"

"What else did DeMarco ask?"

"The only other thing he asked was if I ever met Eric Doyle, the president's national security advisor."

"And what did you tell him?"

"That I never met Doyle. And I haven't."

Doyle knew she was telling the truth about that. He'd never met her or spoken to her. He'd only spoken to Cartwright. He hadn't even known she existed until DeMarco went to see her. But Doyle knew the problem with torturing people for information was that at some point they'll tell you what you want to hear whether it's the truth or not. He needed to ask a couple of questions to confirm she was telling the truth.

"You said you arranged women for Cartwright's special friend. How many women?"

"Three. "

"And where did the women come from? What countries?"

"How did you know they came from foreign countries?"

"Answer the question. What countries were they from?"

"Costa Rica, Brazil, and Mexico."

Doyle exhaled. Now he had proof that she'd told the truth.

"Is that all? Did DeMarco ask you anything else?"

"No, I swear. And when I wouldn't admit to the things he was accusing me of, he said he was going to tell the FBI about me."

"Okay. I believe you. Give the phone back to the man who gave it to you."

"No, please, please. Don't hurt me anymore. I'm telling you the truth. I swear."

"I told you I believe you. And don't worry, I'm not going to tell him to do anything else to you. I just need to talk to him."

Barkley held out the phone to Shaw.

Shaw took it and said, "Yes, boss."

"Make her disappear."

"Yes, sir."

Shaw disconnected the call and nodded to Burkhart, who put the bag back over Barkley's head.

22

Doyle had been sitting in his office when he interrogated Barkley. The room was mostly dark, as all the lights were off except for a small lamp on his desk. It was after midnight and the White House was silent. There were people on duty, of course, but the building wasn't humming with activity as it did during the day. The president was sleeping on the floor above him and probably sleeping soundly because he had no idea of the potential disaster that was looming.

How in the hell could DeMarco have known about Cartwright asking for a pardon? The only people who should have known about the pardon were Doyle and the president and Cartwright—and Cartwright was dead. And he hadn't told anyone, and he was sure the president hadn't either. So how in the hell had DeMarco known?

When Shaw and Burkhart raided Cartwright's house, they hadn't found anything that Cartwright could have used to blackmail the president. Doyle knew this because he'd spent a night going through everything they'd retrieved from the house. He'd concluded that if Cartwright had something physical, like a recording or document summarizing what he knew, he must have hidden it somewhere. Or he might not have had *anything* physical and had been bluffing about having proof. He hadn't been too concerned, however, because Cartwright was dead and there was no evidence that Cartwright ever knew DeMarco or spoke to him, nor would DeMarco have had access to anyplace Cartwright had hidden something, like his house or a safe-deposit box. But DeMarco had somehow found out about Cartwright's attempt to blackmail the president, which was inexplicable. *Christ, what a mess.*

Doyle drank alcohol sparingly, but now he pulled a bottle from his desk and splashed two fingers of bourbon into a glass. Then he turned off the light on his desk and sat in the dark, sipping the bourbon, reflecting on the past and the quagmire he found himself stuck in—one that was totally due to the fact that the leader of the free world couldn't stay faithful to his wife.

The booze he was drinking was Pappy Van Winkle's Kentucky bourbon whiskey, Pappy's being one of the most expensive bourbons in the world. He had the bottle in his desk for those occasions when the president would come to his office at the end of a long day—instead of calling Doyle to the Oval Office—and, to relieve the pressures of their jobs, they'd drink and bullshit like the old friends they were. It was during one of those late-night drinking sessions that the president said, "This fuckin' job. Eric, if I don't get laid soon, I'm gonna explode." And Doyle knew that the president didn't mean getting laid by his wife of thirty years.

When Doyle met the president at Harvard—the president finishing up law school, Doyle getting a postgraduate degree in economics the Army wanted him to get—they were assigned to a room together and they quickly became friends, two bright, ambitious, charming young men for whom the sky was the limit. At the time, the president was engaged to be married to a girl in his hometown in Texas, but that didn't stop him from chasing after every nicely filled skirt in Cambridge and

Boston. And Doyle and the president, both being good-looking, appealing young fellows, had no problem at all finding women to go to bed with them. But of the two of them, it was the president who had the greater need for sex. It was as if he had an addiction.

Doyle had figured that after the president got married, he'd settle down—but he didn't. When Doyle was assigned stateside, and a couple of times when he was stationed in Europe, he and the man who would later become president would take short vacations together where they'd hunt, fish, rock climb—and fuck pretty women. The president just couldn't help himself. He was married to a beautiful woman, but for whatever reason she just wasn't enough for him. And back when the president was a mere lawyer, if he'd been caught cheating on his wife, there wouldn't have been any serious ramifications—other than pissing off his wife. But then he went into politics, and it wasn't long before he became a nationally recognized figure and chasing after women became a potentially career-ending activity.

Doyle suspected the president's wife knew that her husband cheated on her, but for whatever reason—because she loved him, because they had kids—she chose to overlook his philandering. But when he was in the Senate, he went and screwed some bimbo twenty years his junior, and the bimbo got her nose out of joint when he refused to see her again and talked to the press. Doyle was in Iraq at the time, but he watched on television as his old friend stood next to his wife and apologized to her and the country for his infidelity, saying he was getting counseling and it would never happen again. His wife, whom Doyle genuinely liked, stood next to him that day looking humiliated but made it clear that she was standing by her man.

Doyle had no doubt that he cheated again after publicly scourging himself—he just couldn't help himself—but he must have been more careful with his choice of extramarital companions because he was never outed publicly again.

But then he went and got elected president.

There was nothing at all unusual about presidents being unfaithful, going all the way back to Thomas Jefferson, who sired children with one of his slaves. In recent times, it appeared as if about half the men who'd occupied the Oval Office had cheated on their spouses. The affairs of Roosevelt, Eisenhower, Kennedy, Johnson, and Clinton were well-documented, and Nixon and both Bushes allegedly had affairs. Doyle often wondered if the type of personality that made a man want to become president played a major role in these same men being unable to remain true to the women they married.

The problem the current president had—which was the same problem past presidents had had—was that he was surrounded twenty-four hours a day by Secret Service agents and had to rely on their discretion. And every time he stepped outside the White House, the media stuck to him like remoras attached to a shark, and these days every person on the planet had a camera in their pocket. Foolin' around on your wife ain't easy when you live in a goldfish bowl.

That night, as they were sipping Pappy's, and the president made the comment about how he was going to explode if he didn't get laid, he added, "I'm serious, Eric. I'm so horny, I can hardly think straight. There's this one gal, one of my secretaries, Madeline something or other. She's got big boobs and legs that go on forever and these pouty lips. Hell, I'm telling you, the last time she was in my office, I almost jumped her. You gotta help me out here."

And Doyle could tell his good friend *was* serious and meant what he said—so help him out he did.

Doyle saw an article on the society page of the *Washington Post* discussing a dinner party that Brandon Cartwright had hosted that included an actress who'd just starred in an NC-17 movie. Doyle, of course, had heard the rumors about Cartwright hosting orgies—and Cartwright himself enjoyed slyly hinting that the rumors were true. But none—not a single one—of the famous people that Cartwright partied with had ever confirmed the rumors. So either the rumors were false—which Doyle doubted—or Cartwright was a master at finding his friends sex partners who kept their mouths shut.

Doyle researched Cartwright—learned about his past, learned where his wealth came from, learned about the celebrities he hobnobbed with, learned that he was gay although he often claimed not to be—and set up a clandestine meeting with him. He told Cartwright that he wanted to arrange a liaison with a woman for himself, saying that because of his position the liaison must take place in such a way that no one would ever know about it. Although he lied and the president's name was never mentioned, he suspected Cartwright knew from the beginning that he was there on behalf of the president. Doyle was single—he'd been married briefly in his twenties—and was one of Washington's best-known bachelors and was often seen in the company of attractive women. Nonetheless, Cartwright pretended to believe the lie, which was all that mattered, and Cartwright would never be able to prove anything when it came to the president. He would never see or talk to the president.

Doyle told Cartwright that the woman had to be young, between twenty-five and thirty, no younger, no older. A woman younger than twenty-five was more likely to be impulsive and do something stupid. As for a woman older than thirty, well, that wasn't what the president would want. She had to be exceptionally beautiful—Playmate, movie star, supermodel beautiful. She had to speak English but live outside the United States. Doyle figured that a foreigner was less likely to have credibility if she talked. Who would believe that someone had flown her to the United States to have sex with the man who occupied the Oval Office? A professional sex worker was expected and preferred; a pro would be used to having clients who demanded that their identities not be revealed. And she would be paid ten times her normal rate and informed that if she proved herself to be a woman who could keep her mouth shut, she might be used again, although she wouldn't. But she would also be told that if she ever discussed the liaison with anyone—her sister, her mother, her best friend—the person she had sex with would know and something dire would happen to her and to whomever she talked to. Lastly, Doyle said to Cartwright, "And if you ever talk about this, I'll have you killed." And he could tell that Cartwright knew he meant what he said.

After meeting with Cartwright, Doyle told the president that his desires were about to become reality. The man was of course delighted. He was like a kid on Christmas Eve barely able to contain himself as he waited to see what Santa had brought him.

Two weeks later, the president and Doyle left the White House in a car driven by a Secret Service agent; another car containing four other agents followed. The president would be meeting the woman at Cartwright's estate near Manassas, but the agent drove the president to a home in Gainesville about ten miles from Cartwright's place.

The home in Gainesville was an architectural monstrosity made of unpainted concrete, with narrow windows and steel doors and surrounded by an eight-foot concrete wall topped with broken glass. The bulletproof windows in the house looked like gunports—because they were. The home was owned by a ready-for-Armageddon survivalist nut whom Doyle had known from his days in the Army. The man, like Doyle, had been a general and Doyle had liked him, but he'd been passed over after his first star because, well, he was a nut.

Inside the house were enough guns and ammunition to hold off a small army and a year's worth of food. On the property was a well to provide water in case of a siege and not one but two generators and enough fuel, batteries, and solar panels to keep the lights on for quite some time while the rest of the world cowered in the dark. Doyle knew all about the house because the man who owned it—his friend, the former general—had invited him for a tour after he finished building it. And the house had one other special feature, this feature being the main reason why Doyle had convinced the owner to let him use the place: there was an escape tunnel that ran under the property and exited three hundred yards beyond the wall surrounding it.

The Secret Service agents were told that the president would be meeting privately with a man who was already inside the house and because of who this man was, and for national security reasons, the agents wouldn't be allowed to see his face. Doyle, who was armed, would go into the house first and verify the man was unarmed; then Doyle would escort the president into the house and stay with him. The Secret Service agents weren't happy with this arrangement—they would have preferred to search the house first and satisfy themselves that the man the president was meeting was harmless—but they were told: *Tough shit. Do as you're told.* Doyle told the agents the president would be meeting with the man for several hours, and while he was with him, the agents were to post a guard around the house and make sure that no one tried to get in.

Once they were in the house, Doyle and the president went to a safe room—a stainless steel vault that would survive a nuclear blast—and raised an invisible hatch in the floor and dropped down into the tunnel. A car was parked at the tunnel exit and Doyle drove the president to Cartwright's mansion. The president could have met the woman in the survivalist's house—which would have made matters simpler—but the interior of the house was as austere as the exterior. At Cartwright's place would be a buffet prepared by Cartwright's cook, bottles of booze, a large bathtub for the president and his companion to use, and a king-sized bed with a mirror on the ceiling. The other reason they went to Cartwright's house was that if the woman should ever talk about having had sex with the president, the president would have five Secret Service agents who would testify under oath that the president never left the house in Gainesville.

The woman was waiting for the president in one of the upstairs bedrooms—but it was Doyle who saw her first. He donned a mask—a simple black mask like the men who screwed Tracy Woods had worn—and went to the bedroom and, using a device provided by the NSA, verified there were no cameras in the room and that the woman wasn't wearing a recording device. Had she been wearing one, it should have been obvious, as all she had on was a sheer teddy made of black lace. Nonetheless Doyle ran the device over her body.

The woman was stunning: long dark hair, perfect features, a flawless complexion, an incredible body. She was from Costa Rica, and Doyle had learned from Cartwright that she came in third in the competition to represent Costa Rica in the Miss Universe contest, making Doyle wonder what number one and two had looked like. The president then put on a mask and went to the room, where he spent three hours with the woman. Before going, he gave Doyle his cell phone so if there was some sort of disaster, Doyle could get the word to him. The disaster, however, would have to be on a scale comparable to 9/11 before Doyle would interrupt the president's tryst.

Doyle spent his time walking through the mansion to make sure there was no one there, checked in periodically with the Secret Service agents outside the house in Gainesville, then sat in Cartwright's den watching a baseball game. When the president finished with the woman, he looked like a man who'd experienced paradise. He patted Doyle on the shoulder and said, "Thank you, my friend." They drove back to the house in Gainesville and entered it through the tunnel, and the president allowed the Secret Service to whisk him back to D.C. as he sat in the back seat with a small, contented smile on his face.

Doyle arranged two other times for the president to meet with women supplied by Cartwright at Cartwright's mansion, and no one was the wiser. But then Cartwright was indicted for prostituting Tracy Woods—after which the dumb son of a bitch called Doyle and threatened the president with exposure unless he was granted a pardon. Doyle knew that Cartwright would never be able to prove that the women had slept with the president. But if Cartwright talked, considering his reputation—and if he identified the women the president had slept with, and if *they* talked—it would be a scandal of earthshaking proportions. So Cartwright had to go. And Doyle had thought that with him gone, and with the Prince William County chief of police essentially doing nothing to catch Cartwright's killers, everything was settled.

But then along comes Mahoney's fucking fixer.

23

Shaw and Burkhart had killed a lot of people, mostly people they'd killed in the Army. But all the ones they'd killed in the past, they'd shot and left them lying where they dropped. They'd never had to dispose of a body before and hadn't known in advance that Doyle would want Barkley's body to disappear.

"What the hell are we supposed to do with her?" Burkhart asked, saying what Shaw was thinking. "Dump her in a river?"

"No. We dump her in a river, if we don't do it right, the body will come bobbin' back up. Or some guy fishing will snag her with a hook. We'll bury her."

"How are we going to bury her? We don't have a shovel," Burkhart said. "Where we gonna get a shovel at two in the morning?"

Good question. Shaw stood for a moment mulling it over, thinking maybe they'd have to dig a grave with their hands or with coffee cans or something similar. But then it occurred to him that they were in New York, the city that never sleeps. He took out his phone and looked for hardware stores that were open twenty-four hours a day, and, sure as shit, there was one. It was a place called Nuthouse Hardware on E. Twenty-Ninth Street. The store apparently catered to do-it-yourselfers who were insomniacs or contractors who worked through the night. He didn't know if the name "Nuthouse" was supposed to be a joke or not.

He told Burkhart about the hardware store and said, "Find her cell phone and her purse and make sure her apartment keys are in her purse."

Burkhart found her purse. Her keys were in it. Her phone was sitting on a table next to her bed. Shaw pried the phone apart with a knife, ripped out the battery, and tossed the pieces into her purse. To Burkhart, he said, "So they can't track her with her phone."

"Yeah, I figured," Burkhart said.

Shaw said, "Find a suitcase. We'll make it look like she took a trip."

Burkhart found a large rolling suitcase in a closet and tossed a bunch of Barkley's clothes into it, leaving gaps and empty hangers in the walk-in closet. While he was doing that, Shaw went to the bathroom and grabbed makeup, her toothbrush, toothpaste, deodorant, and a couple of prescription vials—she had prescriptions for blood pressure and cholesterol—and placed those items in the suitcase.

Shaw said, "Look for anything else she might take on a trip."

They walked through the apartment and found the charger for her phone and an iPad, and into the suitcase they went.

Shaw said, "Okay, what else? What else do you do when you take a trip?"

Burkhart shrugged. "You turn down the temperature. You empty the shit that'll spoil out of the refrigerator.

"Do that," Shaw said. "I'm going to go make her bed. She looked like the type who would make her bed."

Burkhart found a garbage bag under her kitchen sink and tossed leftovers and sliced deli meats and cheeses that were in the refrigerator into the garbage bag and poured a carton of milk and coffee creamer down the sink.

When Shaw returned from the bedroom, Burkhart said, "Passport?"

"Good," Shaw said.

It took them a few minutes to find her passport in a drawer in a desk in a room she used for an office. On the desk, he also found DeMarco's business card. That went into her purse along with the passport and a wallet that contained her driver's license and credit cards.

They stood a moment in the living room, trying to decide if there was anything else they should do, the body sitting on the couch, the eyes wide-open, the tongue protruding. Unable to think of anything else, Shaw went to a linen closet and removed a bedsheet. He put the sheet on the floor, placed Barkley on it, and rolled the sheet around her body.

"Okay," Shaw said, "let's get out of here."

Shaw flung Barkley's body over his shoulder. Burkhart pulled the suitcase with one hand and held the garbage bag containing the stuff from the refrigerator in his other hand. It was now half past two. If they encountered some poor bastard in the elevator while they were taking the body to the car, they'd have to bury two bodies instead of one. Luckily, they didn't encounter anyone. They tossed the garbage bag in a dumpster near the loading dock, put the body in the trunk of their car, and put the suitcase and Barkley's purse on the back seat.

Shaw plugged the address for Nuthouse Hardware into his phone. He was surprised at how many customers were in the place at three in the morning. Fucking nuts for sure. Shaw purchased two shovels and a pick from a sleepy-looking clerk, paying in cash.

"Where we going?" Burkhart asked.

"New Jersey," Shaw said. "Where else would you dump a body?"

They drove through the Holland Tunnel into Jersey, drove a dozen more miles, took an exit, and found what Shaw had been looking for: a strip mall that was closed for the day, and behind the mall were a bunch of dumpsters. They tossed Barkley's clothes into four different dumpsters after making sure nothing had name tags on it and dropped the rolling suitcase off on a corner where Shaw figured some bum would steal it. They kept driving, heading mainly southwest, having no idea where they were, until they came to a bridge passing over a fairly wide river. There wasn't any traffic around at four a.m., so they stopped on the bridge and tossed Barkley's phone and iPad into the river, then opened her purse and dumped everything in it into the river, too, then the purse itself.

Now all that was left to deal with was the body.

They were in an area that was semirural. They didn't see any houses near them—just fields and forests—although they'd passed a couple of large sheet metal buildings that might be warehouses. Shaw stopped the car on a road that had trees on one side. He said, "Maybe this'll do." He pointed to the trees and said, "See how far back those trees go."

Burkhart got out of the car and walked a hundred paces into the woods, using his phone light to guide him. There was nothing but trees in front of him. He came back to the car and said, "The trees go a ways. At least a couple hundred yards. This will work." Shaw hauled the body fifty yards into the woods where they wouldn't be seen if a car came down the road. Burkhart carried the shovels and the pick. They dropped the body and started digging a grave.

"How deep should we go?" Burkhart asked.

"Hell, I don't know. Three feet? Maybe four?"

The digging wasn't easy, as they kept hitting tree roots, but they eventually managed a hole that was six feet long, three feet wide, and three and a half feet deep. They rolled the sheet-enclosed body into the hole and shoveled dirt over it, flinging the extra dirt around the area. When they were finished, they shined their phone lights on the grave to see what it looked like—and it looked just like what it was: a freshly dug grave. Burkhart used his pocketknife to cut a few branches off nearby trees, used the branches to sweep the dirt over the grave, and then spread the branches on the grave and stomped on them.

"That's better," Shaw said.

"Fuckin' good enough," Burkhart said. "Let's get out of here."

Shaw figured Burkhart was right. What they'd done should be good enough. There were no nearby homes and there was no obvious reason why anyone would want to walk in these woods. They hadn't seen any walking trails.

They headed toward the airport to turn in the rental car and catch a flight back to D.C., dropping the shovels and the pick off on the side of some road.

They got back to D.C. about nine in the morning, exhausted and looking like a couple of construction workers who'd just gotten off work. Their T-shirts were sweat-stained, their jeans and boots covered with the dirt from the grave. As soon as they got off the plane, Shaw called Doyle. He said, "We're back in town. No problems."

"Reacquire DeMarco," Doyle said. "Go to his house. If he's not there, wait until he shows up, then stay on him."

"Yes, sir," Shaw said.

He almost told Doyle that they were exhausted and needed to change clothes and shower—but didn't. A good soldier doesn't whine, and Shaw and Burkhart had endured much worse in Afghanistan. But still—

24

The morning after talking to Emma, DeMarco called Mahoney's office and told Mavis that he needed to speak to the man.

She said, "He's over at the DNC, screaming at people. I don't know when he'll be back."

DeMarco said, "Well, text him and tell him I need to talk to him about Doyle—he'll understand—and when he can take a break from the screaming, I'll be waiting for him outside the building."

Mahoney had only one reason for living these days, and that was to regain his job as the Speaker of the House. He had no interest in governing, and, with Republicans in control of the House and the Democrats holding the Senate, no meaningful legislation was being passed anyway. The Democrats lost the House in the last midterm elections by only nine seats, and Mahoney spent every waking moment scheming to win back those seats. He was analyzing every congressional district in the country, examining potential candidates, weeding out the weak ones, trying to figure out the best places to spend money, trying to see what states could be gerrymandered to the Democrats' advantage, trying to find dirt on Republican incumbents. This was supposed to be the job of the Democratic National Committee, but Mahoney had no faith in their ability, considering the way they had blown the last election, so he was hounding them relentlessly.

The DNC resided in a block long, three-story, sand-colored office building on SE Capitol Street, less than half a mile from the U.S. Capitol. DeMarco walked over there, picking up a cup of coffee on the way, and took a seat on the low wall in front of the building. As he waited, he read articles from *Golf Digest* on his phone. He was reading about how the key to increasing his driving distance was rotating his body when Mahoney came out the front door of the building. Mahoney had his suit jacket off and was wearing a white shirt with red suspenders, the color of the suspenders matching his complexion, which was also red from the exertion of yelling at people.

He walked over to where DeMarco was sitting and said, "These fucking people don't seem to understand that when you're fighting a war, there's gonna be some casualties."

DeMarco had no idea what he was talking about and didn't ask.

"So what do you got?" Mahoney asked.

DeMarco hated talking to Mahoney when Mahoney was in a foul mood. It was like dealing with a polar bear with an infected molar. And he suspected Mahoney was going to be in an even fouler mood after he talked to him.

DeMarco told him what he'd been up to and who he'd spoken to. He told him how the lead detective assigned to Cartwright's murder had been undermined by her boss and that he suspected that her boss was being pressured by someone to drag his feet on the murder investigation.

"Doyle?" Mahoney asked.

"Don't know," DeMarco said.

"So what *do* you know?"

DeMarco said, "The main thing I got that nobody else has is I've identified the woman who recruited and paid Tracy Woods to have sex with those two guys. Her name's Maxine Barkley and she was a close friend to Cartwright. So I went to see her and told her if she didn't talk to me about Cartwright blackmailing the president and everything else she knew, I was going to hand her over to the Bureau for Woods and she'd go to jail. But she told me to go to hell. I know she knows something, but at this point she's more afraid of talking than going to jail."

"So what are you going to do?"

"Give her to the Bureau," DeMarco said. "There's nothing else I can do. Maybe when she's looking at jail time for sex trafficking a minor, she'll have a change of heart and spill her guts."

"*Maybe?*" Mahoney shrieked. "Doyle and the president had Cartwright murdered, and the best you can do is *maybe*? Goddamnit, do your fuckin' job!"

"Hey, I'm not going to be able to prove the president had Cartwright killed. Get real. You need to tell DOJ about the note in Archives, and DOJ needs to assign a special prosecutor and the prosecutor can subpoena the note. And the FBI needs to take over the Cartwright murder investigation. They're the ones who should be investigating, not me."

Mahoney said, "I'm not going to tell the Bureau about the damn note without some kind of actual evidence that the president or Doyle committed a crime. And there's gotta be some evidence. You just need to get off your ass and find it. Goddamnit, I'm surrounded by incompetents."

DeMarco assumed the other incompetents he was referring to were the ones in the DNC building.

And with that, Mahoney stomped away

DeMarco sat for a moment fuming. He had Emma on one side and Mahoney on the other, both of them unsatisfied that he hadn't done enough and demanding the impossible. He finally decided that the only thing he could do was tell the FBI about Barkley and let things play out from there. Mahoney hadn't told him *not* to tell the Bureau about her. And maybe there was a way to point the FBI in the right direction when it came to Cartwright's murder. He doubted that, but maybe.

He wished he could stop using that word.

DeMarco met with Burton in the same coffee shop where they'd met before. And Burton looked just as he had the last time DeMarco saw him. In fact, it looked as if he was wearing the same clothes. Burton dropped heavily into the seat across from him and said, "So what is it now? More flak from the congresswomen?"

"No," DeMarco said. "I learned something you need to know. I found the woman who was at Cartwright's house the night Tracy Woods was there. The woman who recruited Woods and paid her."

"How did you find her?" Burton asked.

"By talking to Cartwright's cook."

"The cook wasn't there that night."

Taking credit for Emma's idea, DeMarco said, "No, but I figured that if Cartwright used a woman to recruit hookers for him, she would have been someone close to him, someone he trusted, and she probably visited him frequently. So I described the woman to the cook and she told me her name. Her name is Maxine Barkley. She lives in New York. I've got her address."

"Well, shit," Burton said. "This is going to make me look pretty fuckin' stupid."

"No it won't. I don't have any interest in taking credit for finding her. Go talk to Cartwright's cook yourself and she'll tell you the same thing she told me, then take it from there. Go question Barkley. Make her tell you who the two guys were that had sex with Tracy. Offer her a deal if she'll give them up."

"Yeah, okay," Burton said.

"And there's one other thing you ought to think about. Barkley might know something about who killed Cartwright and you should squeeze her about that too. I mean, you can be a real hero here, Burton, if you solve the murder. Hell, maybe you should offer her total immunity if she can lead you to Cartwright's killers."

"Huh," Burton said.

What DeMarco was hoping was that Barkley might start talking about Cartwright blackmailing the president. He knew she knew more than she'd told him and maybe she'd tell Burton and maybe he'd do something about it, like get the FBI's resources focused on the murder. He doubted that would happen, but it was worth a shot.

Then Burton asked the question DeMarco had been hoping he wouldn't ask. "How come you're giving me a break here? Wouldn't it be better for you to tell the congresswomen I fucked up and then they'd score points by coming down on the FBI for being incompetent?"

DeMarco said, "Yeah, well, some things transcend politics."

He had no idea what that meant when it came to the current situation, but, thankfully, Burton didn't either.

After talking to Burton, he drove home. He was going to finish building his fence.

He didn't notice the two men in a black Jeep parked half a block from his doorstep.

25

DeMarco didn't hear from Mahoney or Burton for the next two days.

Mahoney was out of town, attending a conference at some rich guy's ranch in Montana, and the attendees were other rich people who favored the Democratic Party. And what Mahoney was most likely doing was promising the rich people anything they wanted if they'd cough up the money to get the Speaker's gavel back into Mahoney's paws.

So, having nothing better to do, or nothing he'd rather do, DeMarco finished his fence. And spent more time thinking about his father.

Shaw and Burkhart were going out of their minds from boredom and getting sick of each other's company. They were good friends, but too much was too much.

They told Doyle that DeMarco wasn't doing anything other than erecting a fence in his backyard.

"A fence?"

"Yeah."

Doyle said, "Well, stay on him."

They spent part of the time they were watching DeMarco trying to decide what they'd do with the cash they'd found in Cartwright's safe. When they'd told Doyle about the cash, he said for them to keep it, not even asking how much there was.

There was forty thousand, which they split evenly. Shaw was thinking about spending his share on a snowmobile, although he didn't know where he'd ride the snowmobile. Burkhart said he was planning to take a trip to the Galápagos Islands. When Shaw asked him why, he said he wanted to see the strange birds and lizards, but mostly he wanted to swim in the sea with the big turtles there. To which Shaw had responded, "You're a weird guy, Dave."

At one point, convinced that DeMarco wasn't going anywhere soon, as he was busy nailing cedar planks to the fence rails, Shaw took the Jeep and went home and showered and packed some extra clothes in a knapsack while Burkhart hung around DeMarco's neighborhood. When Shaw got back, Burkhart took the Jeep and did the same thing. They hadn't had any sleep other than catnapping in the car, but they felt better now that they'd showered. They just wondered how long they were going to have to keep this up.

Doyle didn't know if DeMarco was finished investigating Cartwright's murder or not. But he might be, as he'd told the FBI about Barkley.

Doyle knew he'd told the FBI about her because, just as he'd inserted himself into the Cartwright murder investigation, he had a supervisor at the Bureau keeping him informed when it came to the Tracy Woods case. And he knew that right now the Bureau was trying to locate Barkley—and he knew they wouldn't locate her. So Barkley wasn't a problem.

Nonetheless he had to keep tabs on DeMarco because he still hadn't figured out how the son of a bitch could have known about Cartwright asking the president for a pardon. And DeMarco hadn't mentioned anything about a pardon to the Bureau. It was driving him insane that he couldn't figure out how DeMarco had gotten that information.

He wanted to tell Shaw and Burkhart to snatch the bastard and make him talk, but he was reluctant to do that. Disappearing Maxine Barkley was one thing. Killing Mahoney's fixer was something else. DeMarco worked for Congress; if something happened to him, Mahoney had enough clout to get the Capitol Police and the FBI involved, and he didn't want that to happen. And he figured that if DeMarco knew about the pardon request, most likely Mahoney did, too, and killing the minority leader of the House was definitely something he didn't want to do. The FBI would pull out all the stops if that happened, and who knew what they might uncover. Then there was that woman, Emma. What had DeMarco told her?

Shit, there were just too many unknowns to make a decision, and the best he could do for now was watch DeMarco and keep his ear to the ground about anyone talking to DOJ or the FBI about presidential pardons. The only good news was that right now DeMarco was building a fence—why he would be doing that, he had no idea—and Mahoney was in Montana, sucking up to billionaires.

26

Another day passed, and DeMarco still hadn't seen anything reported about Maxine Barkley being arrested. Considering how slowly Burton had worked the Tracy Woods case before arresting Cartwright, maybe that shouldn't have been surprising. Nonetheless, he decided to call Burton, who was now a buddy, and ask what was happening.

"Barkley's disappeared," Burton said. "We got a warrant to get into her apartment and found that she'd packed up about half her clothes, like maybe she took a trip. But she didn't make a train or airplane or cruise ship reservation, and she doesn't own a car and she hasn't rented one. And she hasn't used her credit cards in three days, and her phone's gone dead. We can't locate her."

"Well, shit," DeMarco said. If Barkley was on the lam, he supposed it was his fault, since he'd warned her that he was going to turn her over to the Bureau. And now he needed to do something before Mahoney got back from Montana, or he'd have to endure another one of Mahoney's tantrums.

And there was only one thing he could think to do, knowing in advance that it was probably futile.

Darcy Adams answered the phone, whispering, "What is it?" She recognized DeMarco's number and he could tell she didn't like him calling her while she was at work.

"Can you talk?" he asked.

"For now. I'm by myself."

He said, "I want to get into Cartwright's mansion."

"Why?"

"Because of what you said about how the guys who killed him maybe didn't find what they were looking for. I want to search the place."

"By yourself? You know how big that place is?"

"Yeah, but I have a friend who's going to help me. And she has a lot of experience conducting searches." He didn't know if that was true or not, but considering that he was talking about Emma, he figured he was probably right. "What's the status of the house right now? Is anyone living there?"

"No. Cartwright didn't have a will and a bunch of people are fighting over the house. He didn't have any children or siblings, but he had cousins—like, second or third cousins—who say they should inherit. At the same time, there are a couple of banks that Cartwright owed money to—like a lot of rich people, he was carrying a lot of debt—and these banks are saying they get first dibs on everything Cartwright owned. So right now the place is empty while all the squabbling is going on and it's still technically a crime scene, so the department has access to it."

"Does that mean you have a key?"

"Yeah. It's in the evidence room. Along with the remote to open the front gate and the code for the security system."

"Can you get me the key?"

Darcy said, "I'd lose my job if I got caught doing that. All you were supposed to do is tell somebody about how Harmon tanked the investigation."

"It's like I told you last time: the guy I work for wants more evidence before he does anything. But I don't want you to lose your job.

I guess I'll have to figure out some other way to get in or forget about the search."

But he didn't hang up. He waited for Darcy to say something. He knew she wanted to help him.

Darcy said, "Let me think on it. I'll get back to you."

Darcy wanted to help DeMarco because she wanted to see Harmon pay for undermining the Cartwright investigation and then pissing all over her. But she didn't want to get fired. She planned to quit as soon as she could line up another job, and if she got fired, no one would hire her.

Getting the key and the remote for the gate wouldn't be a problem, however. The guy in charge of the evidence room was a drunk named Crenshaw who was four months away from retiring. The department should have fired him years ago, but now it was less of a hassle to let him finish out his time sitting in the evidence room where he couldn't do any damage.

But should she take the risk? She figured no one would know if she took the key. The Cartwright case wasn't being actively worked, so she doubted anyone would go looking for it. And if DeMarco got it back to her quickly—like, the day after she gave it to him—she could get it back into the evidence room and no one would be the wiser.

Yeah, she was going to do it.

She looked up a case in her computer and then walked down the steps to the basement where evidence from active cases was kept. The storage area was a big wire cage and the evidence for individual cases was in lockers, which were small, locked wire cages. Crenshaw was on a stool behind the locked door that permitted entry into the area. He appeared to be sleeping, making Darcy wonder if he ever fell off the stool. She banged on the evidence room door with her hand and Crenshaw slowly opened his boozer eyes.

She said, "One of the detectives on the Winslow case asked me to check something."

Ronnie Winslow was an idiot junkie currently sitting in the county jail, awaiting trial, as he didn't have the money to post bail. He'd robbed five houses in the neighborhood where he lived and everyone in the neighborhood knew he was the thief. And when he was arrested, he was caught with the loot he hadn't gotten around to pawning. That was the stuff in the evidence locker. But Ronnie had a bigger problem than being convicted of burglary: when he robbed one of the houses, an old lady had a heart attack, and the detective assigned to the case suspected the heart attack was a result of Ronnie scaring her to death, so Ronnie had also been charged with involuntary manslaughter.

"I don't have to remove anything," Darcy told Crenshaw. "I just need to check a serial number. Don't ask me why."

Crenshaw didn't ask. He didn't care. He yawned and said, "Sign the log."

She printed her name in the log, wrote down the Winslow case number—which she'd looked up before going to the evidence room—signed her name and dated it. She hated that there'd be a record of her entering the storage area, but there was nothing she could do to avoid that. But the reason she'd picked the Winslow case was that the detective working the manslaughter charge was her old partner, Jim Stratton, and if she absolutely had to, she'd ask Jim to cover for her. She didn't know if he would, but she'd cross that bridge when she came to it.

She said to Crenshaw, "What's the box and combo number?"

The individual evidence lockers were numbered and locked with combination padlocks and Crenshaw, as the custodian, had that information. Acting as if she'd asked him to roll a boulder up a hill, Crenshaw pulled out a notebook, one with a green cover like an accounting ledger, flipped the pages, and said, "Four twelve. Nine fifty-six."

"Thanks," Darcy said. Crenshaw unlocked the door to the room and she stepped inside. She said, "I know where 412 is. You don't need to show me." She walked away and down a row of lockers behind Crenshaw's stool, turned a corner, and walked over to another row.

Instead of going to the Winslow case locker, she went to one near it: the Cartwright evidence locker. She knew the combination to the padlock because she'd been in the locker numerous times when she was working the case. She spun the dial on the lock, opened the locker door, and pulled out a small cardboard box. Mostly all that was in the box were bits of material that had been used to identify the explosives used on Cartwright's safe and the shell casings from the bullets used to kill him and Margate. There was also a quart-sized plastic bag that contained a key, the remote that opened the front gate, and an index card with the code number for the security system written on it. Darcy grabbed the bag and shoved it into her blouse. She put the box back in the locker and thanked Crenshaw as she left the evidence room. Crenshaw didn't reply; it looked as if he was sleeping again.

She returned to her desk, surprised how hard her heart was beating. *Please, Dear God, don't let me get caught for doing this.*

She called DeMarco and said, "Okay, I got the key and the remote for the gate. And also the PIN for the security system, which you'll need. The key is for the door on the side of the house where the garage is because the front door was damaged and it's nailed shut."

DeMarco said, "Thanks, Darcy. I really appreciate you doing this."

"You need to do the search tonight. I want to put the key back tomorrow. I don't think anyone will notice it's missing but I don't want to take the chance."

"Okay," DeMarco said. "When and where can I meet you?"

"Meet me at six thirty. There's a 7-Eleven on Old Bridge Road, off I-95, a couple of blocks from my house. Get there before me, stand over by where they keep the soft drinks in the cooler, and I'll pass everything off to you."

"Sounds good," DeMarco said.

"Tomorrow morning, I'll stop in the same store to get coffee on my way to work at seven and you pass it back to me."

"Got it," DeMarco said.

"And you gotta tell me if you find anything in Cartwright's house."

"I will," DeMarco said.

Maybe.

27

"Maxine Barkley's disappeared," DeMarco said. "I sicced the FBI on her and when they went to arrest her, she was gone, and they can't locate her."

"Why are you calling me?" Emma said. He could tell by her tone that she was still annoyed with him. But then, that was nothing new.

"Because I want to search Cartwright's house like you suggested," DeMarco said, "and I want you to help me. I got ahold of the detective who worked the case, and she'll give me a key this evening, so we don't have to break in. But there's something I'd like you to do first."

"What's that?"

"I want you to see if I'm being followed. When I talked to the detective the first time about the Cartwright investigation, she said there were a couple of times she saw people and didn't tell her boss who she was seeing. Like the lawyers representing Cartwright. But somehow her boss found out she talked to the lawyers, and she couldn't figure out how he knew. I think it's possible she was being followed because whoever killed Cartwright wanted to keep tabs on what the cops were doing.

"And then I go see Barkley. And right after I see her, she disappears. Now, it's possible Barkley split because she didn't want to get arrested, but I find it hard to believe she could disappear in a manner that the FBI can't locate her. It's not like she's some kind of spy with fake identities. I can't help but wonder if she disappeared because someone found out I was talking to her and made her disappear. And the only way that could have happened is if I was followed."

"Huh," Emma said.

"I'm at home. What I'd like you to do is come over here. Exactly an hour from now I'm going to take a drive, and I want you to see if I'm being tailed."

"Okay."

He'd known it wouldn't be hard to convince her. Emma lived for this sort of thing.

DeMarco waited an hour, and since he had to buy some stain for his fence, he drove to the Home Depot on Rhode Island Avenue, taking an indirect route, making three or four unnecessary turns, and stopping on the way to fill up his gas tank. The traffic was heavy, and he didn't spot anyone following him. Nor did he see Emma. He bought two gallons of the stain he wanted and drove back home.

DeMarco's phone rang. It was Emma.

"You're being followed. Two guys in a black Jeep SUV. I called Neil and gave him the plate number. I'm waiting to hear back from him."

"Son of a bitch," DeMarco muttered.

"I'll call you when I hear from Neil."

Less than half an hour later, Emma called again.

She said, "The Jeep is owned by a man named Wayne Shaw. He's ex-Army, ex–Special Forces. He served under Doyle when Doyle was stationed in Afghanistan, and he's now employed by Doyle's security company. I don't know who the other guy is, but it's probably safe to assume that he's someone like Shaw."

"Well, there you go," DeMarco said. "Now we've got proof that Doyle was involved in Cartwright's death. Why else would he have two of his guys following me?"

"The only thing we have proof of is that two people are following you, and that's not a crime."

"I still want to search Cartwright's place tonight. But I don't want these guys to see me going there. I'll figure out a way to lose them and meet you at Cartwright's at eight."

"Are you sure you can lose them?"

Her confidence in him was underwhelming. He said, "Now that I know they're behind me and what they're driving, I'll lose 'em."

There was a pause, then Emma said, "Maybe you shouldn't lose them. Maybe you should let them follow you to Cartwright's."

"And why on earth would I want to do that?"

"Joe, the likelihood of us finding anything in Cartwright's house is small. We need to make something happen. We need to provoke Doyle into doing something."

"Like what?" DeMarco said.

Before Emma could answer, the pin dropped. DeMarco said, "No fucking way. You're saying that maybe these guys will come after me if they see me go into Cartwright's place. That maybe Doyle will order them to snatch me to find out what I'm up to or maybe just kill me. But you, Wonder Woman, will somehow manage to stop them before they kill me, and they get arrested and give up Doyle. Is that your plan?"

"Basically," Emma said. "And it wouldn't just be me. To make sure nothing happens to you, I'll bring in a couple of people to help. I know a guy who runs a security company. He used to work for me, and his company provides bodyguards for big shots. I'd have his people follow Doyle's people when they follow you, and if they try something—"

"No way. I'm not going to do it. For one thing, this is just too half-assed. You're making up this plan on the fly and there's no time to iron out all the details before I have to pick up the key from Darcy. The other thing is I don't want these guys to see me meeting her. That'll put her in danger. No, I'm not going to do it—not today anyway. I want to search Cartwright's place, and if we don't find something, then maybe I'll do what you want, but not yet."

Before Emma could object, he said, "Meet me at Cartwright's place tonight at eight." And hung up.

Fucking Emma. She was dangerous.

He thought a bit about how he was going to lose the guys tailing him and came up with an idea. He called Hertz and reserved a car, then called Fredo's, the restaurant where Mahoney had met with Porter Hendricks. He spoke directly to Fredo and not the hostess.

DeMarco's plan for ditching the guys following him was to walk to Fredo's, enter through the front door like a customer, then leave via the kitchen back door and the alley that Hendricks had used when he met with Mahoney. From the restaurant, he'd walk to a car rental agency that was in a hotel only a couple of blocks away, pick up a car, and be off before the guys following him even knew he was gone. The only potential flaw in this plan was the guys following him deciding to shoot him or kidnap him before he made it to Fredo's.

Shaw nudged Burkhart, who was sleeping in the passenger seat. DeMarco had just come out the front door. He walked down the steps and headed on foot in the direction of M Street, Georgetown's main thoroughfare.

Burkhart waited until DeMarco was a block away, then got out of the car and took off on foot after him. Shaw started the car and turned a corner, heading down a street parallel to the one DeMarco was walking on.

The sidewalks on M Street were crowded and Burkhart blended in with the other people walking, having no problem keeping DeMarco in sight. DeMarco finally entered a restaurant called Fredo's and Burkhart couldn't see him after he went inside. He didn't sit at a table near a window. Burkhart called Shaw and told him where he was.

Shaw drove up next to him and Burkhart hopped into the car. Burkhart said, "Looks like the fucker's having dinner. I'm going to go into that place across the street and take a shit and pick us up a couple of sandwiches. Be right back."

DeMarco stepped into Fredo's and saw Fredo standing behind the bar as usual. The whole time he'd been walking from his place to the restaurant, he'd felt as if he had a target on his back. He nodded to Fredo, Fredo nodded back, and DeMarco walked through the kitchen and out the back door and headed down the alley. Fifteen minutes later he was driving away from the rental car outfit in a Prius and on his way to Woodbridge.

At six thirty he picked up the bag containing the key and gate remote from Darcy Adams. She walked past him as he was standing near the soft drinks cooler and handed him the bag without looking at him or saying anything to him. As she'd just come from work, she was dressed in her uniform. She looked nervous and not at all happy about what she was doing.

Now he had an hour to kill before heading to Cartwright's place and hooking up with Emma. He'd told her to meet him at eight because it would be dark by then. He spent the time in a bar in Manassas where he had dinner and watched a girls' college basketball game. He noticed that two of the girls playing were six foot eight and towered over the other players and figured they'd probably been offered full-ride scholarships when they were freshmen in high school.

At seven thirty he left the bar and drove to Cartwright's mansion, used the remote to open the gate, and drove up the winding driveway to Cartwright's front door. He figured it was best to park his car near the house where it couldn't be seen from the road because of the wall around the property. If he parked on the road near Cartwright's abandoned mansion and a cop on patrol saw his car, the cop might investigate.

As he drove up the driveway, he noticed there were some lights on in the house. He figured that the cops had left the lights on when they'd been investigating and forgot to turn them off, or maybe the lights had been left on deliberately to give the impression the place wasn't abandoned. The lights being on was good, as he and Emma wouldn't have to search the place using flashlights. Well, it was good unless there was someone in the house.

He used the key to unlock the side door and heard the security panel in the foyer near the front door beeping. That was also good, as it meant the house wasn't occupied. He hustled to the front door, worried that he wouldn't get there before an alarm sounded, and entered the security code into the keypad. The code was written on an index card in the evidence bag that Darcy had given him.

He called Emma and said, "When you get here, call me and I'll open the front gate."

28

"How in the hell are we supposed to search this place? And we don't even know what we're searching for."

He was standing with Emma, looking at Cartwright's enormous sunken living room with all its couches and chairs, coffee tables, and end tables. He'd seen hotel lobbies that were smaller than Cartwright's living room.

"We know what we're searching for," Emma said. "We're searching for something Cartwright could use to blackmail the president."

"Yeah, but if it's a photo or video on a phone or a flash drive, something small like that, how in the hell would we ever find it in a place this size? And keep in mind that whoever killed Cartwright already took everything from the house that was likely to have a video in it and they took everything from his safe. I mean, what if Cartwright buried whatever he had outside? This place must sit on at least five acres. And how many rooms do you think there are? Thirty? Fifty?"

"You're right, there's no way to search the whole house. So we have to make a couple of assumptions. First, we'll assume that if Cartwright had something important, something his future and his freedom depended on, he'd have put it someplace that wouldn't be found if law enforcement executed a search warrant, which was possible due to the Tracy

Woods mess. And he would have realized that if a search warrant was executed, the cops would get into his safe, so he probably wouldn't have put whatever he wanted to hide in there. And if the cops searched a place this size, they'd bring in a dozen people. They'd look in toilet tanks and closets and freezers. They'd open every drawer. They'd look under mattresses. They'd look in every pocket of the clothes in his closet. They'd look in ventilation grilles, in every cannister and cereal box in his kitchen. They'd search every vehicle he had. So we're not going to bother looking in those places."

"So where are we going to look?"

Emma said, "We'll start with the master bedroom."

"Why?"

"We'll make a second assumption. We'll assume that whatever he hid, he'd want it close at hand, somewhere he could get to it quickly, somewhere he could grab it fast in case of a fire or if he got a call in the middle of the night saying someone was coming for him. That's why he wouldn't bury it in his backyard. So his bedroom is a logical place to search first."

Emma went up the stairs, DeMarco following. When he worked with Emma, he was always the one following. They had no problem finding the master bedroom. It was the one with the king-size four-poster bed—and with bloodstains on the wall on the side of the bed where Cartwright had slept. There was a walk-in closet that held more clothes than DeMarco could ever imagine one man having. There had to be a hundred pairs of shoes. A love seat and a couple of armchairs sat near a large fireplace. Half a dozen paintings were hung on the walls in gilded frames. An attached bathroom held an enormous tub and a glass shower stall. Against one wall, near a window, was a small, ornate table and two fragile-looking antique chairs. On the table was a chessboard, the pieces lined up, ready to begin a game.

"The outlets?" DeMarco said. "All you'd have to do is remove the plate over an outlet and you could stash something small in one of them, like a flash drive."

"Too obvious," Emma said, "but look in the drawers and see if you can find a screwdriver."

She walked over to Cartwright's side of the bed and opened the drawer in the nightstand next to the bed. It was the nightstand where Cartwright had stored the gun that he'd fired at his killers. DeMarco went to the other nightstand, the one on Margate's side of the bed. In a drawer were reading glasses, a couple of paperbacks, a tube of lubricant, cough drops, and what looked like two hand-rolled marijuana joints. No screwdriver.

He looked over at Emma. She was studying a small, clear plastic tube, one about three inches long and half an inch in diameter, sealed with a red plastic stopper.

"What's that?" DeMarco asked.

"It's a kit for repairing eyeglasses," Emma said. "A couple little screwdrivers and a bunch of tiny screws, but there's something else." She shook the contents of the tube into her hand. "I wonder what this is," she said.

She was holding a small piece of metal, maybe an eighth of an inch in diameter and two inches long. There were two narrow slots cut into one end.

She said, "This could be a key. It's not for fixing glasses." She looked around the room. "Cartwright was a rich man who could afford to have something clever built that he could hide things in. Look for something that looks like a keyhole that this thing will fit into. Check the lamps, those statues over on the fireplace mantel. Look in the closet and see if you see a box, like a jewelry box that might have a hidden drawer that this tool will open. See if any of the picture frames have a small hole in the side or on the bottom."

They started doing those things—and found nothing.

Emma walked over to the chessboard. The chessboard was about two inches thick, made from some exotic wood, inlaid with squares of black and white stone. The pieces were also carved from stone. She knelt next to the table the chessboard was resting on and turned the chessboard slowly so she could see each side. Then she picked up the board, scattering chess pieces all over the floor.

She inserted the piece of metal she'd found in the bedside table into a small hole in one side of the board and twisted it, and the bottom of the board fell open. It was hinged on one side, the hinges invisible.

Three photographs fell onto the carpet at Emma's feet.

———◆———

The photographs that had been hidden in Cartwright's chessboard were headshots of three gorgeous women. They were the sort of photos a model or an actress would have taken by a professional photographer to include in her portfolio. They weren't selfies. On the back of each photo, written in ink, was a first name and the name of a city. Also, what appeared to be a date, but just the day and the month and not the year.

Camila, San José, Costa Rica, 7/16

Gabriela, Mexico City, 9/23

Elena, Rio de Janeiro, 2/9

DeMarco said, "These could be the women the president had sex with."

"But these photos aren't proof of that," Emma said. "They're just photos of three beautiful women."

"Cartwright wouldn't have hidden them if they weren't important."

"No, but the fact that they were hidden doesn't conclusively connect them to the president or Doyle. We need to find out who these women are."

"And how are we going to do that?"

"We're not. Neil is. We'll make the assumption that these women work for escort services and most escort services have photos of their employees on their websites."

DeMarco wondered how she knew that but decided not to ask.

Emma said, "Then Neil will do what he does, probably using facial recognition software, to identify these three women."

"Just a minute," DeMarco said. He took out his phone and typed "Escort Services, Mexico City" into Safari. He hit return and showed the result to Emma. "I got more than eleven million hits."

"That's Neil's problem. He'll have to refine the search to focus on high-end escorts, ones working for reputable companies with a track record for discretion, ones that charge a lot of money. Cartwright wouldn't have used women working on their own, posting nude photos on OnlyFans."

"I guess," DeMarco said, although he wasn't sure even Neil could do it. But, as Emma had said, that was Neil's problem.

DeMarco looked at his watch. It was only nine. He said, "I'm going to return the house key to Darcy tonight. I don't want to have to drive back here in the morning. You can take the photos to Neil and get him started working on them and I'll meet you at his place as soon as I can get there."

He had no doubt that Emma wouldn't hesitate to wake Neil up if he was sleeping and order him to go to his office. And he had no doubt that Neil would do as he was told.

DeMarco called Darcy and said, "I finished searching Cartwright's place."

"Already?"

"Yeah. Meet me at the same store where we met before and I'll give the key back to you. I don't want to have to drive back up here in the morning because I've got other stuff to do. I can meet you in half an hour."

"What did you find?"

DeMarco didn't want to tell her what he'd found because he couldn't be sure she'd keep the information to herself. She was so pissed at her boss that if DeMarco didn't do something or make something happen, she might decide to do something on her own.

He said, "I found a flash drive. It was in a hidden compartment in a fancy chessboard in Cartwright's bedroom. But—"

"How did you figure out—"

"It doesn't matter. But the drive's encrypted, so I don't know what's on it. It might not have anything to do with Cartwright's murder. It could be banking information or something like that. I'm going to take the drive to a computer guy I know. He's good but he told me he might not be able to get around the encryption and won't know until he sees the drive. He also told me that even if he can get around the encryption, that's a process that could take days. Anyway, meet me at the store and I'll pass the key back to you, and if my guy can get into the flash drive, I'll let you know what's on it."

"You promise?"

"Yes."

29

Neil looked exhausted—which was understandable, as he'd been up all night.

He started working to identify the women in the photos at ten p.m. and it was now seven a.m. While he'd been working, DeMarco slept on a couch in his office. Emma dozed off periodically in a chair—when she wasn't pacing behind Neil, telling him to hurry up.

But Neil worked his magic and at seven he handed Emma short bios of three women who lived in Costa Rica, Mexico, and Brazil.

Neil had written a program to refine the search as Emma had said, and his machines hummed through the night, comparing the three photos they found in Cartwright's chessboard to millions of others online on escort agency websites. He eventually found the escort agencies the women worked for, and their photographs on the agencies' websites were identical to the photos Cartwright had hidden. And once Neil had the names of the escort agencies, he was able to identify the women.

DeMarco didn't know how Neil did it—he suspected the cyber-security programs used by the escort agencies were nowhere near as sophisticated as those of other organizations Neil had penetrated in the past—and the escort agencies, like all well-run companies these days, had the information Neil needed stashed in their computers. The escorts employed by these agencies weren't being paid fifty bucks in cash to give a guy a blow job in his car and passing the cash on to a pimp. The agencies accepted credit cards for payment. They paid taxes. Their databases provided employee and billing information.

For example, Gabriela, of Mexico City, was Gabriela Lopez. She was twenty-nine years old. Last year she'd billed $240,000. The escort agency took a thirty percent commission for her services. The most important thing Neil learned had to do with the date on the back of Gabriela's photo: September twenty-third.

Once Neil had Gabriela's full name, DeMarco asked the question: Could she have been in Washington, D.C., on September twenty-third? Neil had said, "I'll need to make a couple of calls." One thing that DeMarco had learned about Neil over the years was that he didn't always have to hack his way into databases. He had a number of contacts in sensitive positions in places like banks and credit card companies and wireless companies, and he paid these contacts to provide him with information he needed. And from one of these contacts, Neil learned that on September twenty-second of last year, Gabriela had flown into Dulles and on September twenty-fourth she flew back to Mexico City.

Neil found similar information for Camila and Elena: their full names, their addresses, the agencies that employed them, and the fact that they'd flown into Dulles on the day before the date listed on the back of their photos and flew out a day later. They could have spent their time in D.C. touring the Smithsonian, but a more likely scenario was that they spent a night with a client, a client DeMarco suspected was the president.

DeMarco asked, "How would Cartwright have used these photos to blackmail the president?"

Emma said, "We don't know what Cartwright told the president. All he may have said was: 'I have proof that you slept with three escorts on specific dates, and if you don't give me a pardon, I'll tell what I know to the media. Or give the media the proof I have.' The president would have to be able to prove he wasn't with the women on the dates in question. And maybe he can do that. Maybe he has an alibi. But maybe he doesn't. And keep in mind Cartwright's reputation for providing sex partners for his pals. Cartwright would have some credibility. Also keep in mind the president's reputation, how he had a well-publicized affair when he was in the Senate. So I think that the president was worried that if Cartwright presented his proof to the media, and no matter what the president said, the public would believe that he did indeed cheat on his wife with high-priced call girls he had flown in to service him."

DeMarco said, "But none of the call girls were minors like Tracy Woods. So he didn't commit a crime, and the most Cartwright would have been able to do was embarrass him."

"And to keep that from happening, the president had him killed," Emma said. "Or Doyle had him killed."

"So what do we do with this?"

Emma said, "We could try to get these women to admit they had sex with the president. If they admitted it, then we'd be dealing with a fact and not an assumption."

"And you think they would admit it?"

Emma shrugged. "I don't know. Would you want to pick a fight with the leader of the free world? I still think the best course of action is to provoke a reaction from Doyle, to force him to do something more than just have his people follow you."

"You mean tethering me to a stake like a goat for the hyenas to eat? Well, before we do that, I'm going to go talk to Mahoney. We have the note in Archives—"

"Which you don't have a copy of and which Porter Hendricks refuses to show anyone."

"—and we have the photos hidden at Cartwright's house."

"Which we obtained through an illegal search."

"And we have the identities of three sex workers. So we have a motive for murder, and we have the fact that Doyle's guys—a couple of guys who could have killed Cartwright—are following me. Like I said before, Mahoney needs to talk to DOJ and convince them to assign a special prosecutor. If you and I went to the FBI with what we have, they'd toss us out of the Hoover Building like a couple of nuts who claimed to have been abducted by aliens. But Mahoney isn't some ordinary citizen. He's the minority leader of the House of Representatives. They'll listen to him."

Emma shook her head. "I'm telling you, Mahoney won't do it. He won't accuse the president of murder based on what we have. He'd never stick his neck out like that unless he was a hundred percent sure it could be proven. We need to make Doyle do something."

"Yeah, well, I'm gonna talk to Mahoney first," DeMarco said.

30

"Elsa, get back here!"

The damn dog was just useless.

Charlie Dunkin didn't know why he even bothered to bring her with him.

Elsa was a pure-bred springer spaniel. Charlie had named her Elsa because he'd made the mistake of letting his granddaughters pick the name. Her full name was Elsa of Arendelle, one of the princesses in the movie *Frozen*, which he'd been forced to watch with his granddaughters maybe fifty times. He'd bought Elsa in part because he'd liked dogs and because he'd always owned a dog. And he'd bought a springer spaniel because he liked the breed and because springers were supposed to be good at finding truffles and shrooms.

After he retired, Charlie took up mushroom hunting. He'd always liked roaming around in the woods, but he was seventy-five now and too old to go on long, rugged hikes like he used to. He didn't golf like his friends did—he thought golf was a stupid, pointless game—and he didn't like walking for no good reason. A neighbor, a young doofus who couldn't hold down a job, had introduced him to mushroom hunting ten years ago. The sport—although he supposed you couldn't call it a sport—appealed to him. For one thing, he liked to hunt. Not for animals but for treasure, which was why he also had a metal detector he used to sweep the beach. And mushrooms were a treasure. A pound of morels could cost as much as twenty bucks, not that he ever sold them. He ate what he found because in addition to being a hunter he was also a decent cook, and he used the shrooms in sauces and stews. His wife was convinced he was going to poison them to death no matter how many times he showed her the pictures that proved he knew what he was doing.

Today he wasn't hunting for morels—they were out of season—but he'd hunted this patch of woods before. It wasn't that far from his house, and you could park on the road and walk into it easily. And as he'd hunted in this area before, he knew there were a variety of edible shrooms if you knew what to look for and kept your eyes peeled. There were honey mushrooms, Entolomas, puffballs, and a variety called chicken of the woods because they kind of tasted like chicken.

Where did that damn dog go?

He could hear her barking but couldn't see her. He walked in the direction of the noise and spotted her. She was frantically digging for something, but he doubted she'd found any truffles. He'd spent hours trying to train her, but it was hopeless. He wondered if she had some sort of genetic defect that affected her sense of smell. Or maybe she was just stupid.

He walked over to her and said, "What are you diggin' for, you crazy mutt?"

There were a couple of dead tree branches close to where Elsa was pawing, but then he noticed the ground in the area where she was digging was slightly depressed in a shape forming a rectangle, one that was about three feet wide by six feet long.

And he said, "Oh, shit."

Charlie had been retired for almost twenty years, but before he retired, he'd been the Essex County coroner. He'd seen his share of hastily dug graves in forests, in marsh areas, in onion fields, in monsters' backyards.

He said, "Stop digging, Elsa."

He put the leash on the dog and had to practically drag her away from the grave. The damn dog couldn't smell truffles, but apparently she could smell a decaying corpse. He took out his phone but didn't call 911. He called the general number for the sheriff's office, which he knew by heart. Whatever was buried here wasn't an emergency at this point.

31

After confirming that Mahoney was back from Montana, DeMarco left Neil's office and drove to the Capitol in his rented Prius, glad, at least for the moment, that he wasn't being followed.

Mahoney sat behind his big desk, suit jacket off, a coffee cup in his big right paw. DeMarco could smell the bourbon in the cup. Fortunately, it was only nine in the morning, and Mahoney was still sober. Whether he was rational or not was yet to be determined.

DeMarco said, "The first thing you need to know is that two guys have been following me everywhere I go. I've confirmed that one of them works for Doyle's company and I suspect the other one does too."

"How'd they get on to you?"

"I don't know."

"You think these could be the guys who killed Cartwright?"

"I think it's possible."

"So is that it? You're being followed?"

"No, that's not it. Emma and I searched Cartwright's house and—"

"Goddamnit!" Mahoney shouted. "Why in the hell did you get her involved?" Mahoney knew how Emma felt about him. He also knew that he couldn't control her, a point he made when he said, "She's a fucking loose cannon."

"I needed her help," DeMarco said. "She's the one who spotted the guys following me and identified one of them. Anyway, when we searched Cartwright's house, we found photographs of three women that Cartwright had hidden."

DeMarco took copies of the photographs out of his jacket that had been folded lengthwise and passed them to Mahoney.

"Whoa!" Mahoney said. DeMarco assumed his reaction was due to how good-looking the women were.

While Mahoney was still staring at the photos—and probably fantasizing—DeMarco said, "On the back of the original of those photos were the women's first names, the name of a foreign city, and a date. We used a computer guy Emma knows—and he's a guy who will keep his mouth shut—to ID the women. They live in Costa Rica, Mexico, and Brazil, and they all work for high-end escort agencies. The dates coincide with days they flew into and out of Dulles." DeMarco paused before saying, "I think those photos are what Cartwright was using to blackmail the president into giving him a pardon."

"So what are you going to do?"

DeMarco pretended he hadn't heard the question. "Like I told you before, you need to turn this whole mess over to the DOJ. DOJ can make Hendricks cough up the president's notes. They can subpoena him. The FBI can question the escorts and ask them what they were doing in D.C. But the main thing is, the FBI can take the Cartwright murder investigation away from a county police chief who doesn't want it solved. They can grab the guys following me and ask why Doyle is having them follow me. They can ask them where they were the night Cartwright was killed and get their phones to see who they've been calling and where they've been."

Mahoney had started shaking his head while DeMarco was talking—and DeMarco could see this discussion wasn't going to end well.

DeMarco said, "Or if you don't want to do that, I can feed everything I got to Rachel Maddow, and she can start bugging Justice to do something on national television."

Mahoney said, "Not yet. You need to get these women to admit they fucked the president."

"Why would they admit it? Why would they put themselves in the president's crosshairs? And proving the women had sex with the president isn't the important thing. The important thing is to get someone competent investigating Cartwright's murder."

"They'll admit it," Mahoney said, "because you'll tell them that you'll give them a shitload of money if they do."

"What do you mean by *a shitload*?"

Mahoney shrugged. "A million. A million will get their attention."

"Where's the million coming from?" DeMarco asked. "Even you don't have the clout to vector three million bucks from the U.S Treasury to three hookers who live in foreign countries."

"It won't come from Treasury. I can name five billionaires off the top of my head who hate the president enough that they'd be happy to shell out a million bucks to screw him over. The money's not a problem. Go see the hookers. I want them on the record as having fucked the president."

DeMarco shook his head. "I don't want to do that."

"Why not?"

"Because the guys who've been following me might try to kill me."

"Yeah, well, be careful," Mahoney said. Then he got up, shrugged into his suit jacket, and said, "I gotta go vote on something. Go see the hookers. Hell, make a date with them. That's what I'd do if I was you."

32

DeMarco called Emma.

"Mahoney told me to go talk to the women and see if they'll admit to sleeping with the president. He's authorized me to offer them a million if they'll talk. The money will come from rich people who aren't fond of the president."

"What's Mahoney's endgame?" Emma said. "What does he plan to do if the women come forward?"

"I don't know that he has an endgame. Or if he's got one, he's not telling me. Maybe he just wants to have something in his back pocket that he can use to control the president."

"That's not good enough," Emma said. "Particularly now."

"What does that mean, *particularly now*?"

"Have you talked to Neil in the last hour?"

"No. He called while I was with Mahoney, but I didn't take the call and he didn't leave a voicemail."

Emma said, "The reason Neil called was to tell you that Maxine Barkley's body was found yesterday. He had an alert set on his machines for any news about her, and after you left this morning he learned that her death had been reported. She was buried in a shallow grave in a wooded area in New Jersey, cause of death not specified, homicide suspected. She was identified by her fingerprints."

"Aw, shit," DeMarco said. He couldn't help but wonder if Barkley had died because he'd tracked her down. And with Barkley dead, she wouldn't be able to testify to her role in the Tracy Woods case, nor would she be able to corroborate his suspicion that she was the one who'd lined up the escorts for the president.

Emma said, "Joe, three people have died. Someone has to go to prison."

"Yeah, well, maybe you can figure out a way to make that happen. But what I'm going to do is go see these women like Mahoney wants, and if they'll admit to anything, then I'm gonna try again to get Mahoney to do the right thing and whistle for the cops."

Emma started to say something, but DeMarco cut her off. "I'll see the one named Gabriela in Mexico City first. She's the closest. The problem is, I have to go home to get my passport, and I think it's possible that the guys who were following me earlier will be waiting there. I think they followed me to the airport when I went to see Barkley and somehow figured I was going to New York and there was someone waiting in New York to follow me when I landed. I don't know how they did it, but I don't want the same thing happening when I fly to Mexico."

"I know how they did it," Emma said. "Doyle is the national security advisor. When his guys followed you to National, he had someone call the TSA to see where you were going."

"Well, I don't want that to happen again."

There was a brief pause before Emma said, "I'll keep them from following you."

"How?"

"I'll figure out a way. When are you leaving?"

"Probably tomorrow morning. I need to make a date with Gabriela. That's the easiest way to meet her, but I don't know how booked up she is."

"All right," Emma said. "Let me know your schedule when you've figured it out. In the meantime, I'll start watching the guys watching you. And I'll make sure when you leave for the airport they're not behind you."

33

The CIA analyst briefing Doyle was humorless, rigid as rebar, and had eyes as cold as ball bearings. If the woman had a heart, it would take a microscope to find it. Doyle liked her.

She was saying, "We believe al Rahman is in Quetta at the home of a man named Qassim Hazara. Al Rahman went to a university with Hazara twenty years ago."

Quetta is a large city in Pakistan close to the Afghan border and al Rahman was an Al Qaeda terrorist the United States had been trying to kill for a dozen years. Normally, Doyle would have been delighted by the analyst's report—but today he was having a hard time concentrating on what she was saying.

Shaw and Burkhart had lost that fucking DeMarco. They followed him to a restaurant yesterday evening and when he didn't come out after two hours, Burkhart went in to see if he was there and found out he wasn't. He'd been gone all night and still hadn't returned home, and Doyle had no idea what he'd been doing or who he'd been talking to. On top of that, Maxine Barkley's body had been found. So far, the Jersey cops hadn't found anything that pointed to Shaw and Burkhart, but that was now one more investigation he needed to keep tabs on.

Forcing himself to focus on the matter at hand, he asked the CIA analyst, "What's the information on al Rahman based on?"

"Snippets of a cell phone conversation and an informant in Quetta we've used before. The informant hasn't been able to positively ID al Rahman, but he's seen a man in Hazara's house who's very tall and wears glasses."

Al Rahman was six foot six.

"Does Hazara live alone?"

"No. He has a wife and two children and his mother lives with him."

"Are there other houses near Hazara's?"

"Yes, unfortunately. He lives in a neighborhood where the houses are close together, no more than a couple of feet apart."

Meaning if they dropped a Hellfire missile on the son of a bitch, there'd be at least four innocent civilian casualties and probably more.

"What's your level of certainty that it's al Rahman?" Doyle asked.

"I'd say eighty percent," the analyst responded.

Eighty percent was more than good enough, but if a couple of kids were killed, the Pakistanis would raise a stink, and right now relations with the Pakistanis were dicey.

"Keep the house under surveillance," Doyle said. "See if there's a time the kids and the wife aren't normally there. Like, does she take them to school or visit someone on a regular basis."

"And the mother?" the analyst said.

Doyle didn't respond, his silence indicating: *Fuck the mother.* The death of one old woman was worth the price of killing al Rahman and the man providing him refuge.

"Okay," the analyst said.

The analyst left and Doyle walked over to a window and was again treated to the sight of sign-waving protesters in Lafayette Square. There had to be some way to keep those bastards from congregating there. He wondered if there was a way to plant a hornet's nest in the park, like those giant murder hornets he'd heard about.

Goddamnit, where was DeMarco? What had he been doing all night?
One of his burner phones rang. It was Shaw.

"Speak," he said.

"DeMarco's back home."

"Good," Doyle said.

He felt like screaming at Shaw for doing a piss-poor job of disposing of Barkley's body, but he didn't. Shaw and Burkhart might not even know the body had been discovered, and they needed to stay focused on DeMarco and not worried about the cops tracking them down for killing the woman.

He said, "Do not lose that son of a bitch again. Do you understand me, soldier?"

"Yes, sir," Shaw said.

34

DeMarco walked home after returning the Prius to the car rental agency in Georgetown. As he approached his front door, he saw the black jeep parked at the end of his block. The bastards were still on him, as he'd expected.

He didn't think Doyle's guys would try anything while it was light out, but once inside his house, he set the security system in the Stay mode and grabbed a sand wedge from his golf bag. The thought occurred to him that if he was forced to defend himself with a golf club against a couple of ex–Special Forces guys, he'd end up dead.

He turned on his laptop and looked at airline schedules and hotels in Mexico City, then called the escort agency that employed Gabriela. It turned out that making a date with her was no harder than making an appointment with any other professional.

A woman said hello in Spanish. In English, DeMarco said, "I'd like to meet with one of your escorts."

"Excellent," the woman said, now in English. "I'm sure you won't be disappointed."

"I want the one on your website called Gabriela. And she's the only one I want. No one else will do."

"I'll have to see if Gabriela is available," the woman said. "She's very popular. When would you like to meet with her?"

"Tomorrow night. Say around seven or eight."

"Let me check her schedule," the woman said. A moment later she said, "You're in luck. She had a cancellation. And where would you like to meet her?"

"At the bar in my hotel. I'll be staying in the Hilton by the Mexico City airport."

He'd been to Mexico City once before on another job for Mahoney, one that had almost gotten him killed. The city was enormous and the traffic was a nightmare, so he'd meet her at a hotel near the airport. After he talked to her, unless there was a reason to do otherwise, he'd fly out the next day. Whether he'd fly on to Costa Rica or Rio would depend on what she had to say.

"Very good, sir," the woman said. "Gabriela's rate is one thousand U.S. dollars per hour. That is, if all you'd like to do is have her accompany you to dinner or some other social event. If you and she decide to do something more than talk, her rate is three thousand per hour."

DeMarco could now understand how Gabriela had billed over two hundred grand last year.

"How do you intend to pay?" the woman asked. "Cash or credit card?"

"Cash," DeMarco said.

"Very good, sir. You need to know that a man will accompany her. He's there for her safety. And if there should be any difficulty when it comes to payment."

"That's fine," DeMarco said. And it *was* fine with him. He didn't know if the woman was lying about Gabriela having a bodyguard, but if she did, that was good. The bodyguard could protect him too.

"The other thing you should know, sir, is that Gabriela has discretion when it comes to her clients. What I'm saying is that if, for whatever reason, she is not comfortable with you, she has the right to leave if she wishes. You won't be charged, of course."

Meaning if she thought he was a creep, she would split.

"Okay," DeMarco said.

"You should also know that there are certain things Gabriela does not do. She will tell you if the subject comes up, and you must comply with her wishes. Do you understand?"

He guessed she meant kinky stuff like S&M or golden showers or God knows what. And no means no.

"Yes, I understand," DeMarco said. "My desires are, uh, conventional."

"Very good. As long as you understand the terms and conditions," she said—making DeMarco feel like he'd just hired a plumber off Angie's List.

The woman asked for his full name and phone number, confirmed the time and place, and concluded the call with "Thank you for calling VIP Services dot com."

DeMarco booked a room at the Hilton and a flight leaving Dulles tomorrow morning at eight thirty and arriving in Mexico City around five p.m.

He called Neil next and told him what he wanted, and less than fifteen minutes later his phone dinged that he had a text message. He looked at the photo accompanying the text and thought: *Perfect.*

His next call was to Perry Wallace, Mahoney's chief of staff. He said he needed ten grand from Mahoney's slush fund deposited into his checking account. Perry knew better than to ask why. DeMarco waited an hour and drove to a bank in Georgetown. Normally he would have walked, but with Doyle's guys parked down the block, he decided that driving would be safer than walking. After he got the cash, he went back home and called Emma.

"Okay, I got a date with a call girl for tomorrow evening," he said.

"Congratulations," she said.

"I'll be leaving my place at six thirty tomorrow morning."

"Roger that," Emma said.

"Roger that"?

Emma was apparently in full commando mode. Then she added, "I'm watching the guys watching you. If they try anything, I'm on them."

Which he was glad to hear. Emma was definitely better protection than a sand wedge.

35

Emma saw DeMarco's garage door roll up and his car back out of the garage.

She'd been there all night, as had the two men in the black Jeep. They were parked half a block from DeMarco's house. She was parked half a block from them. She imagined they'd taken turns sleeping, something she hadn't been able to do. Nonetheless, she felt good. She'd spent sleepless nights before, in worst places than Georgetown.

When DeMarco's car started down the street, she started her car and headed toward the Jeep. The Jeep's engine was running; she could see the exhaust. They were probably waiting for DeMarco to get a block or so ahead of them before they took off after him. The Jeep's front wheels turned as she was approaching it. It was starting to pull away from the curb.

She parked right next to the Jeep, blocking it in.

She'd decided that whether DeMarco liked it or not, she was going to make something happen.

The man in the passenger seat looked over at her, made an irritated motion with his hand for her to move. When she didn't, he yelled something she couldn't hear as his window and hers were both closed. She just looked at him, smiling slightly.

The man in the passenger seat couldn't open his door because Emma's car was too close. The driver, Shaw, opened his door and got out of the car.

Emma rolled her window down. Her Beretta was in her lap.

Shaw, looking over the roof of the Jeep, pointed at her and started to say something, then stopped—and Emma got the distinct impression he recognized her. And she wasn't surprised. She'd figured that if they'd been following DeMarco, they'd seen him come to her house. She waited to see if he was going to draw a weapon or approach her car. He didn't. He said, "Move your fuckin' car. You're blocking us in."

Emma said, "Mr. Shaw, tell Doyle to leave DeMarco alone."

"What?" Shaw said, clearly shocked that she knew his name.

Emma drove off, knowing there was no way they'd be able to catch up to DeMarco and follow him to the airport.

She had no idea what Doyle would do.

But she was confident he'd do something.

———◆———

Shaw hated to do it, but he called Doyle.

"Yes," Doyle said.

"Boss, I'm sorry but DeMarco lost us again."

"Goddamnit!" Doyle screamed. "What in the hell—"

"Sir, wait a minute, I'm not through. We were parked outside his house, and when he left in his car, we started to follow him, but that woman who DeMarco went to see in McLean blocked us in to keep us from going after him."

"Son of a bitch," Doyle muttered.

"And that's not all," Shaw said. "When I told her to move her car, she said, 'Mr. Shaw, tell Doyle to leave DeMarco alone.' Those were her exact words. She knew my name and she knew we worked for you."

Shaw heard Doyle inhale. After a moment, Doyle said, "Where are you now?"

Shaw said, "In Georgetown, just driving around to see if we can spot DeMarco's car."

"Go back to his house and wait until you hear from me."

"Yes, sir."

The situation was getting totally out of control. It appeared as if DeMarco had used the ex-DIA superspy to watch his back and she'd ID'd Shaw in some way and then learned that Shaw worked for his company. And now DeMarco was on the loose again and only God knew what that son of a bitch was up to. He had to find DeMarco. And he had to find out what he and the woman in McLean knew. He could use the NSA to locate DeMarco with his cell phone, but that would mean there would be more people who knew he was interested in DeMarco and there were already too many people who knew. There was the Prince William County chief of police and Albright and if he used the NSA—

The phone on his desk rang. It was Albright.

He answered, saying, "What is it?"

"Sir, I thought you might want to know that DeMarco booked a flight to Mexico City. Because I knew you were interested when he traveled to New York, I told TSA to let me know if he booked any other flights."

God bless you, Albright. "When does his flight land in Mexico City?"

"At four forty-five. He has a layover in Houston."

"What's the flight number?"

"United 1090."

"Thank you, Albright. Good job."

He thought about what to do for less than a minute and called Shaw.

"Yes, sir," Shaw said.

"DeMarco is headed to Mexico City. Go to Reagan National. A company plane will fly you to Mexico. He's on United Flight 1090, landing about five, and you should beat him there because he has a layover in Houston. Follow him when he leaves the airport and report back. And take a weapon." There'd be no problem in Shaw taking a weapon on the company's private jet.

"Yes, sir," Shaw said.

"You'll go alone. I want Burkhart to go to the woman's house in McLean and watch her."

He hated to split Shaw and Burkhart up. It was going to be harder for them working solo to follow DeMarco and Emma, but he still didn't want to get more people involved in this mess unless he absolutely had to. It bothered him that Albright knew as much as she did, and he'd have to figure out what to do about her if the situation escalated.

Doyle said, "And tell Burkhart he needs to be careful. The woman is ex-DIA and she's good."

"Yes, sir," Shaw said.

Doyle called his company's headquarters in Reston and said he wanted the company's jet based at National to be ready to leave within the hour for a flight to Mexico City.

Now all he could do was wait. He'd have to wait until Shaw could tell him what DeMarco was doing in Mexico and wait for Burkhart to acquire Emma and see what she was up to. He hated the situation he was in. He was in an information vacuum and couldn't decide his next move until he knew more.

36

Shaw watched as DeMarco headed for the airport terminal exit, pulling a carry-on bag behind him.

Shaw was dressed in jeans and a dark blue sport shirt that was untucked and hid the Glock in the back of his pants. He was also wearing a baseball cap and sunglasses to somewhat disguise himself. Fortunately, the airport was crowded, and he easily blended in with other people leaving the terminal.

DeMarco walked over to the curb and waved at a passing cab. The cab didn't stop for him but the next one did. Shaw had expected DeMarco to either catch a cab to wherever he was going or rent a car. So when he arrived at the airport, the first thing he did was rent a car for himself and then leave it parked in the rental car lot. All the major car rental companies were located in the same area, and if DeMarco rented a car, Shaw would have one available and be able to follow DeMarco when he left the rental lot. DeMarco taking a cab made things easier and it probably also meant that DeMarco wasn't going far. He ran over to the same place DeMarco had stood and caught a cab.

The cabdriver said something to him in Spanish.

And Shaw thought: *Oh, fuck.* "Do you speak English?"

"Yes," the driver.

"Catch up to that green cab ahead of you. Go."

The driver hesitated.

Shaw said, "Go! If you don't lose the green cab, I'll give you fifty dollars over whatever is on the meter."

The cabbie stomped on the gas pedal.

It was a short cab ride. DeMarco's cab dropped him off at a Hilton near the airport.

As soon as DeMarco entered the building, Shaw paid his driver and walked over to the hotel's entrance. Through the glass in the front doors, he could see DeMarco at the front desk, checking in. A couple of minutes later, DeMarco got into an elevator.

Shaw went to the gift shop off the lobby and bought a *Wall Street Journal* and a Coke. Then he found an armchair where he could see the elevators; the chair was partially hidden by a small, artificial broad-leafed fern. When DeMarco came off the elevators, he'd use the newspaper to shield his face. He left his baseball cap on but took off his sunglasses, thinking they would look odd if he was reading. He didn't know how long he'd have to sit there, but if one of the hotel employees asked what he was doing, he'd say he was waiting for a friend whose flight had been delayed.

—◆—

DeMarco had packed a suit and a dress shirt in his carry-on bag, along with a couple of changes of underwear and some casual clothes. He hung up the suit and the shirt to get the wrinkles out, then showered and shaved.

He had a couple of hours to kill before his date, so he flopped on the bed wearing only a sleeveless T-shirt and boxer shorts and looked for something to watch on TV. The only sporting event he could find was a soccer match between two Mexican teams he'd never heard of.

Soccer bored him to tears, and he couldn't for the life of him understand what made it the most popular sport on the planet. The problem
with soccer, as far as he was concerned, was the lack of scoring. A typical
soccer game could go a full ninety minutes with only one or two goals
being scored, and about half the time they ended in 0–0 ties. He didn't
understand the nuances of the game, and all he could see were a bunch
of guys kicking a ball back and forth—unless they bounced it off their
heads—until one of them, almost miraculously, managed to kick or
head the ball into the net. He'd always thought the game would be more
interesting if they reduced the number of players on each team by half
so they'd score more often.

At seven thirty—the game still 0–0—he put on his suit and a blue
dress shirt that matched his eyes. For whatever reason, he wanted to look
his best. Most likely because the woman he was meeting was so beautiful. He took the elevator to the lobby, and when he asked where the bar
was located, he learned there were two bars, one off the lobby and one
outdoors, near the swimming pool. The swimming pool bar had about
twenty tables, and lights were strung on wires overhead. There were no
kids in the pool making noise and only three couples were in the bar.

———— ⬦ ————

Shaw saw DeMarco step off the elevator and thought: *Finally*.

DeMarco didn't look his way. He noticed DeMarco was wearing a suit
and wondered if he was planning to leave the hotel. He glanced outside
and saw several cabs lined up, so catching a cab wouldn't be a problem. But DeMarco didn't go outside. He went up to the front desk and
spoke to the clerk, and the clerk pointed to the back of the hotel. When
DeMarco walked in the direction the clerk pointed, Shaw dropped the
newspaper he'd been reading and followed him.

DeMarco went out a door where Shaw could see a pool and what looked like an outdoor restaurant. DeMarco stood for only a minute, then turned abruptly to head back into the hotel. Shaw spun around quickly so DeMarco wouldn't see his face and walked back the way he'd come. He decided to go outside rather than sit down in the lobby again. He went and stood by an area where people could smoke and looked through the windows. DeMarco was just standing near the front desk as if he was waiting for someone.

At five before eight, a black Lincoln Town Car pulled up to the hotel entrance. A woman stepped out of the back seat. A big guy emerged from the front passenger seat. The woman looked like a damn movie star; she was, without a doubt, the best-looking woman he'd seen since arriving in Mexico. He had to force himself to stop gawking at her and look back into the lobby to make sure DeMarco was still standing by the front desk.

<hr />

DeMarco saw Gabriela walk into the lobby and thought: *Wow.*

She had long dark hair touching her shoulders, a fashion model's cheekbones, a perfect straight nose, and full lips covered with glossy red lipstick. She was wearing a shimmering black dress that clung to her body and four-inch stilettos. The dress was asymmetrical. The hem stopped above her knee on the right side but on the left side it was cut shorter, exposing one long, bare leg to the middle of her thigh.

A guy walked in after her. Short black hair, thick black mustache. He was six three or six four and had shoulders that barely fit through the door. DeMarco couldn't tell if the guy was with her or if he'd just walked in after her. But her having a bodyguard made sense. He'd heard about women being kidnapped in Mexico, some disappearing forever, some returned for ransom. A woman like Gabriela would be a valuable commodity for her company, and he could see the company paying someone to protect her.

DeMarco walked up to her and said, "Gabriela, I'm Joe. I decided to meet you in the lobby because this place has two bars, and I didn't want you to have to hunt for me."

The big guy who'd been behind her walked past DeMarco and DeMarco didn't bother to see where he was going.

Gabriela smiled at him. Perfect white teeth. Everything about her was perfect. She said, "Well, that was very thoughtful of you." She spoke English with only a slight accent.

DeMarco said, "I thought we might have a drink in the outside bar. It's a pleasant evening."

"That would be delightful," she said.

Shaw saw DeMarco talking to the gorgeous babe from the Town Car. The big guy who'd come with her was standing by the front desk, looking around the lobby. Shaw wondered if he could be her bodyguard. But why would she have a bodyguard? Was she somebody famous? A Mexican celebrity? She didn't look like a politician.

DeMarco and the woman headed in the direction of the outdoor bar by the swimming pool. The big guy trailed along behind them.

Shaw waited a few minutes and followed. DeMarco was sitting with the woman at a table on the perimeter of the restaurant, close to the small fence that separated the bar from the swimming pool. The bodyguard was at a table behind theirs, ten feet or so away. The woman had her back to Shaw.

Shaw went back into the lobby and called Doyle.

Doyle answered immediately. He said, "Hang on."

It sounded as if Doyle was in a restaurant; Shaw could hear people talking and the noise silverware makes when it strikes a plate. He heard Doyle say, "Excuse me, gentlemen. I have to take this call."

———◆◆◆———

Doyle was having dinner with two senators who sat on the Armed Services Committee. The senators were two of his biggest supporters and they thought like he did when it came to dealing with the country's enemies. He'd decided to let them know that he was thinking about dropping a bomb on a house in Quetta to kill al Rahman, that there'd most likely be a little collateral damage, and he wanted to know if he and the president would have their support. But finding out what was happening with DeMarco was more important.

Doyle left the restaurant. Standing on the street outside, he said to Shaw: "What's going on?"

Shaw said, "DeMarco is staying at the Hilton near the Mexico City airport. Right now, he's sitting in a bar with a woman. And the woman has a bodyguard, a big, hard-looking bastard."

"Who's the woman?"

"I don't know. But she's a fuckin' knockout. She looks like a movie star. And maybe she is, and that's why she's got the bodyguard."

"Aw, shit," Doyle said. He had an idea who the woman was. "Can you take a photo of the woman? I think I know who she is, but I need confirmation."

Shaw said, "I suppose I could if I went and sat in the bar. The problem is, I don't know if DeMarco knows what I look like. He's never seen me before, but since that woman from McLean knew my name, he might know who I am."

Doyle was silent for a moment. "Don't worry about DeMarco. Take her photo and text it to me right away."

If DeMarco recognized Shaw, so be it. But he had to know if the woman was who he thought she was.

"Yes, sir," Shaw said.

Shaw left the lobby and walked toward the outdoor bar. He glanced over at DeMarco and could see that DeMarco wasn't paying attention to him. He was too busy chatting up the woman. The woman's bodyguard, however, *did* look at him—bodyguards pay attention to everyone—but the big guy didn't react in any way.

Shaw took a seat at the bar, rather than at a table, and ordered a beer. All DeMarco would be able to see was his back if DeMarco looked over at the bar. After his beer arrived, he took his phone and held it down at the side of his leg, pointed the camera in DeMarco's direction, and took half a dozen photos, hoping the woman would be visible in one of them.

He looked at the photos. Two of them showed her clearly.

He texted one of the photos to Doyle.

Doyle's phone beeped that he had a text. It was from Shaw.

To the senators, he said, "I'm sorry, but it's the president. I need to see what he wants."

"Give him our best wishes," one of the senators said.

Doyle walked outside the restaurant again and looked at the photo Shaw had sent.

It was her.

How the fuck had DeMarco found her? It was just like him knowing that Cartwright had asked the president for a pardon, something he never should have known. But the son of a bitch seemed to know every-thing. Where in the hell was he getting his information from?

A server came to the table as soon as DeMarco and Gabriela sat down. To Gabriela he said, "What would you like to drink?"

Gabriela said, "A glass of champagne would be lovely."

DeMarco told the server to bring them a bottle of Dom Pérignon. He was supposed to be a big shot, one who could afford her rate, one who might offer her a million dollars, so he figured he might as well act the part. And the taxpayers, the poor suckers, were paying for the bottle of Dom.

They made small talk as they waited for the champagne to arrive. She asked if he'd been to Mexico City before. He had, he said. She asked if he would be in town long. Not long, he said. Was he here on business or pleasure? Unfortunately, business, he said.

"If you don't mind me asking, what sort of business?"

The bottle of bubbly arrived at that moment. The server filled their glasses, placed the bottle in an ice bucket, and left.

———◆———

Doyle called Shaw, who was still sitting at the bar.

Shaw said, "Yes, sir."

Doyle said, "Wayne—"

Doyle rarely called him by his first name.

"—DeMarco and the woman he's with pose a significant danger to the United States. I'm not exaggerating when I say they could bring down the government. Do you understand what I'm saying, Wayne?"

"Yes, sir," he said—although he didn't.

"You need to take them both out. Right away. Can you make that happen?"

"I don't know, sir. Like I said, they're sitting in a bar."

"Wayne, the cartels kill dozens of people every day in Mexico. It's a slaughterhouse down there, and if something happens to DeMarco and the woman, it will look like another cartel murder. All you have to do is deal with them and get back to the airport. You'll be back home before the Mexican cops can do anything about it."

Shaw didn't say anything. He wanted to please Doyle, but he didn't want to spend the rest of his life in a Mexican prison. But if Doyle said DeMarco and the woman were a national security threat, he had to try. It was his duty to try.

"Wayne, can you do it?"

"I'll do my best, sir."

"I know you will, son," Doyle said and hung up.

Doyle had decided it was time to put an end to the entire Cartwright debacle. He didn't know for sure what DeMarco and Emma knew, but they knew too much. He didn't know how they'd done it, but it appeared that they'd found the proof that Cartwright claimed he had when he tried to blackmail the president into giving him a pardon. They'd identified one of the women the president had had sex with, and they probably knew the names of the other two. And they knew that Shaw had been following DeMarco and that Shaw worked for him. It was time to sweep all the pieces off the game board. It was time to get rid of everyone who could damage him and the president, and it had to be done before DeMarco and Emma had a chance to pass on what they knew to anyone else.

He called Burkhart.

37

Shaw examined the killing field.

The area where DeMarco and the woman were sitting was enclosed by a low wrought iron fence and was elevated a couple of feet above the tiles surrounding the swimming pool. There were gaps in the low fence for people to walk through to get to the pool. The pool itself was surrounded by a six-foot fence, and behind the fence was a hedge that obscured the hotel's parking lot from the pool and the bar. In the fence surrounding the pool was a gate that led to the parking lot, and the distance from the gate to the table where DeMarco and the woman were sitting was less than thirty feet.

Shaw needed to see if the gate was unlocked.

At that moment, the bartender asked Shaw if he wanted another beer. Shaw could see the outline of a pack of cigarettes in the bartender's shirt pocket. He said, "Yeah." He took out his wallet and placed a ten on the table. The first beer had cost him five bucks. "Keep the change, but can I bum a cigarette from you?"

"Of course, sir," the bartender said, then shook a cigarette partway out of the pack and held the pack out to him. "And can I borrow your lighter?" Shaw said. The bartender reached under the bar and handed him a book of matches. The bartender was going to be able to describe him to the cops, but there wasn't anything he could do about that other than kill the bartender if the opportunity presented itself.

"I'll be right back," Shaw said to the bartender.

Gabriela raised her glass and they toasted, Gabriela saying, "To a wonderful evening."

"Yes," DeMarco said.

"I was asking about your business," Gabriela said.

DeMarco said, "I'm a lawyer who represents a very powerful man in the United States. He's the one who sent me to talk to you."

"To talk to me?"

"Yes." DeMarco pulled an envelope from the inside pocket of his suit coat and slid it across the table to her. "That contains five thousand dollars. More than enough to cover your fee for spending an hour with me. And as much as I wish otherwise, all I want to do is talk."

Gabriela arched an eyebrow in surprise but then took the envelope, glanced inside it, and placed it in her purse.

"What is it you wish to talk about?"

DeMarco said, "Last year, you flew to Dulles Airport in Washington, D.C. Two days later, you flew back to Mexico City. All I want you to do is confirm what you did while you were in Washington."

Gabriela frowned and looked over her shoulder at the bodyguard. The bodyguard could see she was in distress, and he started to get up, but then she shook her head and gestured for him to stay where he was. To DeMarco, she said, "I've never been to Washington."

"Yes you have, Gabriela. I can prove you were there."

She closed her eyes briefly.

DeMarco said, "Don't worry. I'm not here to cause you a problem. And you didn't do anything illegal, and you're not in any trouble. But I know you went to Washington and had sex with a very important man." He didn't know that for sure, but if she hadn't, he'd wasted his time coming to Mexico. "Now, the person that I represent doesn't care if you and the man had sex. You're both adults. But I need you to confirm the identity of the man."

Gabriela shook her head. "I never discuss my clients."

DeMarco said, "If you're willing to confirm the man's identity, the person who sent me is willing to pay you a considerable amount of money. A lot of money. And the company you work for wouldn't be involved at all. The money would be all yours and your agency wouldn't know anything about it."

She looked at him and those beautiful eyes turned from seductive to calculating. "How much money are we talking about?" she asked.

"Half a million U.S. dollars."

Her eyes widened. But then she said, "That's not enough."

DeMarco had to stop himself from smiling. She was negotiating. She was bright enough to know you never accepted the first offer.

"What if it was a million?" DeMarco said. "I believe I can get the man I represent to authorize that, but no more than that."

She didn't respond. But she didn't say no either.

He said, "Like I said, we already know who the man is. We just need you to confirm it. And you should know that the man slept with two other women—women who are in the same profession as you—and if you're not willing to help me, one of them probably will."

"How would I be paid?"

DeMarco shrugged. "However you want. Cash. Wire transfer. It's up to you. We'll set up another meeting, one that your company won't know about, and I'll video you confirming the man's identity. We have to have you on the record. And I'll pay you at that time."

"How do I know you won't try to cheat me? That I tell you what you want to know and then you don't pay?"

"You'll have to trust me, and I'll have to trust you. You could claim that you had sex with the man and be lying. Although I'm going to ask you a number of questions and I think I'll know if you're lying. But if I'm sure you're telling me the truth, I'll give the money to you or have it transferred to your account before I record your statement."

What DeMarco meant was that he'd ask about Maxine Barkley, certain that Gabriela would confirm that Barkley had recruited her.

DeMarco said, "We can work out the details later, when we meet again, preferably tomorrow."

Gabriela sat back and sipped her champagne and studied him.

DeMarco wondered about her background. He suspected she'd been poor before becoming a prostitute. She now made an outstanding salary, but she had to know that she'd grow older and her looks would fade, and he doubted that an escort agency offered a pension. A million dollars could change her future, and that was most likely what she was thinking about.

But she still hadn't agreed to do what he wanted.

DeMarco took out his phone, tapped it a couple of times, and showed her a photo. It was a photo he'd asked Neil to produce, the one that Neil had texted him. Neil had photoshopped a photo of the president wearing a black Lone Ranger mask. DeMarco didn't know for sure that the president had worn a mask when he'd had sex with Gabriela, but as the men who'd had sex with Tracy Woods wore masks, he suspected that he might have. And the president, even wearing the mask, was identifiable. He showed the photo to Gabriela.

"This is the man you had sex with. I know it. And all you need to do is allow me to video you confirming what I know."

She looked at the photo, then raised her eyes to meet DeMarco's and her lips parted to speak.

Shaw passed within five feet of DeMarco's table as he walked over to the gate leading to the parking lot.

He didn't notice the bodyguard following him with his eyes.

The gate was latched but not locked. Near it was a trash container. He lit the cigarette the bartender had given him. He didn't know if he was allowed to smoke in the pool area or not, but he was far enough away from the bar that he doubted anyone would object.

He looked through the gate at the parking lot, which was filled with vehicles. It was dark out, but there were streetlights in the lot, and he'd be visible running through the lot. But at the far end of the lot, he could see a busy street, cars streaming down it. He guessed the distance from the gate to the street was about two hundred yards. Sprinting, he could reach the street in less than a minute.

As he smoked, he turned and glanced at DeMarco and the woman. If this were an exercise, like the ones he'd passed in Special Forces training, he could easily hit two stationary targets thirty feet away. And if he fired half a dozen shots at DeMarco and the woman—he'd shoot the woman first because she was on his left side and it would be easier to swing the pistol from left to right—the people in the bar would panic and start screaming and running, and he doubted any of them would follow him. After he fired, he'd burst through the gate and run like hell over to the busy street. He'd strip off the baseball hat and the blue shirt he was wearing over a white T-shirt to change his appearance, then either catch a cab back to the airport or hijack a car if he had to. It was risky but it was doable.

He dropped the cigarette on the ground near the trash can, took a breath to center himself, and turned toward the bar.

He pulled the Glock from the back of his pants, aimed at the woman, and fired twice. And although he was focused on the woman, he saw the big bodyguard rising from the chair where he'd been sitting, and he had a gun in his hand. Shaw swung the pistol toward DeMarco, fired twice more—he fired four shots in less than three seconds—and then the bodyguard opened fire. Shaw was sure he'd hit the woman but wasn't sure he'd hit DeMarco; the bodyguard had distracted him enough to affect his aim. This wasn't a training exercise.

Gabriela looked at the photo, then raised her eyes to meet DeMarco's and her lips parted to speak—and blood exploded from the exit wound in her left temple.

DeMarco heard a bullet whiz by his head and then felt a sharp pain in his left shoulder and threw himself to the floor. He had no idea how many shots were fired. It sounded like at least a dozen and people were screaming, knocking chairs over, and running from the bar.

Shaw felt a bullet strike his chest but he kept on firing.

He didn't know how many shots he fired after he was hit. He kept squeezing the trigger until he couldn't.

But he'd done his duty.

He'd done the best he could.

And now he was dying.

The last thought he had was: *God, that big bastard was fast.*

38

When all the shooting stopped, DeMarco rose to his feet and then, not knowing what else to do, collapsed back into the chair where he'd been sitting. Gabriela was still sitting in her chair. Blood had poured down the left side of her face and there was another bloody spot in the middle of her chest. Her eyes were wide-open. She was dead. The big bodyguard was standing, breathing heavily, holding a gun down by the side of his leg. On the floor was the waiter who'd served the champagne. It appeared that he was dead too.

DeMarco's left arm ached and blood was flowing from his shoulder, soaking into his suit jacket and dripping onto the floor. He looked down at the blood on the floor and saw his cell phone lying there, the photo with the president wearing a mask on the screen. He picked up the phone, tapped the screen to make the photo disappear, and put the phone in a pocket. Then he didn't know what to do next. He could tell his mind wasn't working right, and he wondered if he could be in shock.

Three men in suits, all armed, ran into the swimming pool area less than a minute after the shooting stopped. Hotel security, DeMarco assumed. The guns in their hands were all pointed at the bodyguard. One of them started screaming in Spanish and the bodyguard dropped his gun on the floor and slowly raised his hands. Uniformed Mexican cops arrived five minutes later.

Before long a young Mexican cop was talking to DeMarco, speaking Spanish, pointing at his bloody shoulder. He ignored the cop. He was looking at Gabriela. A moment ago, she'd been a beautiful young woman thinking about how a million dollars could change her life—and now she was dead. The cop speaking to him turned and yelled to someone and a man wearing a white short-sleeved shirt and carrying a medic's bag walked over to him. The medic said something to him in Spanish and when DeMarco didn't answer, he touched DeMarco's throat to feel his pulse, then took a pair of scissors from his bag and cut off the left sleeves of DeMarco's suit coat and his shirt so he could examine the wound. DeMarco didn't say anything. He just sat there. The medic took a wad of gauze from his bag and taped it over the wound, then said something in Spanish, and when DeMarco still didn't respond, he said in English, "Can you stand up?"

DeMarco had to think about the question. "Yeah," he said.

DeMarco was taken by ambulance to a hospital, a cop accompanying him. By the time he got to the hospital, he was thinking clearly again. His arm ached, but he could tell the wound wasn't serious. A doctor, a short guy with a mop of curly dark hair and black Buddy Holly glasses who spoke perfect English, tended to him. He gave him a local anesthetic, cleaned out the wound, taped a large bandage over it, and gave him an injection to ward off infection.

He said, "The bullet just took a small chunk out of your arm. It didn't break the humerus or cause any muscle damage. I doubt there will be any long-term side effects provided you don't get an infection. I'll give you a prescription for the pain. When you get back home, you need to see your regular doctor. Now stand up and let's see if you get dizzy. You didn't lose much blood."

DeMarco stood. "I'm okay," he said.

The doctor said a few words in Spanish to the policeman who'd been standing nearby while DeMarco was being cared for. To DeMarco he said, "Go with the officer. I've told him to take you to the pharmacy to fill the prescription and then to the cafeteria. Drink a big glass of orange juice. A detective will meet you in the cafeteria."

"Can I get something to wear?" DeMarco asked. All he had on his upper body was a sleeveless white T-shirt that was splattered with blood. His suit jacket and shirt, both missing left sleeves, were on the floor near him.

The doctor spoke to the nurse who'd been assisting him. She left the room and came back a minute later with a red short-sleeved shirt. She handed it to DeMarco and the doctor said, "The man who owned that shirt died a couple of hours ago and doesn't need it."

The man who'd died must have been a big man. The shirt was an XXL.

As DeMarco sat in the cafeteria drinking orange juice, he thought about what he'd tell the cops. And what he wouldn't tell them.

Twenty minutes later, a slender woman dressed in a dark pantsuit and a white blouse walked over to him. She was in her forties, had short dark hair streaked with gray, a long, straight nose, and thin lips. She made him think of an Aztec priestess, one who would plunge a stone knife into the heart of a human sacrifice. She introduced herself as Valeria Ortiz. She didn't state her rank, but it was apparently high enough that the cop who'd been watching DeMarco brought her a cup of coffee.

She said, "Can you tell me your name and where you're from?"

"Joe DeMarco. I live in Washington, D.C."

"And can you show me some identification?"

She'd asked his name before asking to see his ID to see if he'd lied to her.

She looked at his driver's license, compared the photo on it to his face, then took out a notebook and wrote down the information on his license.

"May I ask what you do in Washington?"

"I'm a lawyer."

"And what are you doing in Mexico City?"

"I can't tell you that. I'm here on behalf of a client but I can't discuss his business with you unless he gives me permission."

"Who is your client?"

"I'm sorry, but I can't tell you that either."

She glared at him, clearly not happy with his response.

DeMarco said, "But I can tell you that I wasn't acting on behalf of my client this evening. This evening was personal."

"Who was the woman you were with?"

"I'm sure you already know the answer to that question. The name she gave me was Gabriela. She worked for an escort service here in Mexico City."

"Why were you meeting with her?"

"For the reason any man meets with a call girl. To have sex. But I didn't do anything illegal. I'd just met her and was talking to her before she was shot. She came with a bodyguard. I don't know his name, but I'm sure he can confirm what I'm telling you."

"Do you know the name of the man who shot you?"

"No. I never saw him. I didn't see him shoot me."

"According to Gabriela's bodyguard, he came into the bar while you were talking to her. He sat at the bar."

"Well, I never noticed him," DeMarco said. And that was true: he'd been preoccupied with Gabriela. "What's his name?"

Ortiz hesitated. "According to his driver's license, his name was Wayne Shaw. We'll take his fingerprints to confirm his identity. Do you recognize the name?"

"No," DeMarco said. "Do you have a photo of him?"

Ortiz took out her phone and showed him a photo of a guy with short dark hair who looked to be in his thirties. The guy's eyes were half-open. He looked dead.

"I don't recognize him," DeMarco said.

And that was also true. The two men who'd been following him had never gotten close enough for him to see their faces.

DeMarco said, "And I don't know why he'd want to kill me. Maybe the target was Gabriela. Or maybe he was some nut who decided to shoot up the bar."

"I don't think so," Ortiz said. "And I think you're lying to me."

"I'm not lying to you," DeMarco lied. "I never met the man and I don't know why he'd want to kill me."

There was no way in hell he was going to talk to a Mexican cop about the president of the United States sleeping with a call girl and trying to cover up what he did by having people killed.

"I don't believe you," Ortiz said.

"Am I under arrest?"

"No. But you're not going to be permitted to leave Mexico until I've investigated more. Where are you staying?"

"The hotel where I was shot."

"An officer will take you back there and you will give him your passport."

DeMarco had no idea what the laws were in Mexico and whether she could legally detain him. He needed to call Mahoney and have Mahoney get the American embassy involved.

But the first person he needed to call was Emma.

If Doyle had ordered Shaw to try to kill him, she could be in danger.

———◆◆◆———

A cop escorted DeMarco to his hotel room and left with his passport. As soon as he was gone, DeMarco called Emma. She didn't answer. He left a voicemail saying: "*Call me right away. Mexico turned into a shit show and you could be in danger.*"

He decided not to call Mahoney as it was close to midnight in D.C. He'd call Mahoney in the morning. He got an airline-size bottle of vodka from the minibar in the room and sipped directly from the bottle as he sat there thinking. Thinking about how a beautiful young woman had been murdered simply to keep a politician from being embarrassed. Thinking about how he would have been killed, too, if it hadn't been for the woman's bodyguard. Thinking about what he was going to do when he returned to D.C.

———◆◆◆———

As he sat there, the pain in his upper arm brought back a memory of his father.

One night, when he was fifteen or sixteen years old, he was awakened by a noise coming from the kitchen. He got up to investigate and saw his father sitting at the kitchen table. His shirt was off and he was wearing a sleeveless T-shirt that was covered in blood, the blood coming from a small hole in his shoulder. On the floor was the shirt he'd been wearing, and it was also bloodstained.

His father was using a dish towel to stem the bleeding. Joe said, "Jesus, Dad, what happened?"

Gino said, "Don't wake your mother. Go get some bandages from the First Aid kit."

Joe got the bandages and helped his father tape a couple of big ones over the hole, which was about the diameter of a pencil.

His father said, "Hand me the phone." They had a wall-mounted phone in the kitchen in those days. His father dialed a number and said to whomever he called, "I need you to come over to my place right away. I need you to take me to see Doc Meyers." Joe knew who Meyers was: he was an old drunk who no longer had a license to practice medicine. His father disconnected the call and said, "Go wait by the front door. A guy'll be here in a couple of minutes, and I don't want him ringing the bell and waking your mother up."

Joe said, "I can drive you."

"No, you just go wait by the door."

Joe started crying and said, "Why do you work for him? Why don't you get a job in construction or something?"

His father just shook his head. "Joe, you don't walk away from the business I'm in. Now, go wait by the door. And after I leave, throw that shirt in the trash, then go wipe the blood off the car seat so your mother doesn't see it."

DeMarco never learned more about what had happened that night. His father wouldn't talk about what happened.

His mother pretended it never happened.

DeMarco shook away the past, got another bottle from the minibar, and called Emma again. And again she didn't answer. Maybe she was sleeping and didn't hear the phone ring. But he doubted that. He left another message, saying: "*Call me, damnit.*"

Then he decided to call Christine, Emma's longtime partner. He didn't know if Christine slept in the same bed with Emma. He'd never asked and never would. Christine played the cello in the National Symphony. DeMarco thought she was a lovely, sweet woman but a bit of a ditz, although she was apparently brilliant as she had a doctorate in mathematics. She also had the type of personality that could tolerate Emma's abrasiveness.

Christine answered the phone sounding as if he'd woken her up, which he probably had.

He said, "I need to talk to Emma. Right away."

"I do, too," Christine said, "but she's not answering her phone."

"Aren't you in the house with her?"

"No. She sent me away. I'm staying with a friend."

"Why did she send you away? Did you have a fight?"

"No. She just told me that I needed to stay somewhere else for a few days but wouldn't tell me why. I called her tonight to see how she was doing, but she didn't answer."

"Well, shit," DeMarco said.

Where the hell could Emma be?

And was she still alive?

39

Burkhart was parked half a block from the woman's house in a black Ford F-150 pickup with illegally tinted windows. He'd been there most of the day.

That morning, after Shaw said that Doyle was sending him to Mexico and that Doyle wanted Burkhart watching the woman in McLean, Shaw had dropped him off on a corner in Georgetown and he'd caught a cab back to his apartment to get his pickup. The pickup wasn't an ideal surveillance vehicle, but it was the only one he owned.

When he arrived at her place, he saw her immediately and texted Doyle that he was on her. She was in her front yard, trimming bushes with pruning shears. She glanced down his way once, but she didn't stare hard or anything like that. And his wasn't the only vehicle parked on the street, and he was too far away for her to see his face clearly even if the windows hadn't been tinted.

He still couldn't get over the way she'd parked next to him and Shaw while they were watching DeMarco and boxed them in so they couldn't follow the bastard. That had taken balls, and he'd noticed that she hadn't seemed the least bit frightened when Shaw started screaming at her to move her car. Doyle had told Shaw that she was former DIA and that she was *good*—whatever the hell that meant. Most DIA people Burkhart had encountered in the Army were pencil-necked geeks who spent their whole career behind a desk, looking at a computer screen. And although she moved like she was in good shape, she was old enough to be retired, and he doubted she posed any kind of serious risk.

She finished trimming the bushes, raked up the leaves, dumped them into a basket, and went into the house. A lot of rich people lived in McLean, and the house where she lived looked pricey, so he was surprised that she didn't pay someone to do the yardwork.

An hour later he saw a red car back out of her garage. The car was a Tesla. The car the woman had been driving when they'd encountered her in Georgetown had been a sleek black Mercedes. He picked up his binoculars and looked at the Tesla to see who was behind the wheel. It wasn't her. It was a good-looking young blonde. As the Tesla was backing down the driveway, she came out the front door and waved at the driver, then just stood there watching the Tesla until it was out of sight. She never looked in his direction.

He spent the day listening to the radio and munching on snacks he'd brought with him. The sun went down and the lights came on in her house. He suspected she was in for the night and wasn't going anywhere and he was going to have to spend the night sitting in the fucking truck, fighting to stay awake. He hated surveillance duty.

At nine, Doyle called.

"Yes, sir," Burkhart said.

"Is she still at her house?"

"Yes, sir."

"Dave," Doyle said, "I need you to do something for me."

Doyle usually called him "Burkhart" or "Mr. Burkhart" or "soldier."

"Yes, sir," Burkhart said.

"That woman has to be eliminated. She poses a clear and present danger to the United States."

A clear and present danger. Burkhart had heard those words before. They sounded legal, as if they provided all the justification needed to deal in any way necessary with someone who posed a threat to national security. He didn't know why this woman posed such a threat, but if the boss said she did, that's all he needed to know.

"Yes, sir," he said.

Burkhart decided to wait until she'd gone to bed, and two hours later the lights went out in her house, but he thought: *Not yet.* The lights were still on in some of her neighbors' houses. He'd let her get sound asleep and wait until the other people in the neighborhood had gone to bed too. He'd been a soldier since he was eighteen years old, and he was used to waiting. As they always said in the military, war is long hours of boredom punctuated by minutes of sheer terror. Although usually he'd been one of the people doing the terrorizing.

By one, it looked as if everyone in the neighborhood had gone to bed. In case there were cameras around that he couldn't see, he put on a baseball hat to partially obscure his face and an old Covid mask he had in the pickup. He drove the truck a bit closer to her place so he could get away quickly, then took his Glock from the glove compartment, screwed the silencer into the barrel, jacked a round into the chamber, and got out of the truck.

He walked to the edge of her property, then along the side of her front yard, skirting around the bushes he'd seen her trimming earlier, and went toward the back of the house. There was a big patio in the backyard and a sliding glass door that allowed entry to the house. He crept up to the door and peered in. The door led to the kitchen; he could see the digital clock on the stove. He thought for a moment about breaking the glass door with the Glock, flipping the latch, and rushing inside. He imagined she'd respond to the noise of the glass breaking and come to investigate, and he'd kill her when she did. But maybe she wouldn't do that. Maybe she'd lock her bedroom door and hide in the bedroom and call the cops. The other thing was she might have a gun—like that asshole Cartwright—and she might try to shoot him.

Then another idea occurred to him, something he'd seen in a movie that he'd thought was pretty clever. It had made him smile when he saw it.

He didn't know where her bedroom was but, judging by the layout of the house, it had to be to his right, to the right of the patio door, because on the left side of the house was an attached garage.

He crept along the side of the house, squeezing behind some bushes until he came to a window. He couldn't see into the house through the window because the blinds were closed, but that was okay.

He raised the Glock and tapped on the window with the barrel of the gun. Tap, tap, tap.

That's what the killer did in the movie: he tapped on the window and the guy he was planning to kill turned on the lights in the room and came over to the window to investigate the noise—and the killer shot him through the glass.

The thing about the tapping was that it was an odd sound and not an alarming one, like the sound of breaking glass. The woman would be puzzled by the sound. She might wonder if the wind was causing a branch to slap rhythmically against the window. Or she might think it was a bird tapping its beak on the window, even though it wouldn't make sense a bird would be doing that at night unless maybe it was an owl. Whatever the case, she'd investigate and probably not be too alarmed, and she'd turn on the lights and raise the blinds—and he'd kill her.

He tapped again. Tap, tap, tap.

He waited a couple of minutes and tapped again. Nothing.

Maybe her bedroom was too far from the window he was tapping on for her to hear the noise. He'd move farther down the back of the house and tap on the next window. Maybe then she'd hear it.

To get to the next window, he had to go around another bush—her damn yard was filled with bushes—so he did that. He stepped away from the window he'd been tapping on and onto the grass in the backyard to skirt the bush.

"Drop the gun."

Oh, fuck. Had she been waiting for him outside the house? That didn't make sense. Or had she heard the tapping and decided to go out the front door and come to the back of the house to investigate? That didn't make sense either. Why would she do that? Whatever the case, the bitch was behind him.

"I said drop the gun. I'm armed, and if you don't drop your weapon, I will kill you."

Burkhart moved the Glock down next to the side of his right leg, the barrel pointing at the ground—but he didn't drop it. He doubted she would shoot him in the back.

He started to turn, intentionally moving slowly.

She said, "Don't turn around! Drop the gun."

He kept turning. He turned until he was facing her.

He could barely see her. She was dressed all in black. She was crouched in a shooter's stance, holding a pistol in a two-handed grip. It looked as if she knew what she was doing, and the pistol was aimed at his chest.

The question was: Would she hesitate?

Most people—unless they were trained professionals or someone like him who'd killed many times before—would hesitate before killing another person. Taking a human life isn't easy, and the hesitation was instinctive. And although it might only be a microsecond of hesitation, it would be all he needed.

She said, "Don't even try it." It was as if she knew what he was thinking. "Drop the damn gun."

He didn't. He flipped his wrist. The way a fast-draw artist does, pulling a pistol from a holster and firing as soon as the weapon clears the leather.

He shot her—but she shot him first.

She didn't hesitate a bit.

Her bullet hit him in the chest as he was squeezing the trigger, and he missed her heart.

She didn't miss his.

"Goddamnit," Emma muttered. "Why did you have to do that?"

Then Emma fell to the ground. He'd missed her heart, but he hadn't missed her completely.

40

Emma was on her back and her left leg was throbbing. He'd hit her in the thigh, and she suspected the bullet had broken her femur. She couldn't believe how fast he'd been. Or how slow she'd been. Maybe she wasn't as good as she thought she was or as good as she'd once been.

Her cell phone was tucked into the front of her jeans, facing forward. She pulled it out and stopped the video and turned on the phone's light and shined it on the man. He wasn't moving. She had no doubt he was dead. She shined the light on her wound. It was bleeding heavily but it didn't appear as if the bullet had struck the femoral artery. The blood wasn't surging out in pulses. As she wasn't wearing a belt she could use for a torniquet, she did the only thing she could do: she pulled a handkerchief from her back pocket and used her left hand to press it hard against the wound. She needed to get to a hospital before she bled to death.

When she had prevented Shaw from following DeMarco and told Shaw that she knew he was working for Doyle, she'd done so to provoke a reaction from Doyle, to force him to do something more than have DeMarco followed. She figured that Doyle didn't know exactly what she and DeMarco knew—for example, he probably didn't know about the photos they'd found in Cartwright's house—but when she told Shaw that she knew he was working for Doyle, that would have shaken Doyle.

Up to that point he'd probably thought he was the wizard behind the curtain and completely invisible. And Doyle would have wondered what else she and DeMarco knew about Cartwright's murder. He would have wondered if they had any proof that could cause him or the president a problem. And although she didn't know for sure that he might try to kill her or DeMarco, she thought there was a good chance that he would, because Doyle solved problems Doyle's way: by having people killed. And if Doyle did decide to have them killed, she figured she'd become the first target because DeMarco had flown to Mexico and Doyle wouldn't know he was there. And it had worked out just as she'd thought. Well, except for the part where she got shot.

When she'd spotted the black pickup with the tinted windows parked in the same spot for hours, she wondered if it might contain one of Doyle's men. She knew the truck didn't belong in the neighborhood. And that was when she'd sent Christine away so she wouldn't be in harm's way.

At eleven she turned out the lights in her house—figuring if whoever was in the truck was going to try anything, he'd wait until she'd gone to bed—and then she went into her front yard and hid behind a bush and waited. At one, the truck moved closer to her house and the driver got out. She saw he was wearing a mask. She saw the gun in his hand. When he crept into her front yard, he walked right by the spot where she was lying on the ground under the bush. And when he walked around her house to reach the backyard, she went the other way, and when she saw him tapping on the window, she started videoing him with her phone and ordered him to drop the gun.

But she hadn't wanted to kill him. That was the last thing she'd wanted. She'd wanted him arrested. She'd wanted a live witness that could be squeezed, one who would have to explain why Doyle had him following DeMarco and why Doyle had ordered him to kill her. She'd wanted to put Doyle in the position of having to explain to law enforcement what he was up to. She'd wanted to spill all the worms out of the can that Porter Hendricks had opened. Now, however, with the man dead, she'd have to come up with another plan.

But the first thing she needed to do was get to a hospital.

———◆◆◆———

She called 911.

"What's your emergency?" the dispatcher asked.

Speaking calmly but gritting her teeth because of the pain, she said, "I've been shot, and I shot a man trying to break into my house. The man's dead and I'm bleeding badly. I'm lying in my backyard. My address is—"

She didn't remember the cops and the medics arriving. She must have passed out. Her next memory was waking up in the emergency room as a nurse was cutting the leg off her jeans. She must have passed out again immediately after that, because the next time she came to, she was lying in a hospital bed, hooked up to machines measuring her vital signs.

Her leg was aching, as if someone were hitting it softly but rhythmically with a hammer. But it was a dull pain and bearable. They'd probably given her painkillers. She looked under the sheets and saw her thigh was wrapped in bandages and there was a device encasing her leg to immobilize it.

She found the call button on a stand next to her bed and pressed it. Seconds later a short, cheerful-looking nurse came into the room.

"Ah, good, you're awake," the nurse said with a smile. "How's the pain?"

"Manageable," Emma said. She wouldn't let them give her any more pain medication until she'd talked to her lawyer and the cops. She couldn't take the chance of saying something she shouldn't, and drugs might affect her ability to think. And to lie.

"Good," the nurse said. "I'll go get the doctor and he can explain—"

"No," Emma said. "I need my phone. Immediately. Give me my phone and then you can go get the doctor."

Looking uncertain yet at the same time intimidated, the nurse said, "Okay." She went to a small closet in the room and took a plastic bag off the top shelf, removed Emma's phone from the bag, and handed it to her.

Emma said, "Thank you. What's the name of this hospital?"

———◆———

Emma looked at her phone and saw it was seven a.m. The shooting had happened at about one. She'd lost six hours. Judging by the bandages on her leg and the way the leg was immobilized, she'd probably spent most of that time in an operating room.

Emma pulled up her contacts list and found Janet Evans.

Janet Evans was one of the most expensive lawyers in Washington, D.C. She billed at about twelve hundred bucks an hour. She didn't usually handle mundane criminal cases, and most murders were mundane. Her clients were typically politicians and celebrities and very wealthy people who committed complex crimes like tax evasion and insider trading and money laundering and defrauding their investors. And normally Janet didn't see clients at seven in the morning, and when she did see clients, it was almost always in her office. Emma was the exception.

Janet answered the phone sounding alert. She hadn't been asleep. She said, "Good morning, Emma. Why are you calling so early?"

"I killed someone."

"Again?" Janet said.

"I need you to come to McLean Hospital right away. I want you in the room when the police question me."

"Why are you in the hospital?"

"I've been shot."

"Oh, my God. How badly are you hurt?"

Emma hung up.

A man wearing blue hospital scrubs showed up a few minutes later and introduced himself as Dr. Werner. He was tall and bald and reminded Emma of a character actor who'd appeared in a lot of movies, but, him being a character actor, Emma couldn't remember his name.

"How's the pain?" the doctor asked.

Again Emma said, "Manageable. What's the extent of my injuries?"

"The bullet shattered your femur. I've put in a rod and some screws. I'll show you the X-rays later so you can see the hardware. You'll recover eventually but you have a lot of therapy ahead of you. And a lot of pain. Right now, the only major concern is infection."

The guy had the bedside manner of an android but that was okay. Emma preferred direct and succinct. He said, "There are a couple of detectives waiting to talk to you. Do you feel well enough to speak to them? If you don't, I'll tell them to come back when you do."

"Tell them I'll talk to them as soon as my lawyer arrives, which should be within the next half hour."

———◆◆◆———

The detectives, two men in their forties, dressed in sport jackets, stay-pressed, off-the-rack slacks, white shirts, and muted ties stood at the end of the bed. One of them was Black, the other white. Their names were Green and Murdock. They didn't look alike except for their eyes. They had the eyes of confirmed skeptics, the eyes of men who expected people to lie to them.

Janet Evans sat in the only chair in the room, and it was placed near the head of the bed, close to her client. There was a notebook in her lap and a pen in her hand. Janet was in her sixties but looked younger, as she could afford to pay surgeons to make her look younger. She was dressed in a suit that cost more than the detectives earned in a month.

Green, the Black detective, said, "Okay. Now that your lawyer's here, I guess we can get started. And since we found a dead man in your backyard, I'm going to read you your rights."

He read the Miranda warning off a card, asked if Emma understood, and she said yes. "Okay," Green said, "now can you tell us what happened?"

Emma said. "I heard a man trying to break into the back of my house. I got a weapon, went out the front door of the house, circled around to the back, and asked him to drop his gun. He tried to kill me, and I shot him. I videoed everything."

"You what?" Green said.

Emma handed Green her phone and said, "Hit play."

Green and his partner watched the video. "Jesus," Green muttered when the shots were fired. Then they watched it a second time.

The man she'd killed was barely visible in the video as it had been shot in the dark, but the sound was clear, as were the flashes when the guns were fired.

"How did you video this?" Green asked. "Were you holding your phone in your hand when you shot the guy?"

Emma said, "No. I turned on the camera and put my phone in the waistband of my jeans, facing forward, before I confronted him."

"You're telling me you get woken up by a guy trying to break in, and you had the presence of mind to set your phone to video things? Why would you do that?"

"First, I didn't say I was sleeping. I said I heard someone trying to break in. And I videoed my encounter with the man so there'd be a record of what happened and no doubt that if I was forced to shoot someone, I'd acted in self-defense."

Green looked over at his partner, who shook his head, then turned back to Emma and said, "Lady, I gotta tell you. I'm having a hard time buying this story."

Janet said, "What are you saying, Detective? That you think my client is lying to you?"

"No, I don't think she's lying about how the guy was killed. The video makes that pretty clear. And the video matches the crime scene. But I think there's more to the story."

"Like what?" Emma said.

"I don't know. But something's off here. Like, if you weren't sleeping, what were you doing?"

Before Emma could answer, Janet said, "What difference does it make what she was doing? She was in her home and a man tried to break in and she armed herself and investigated. The video shows she gave that man every opportunity to drop his weapon, but he fired, and she was forced to kill him."

"Did you know the man you killed?" Green asked.

"No," Emma said. That wasn't exactly a lie. The man was Shaw's partner, but she didn't know his name. "Who is he?"

Green hesitated.

Janet said, "We'll get his name eventually, so you might as well answer the question."

"His name is David Burkhart. Does that name mean anything to you?"

"No," Emma said. Emma was certain that Burkhart, like Shaw, had worked for Doyle but there was no reason to tell Green that. Instead, she asked, "Does he have a record for robbery or breaking and entering?" She wanted to know what Green had learned about the man she'd shot.

"I don't know," Green said. "We haven't had time to do a records check."

"Bullshit," Emma said. "You've had all night to do one."

Green said, "Yeah, all right. No, he doesn't have a record. He's ex-military and he used to work for Doyle Logistics. But they fired him a couple of months ago. And that's all I know about the guy so far."

Fired him? Emma thought. That didn't make sense, but she didn't say anything.

Green said, "Okay. I guess we're done for now, but I want your phone so I can examine that video more closely."

"No," Emma said. "I need my phone. But give me your number and I'll text the video to you."

Green paused, then said, "Okay. For now. But I think I might ask one of our lawyers to force you to give me your phone with a subpoena."

"Why would you do that, Detective?" Janet said. "My client is willing to give you a copy of the video. What more do you need?"

"I don't know. But I want the original, assuming that's an original. I want to make sure it hasn't been doctored in some way."

Janet said, "Are you planning to arrest my client?"

"No. Not yet, anyway. But something isn't right here. I need to talk to my boss and the lawyers."

"Detective, my client is a highly respected former civil servant who spent thirty years protecting this country. And you have unimpeachable evidence that she acted in self-defense. If you cause my client any sort of aggravation, I will sue the ass off Fairfax County."

The unhappy detectives left a few minutes later.

Janet said, "Are you going to tell me what's going on here?"

"No," Emma said.

Janet looked at her and said, "You don't look good at all, Emma. How are you feeling?"

"Just tired. Thanks for coming, Janet."

It was time to call DeMarco back.

41

After a fitful night's sleep—he kept rolling over on the arm that had been wounded—DeMarco got out of bed at six, and the first thing he did was call Emma again. No answer.

He called Mahoney's office next. It was seven in D.C. and Mahoney most likely wouldn't be there. But Mavis would be.

He said, "I need to speak to him. It's urgent."

"He's not here. He's attending a prayer breakfast sponsored by the Black Caucus."

"A prayer breakfast? Are you shitting me?"

Mahoney had been raised Catholic and at one time had been a pudgy, irreverent altar boy, one who stole the sacramental wine. These days he wasn't the least bit religious and only attended Mass when he was campaigning. For Mahoney, religion was a political prop and an opportunity to meet voters—or, in this case, an opportunity to stay on the good side of the Black Caucus.

He said to Mavis: "You need to call him and tell him to stop praying. I've been shot and I'm being detained by the police in Mexico."

"Oh, my God," Mavis said.

"Who the hell shot you?" were the first words out of Mahoney's mouth.

A normal person might have asked: *How badly are you hurt?*

"It was one of the guys Doyle had following me," DeMarco said.

"Did the cops catch him?"

"Yeah, in a way. He's dead."

"What the hell happened?"

"Last night I met with one of the call girls who probably slept with the president. In fact, I'm sure she slept with him, but before she would confirm it, she was killed. We were sitting in a bar and Doyle's guy opened fire. He killed the woman, wounded me, and killed a server. He was killed by the call girl's bodyguard."

"Jesus," Mahoney said.

"Look, I can explain all this to you later. Right now, I need to get out of Mexico and the cops have taken my passport and won't let me leave. I need you to call the embassy here and tell them to do whatever they have to do to make the cops let me go. I haven't committed a crime."

"Yeah, all right," Mahoney said. "Oh, how bad were you shot? You sound all right."

"I'm all right. It was just a flesh wound. But thanks for asking."

An hour later—folks tended to jump when Mahoney wanted something done—DeMarco was called by a guy from the American embassy. The guy said he was an assistant something or other, sounding as if DeMarco should be impressed by his title. He told DeMarco that he had his passport and would drop it off at the hotel shortly and DeMarco was free to leave the country. He added that the detective in charge might call him later if she had more questions and the embassy guy had promised her that DeMarco would be cooperative and answer her questions and would return to Mexico if necessary.

"You bet," DeMarco lied.

DeMarco took a shower, shaved, packed, and made a reservation on a flight to Dulles.

He didn't feel safe until he'd gone through security at the airport.

———◆◆◆———

His phone rang as he was about to walk down the jetway to board the plane. It was Emma. Finally.

DeMarco answered saying: "Where are you? That guy Shaw who works for Doyle tried to kill me last night."

"Doyle had someone try to kill me too," Emma said. "I killed the man but I'm in a hospital in McLean."

"A hospital? Jesus, what happened?"

"We'll talk about what happened to me later. What happened in Mexico?"

"While I was talking to Gabriela, Shaw killed her and shot me in the arm. I'm okay. Shaw's dead. Gabriela's bodyguard killed him."

"Where are you now?"

"At the airport in Mexico City, about to catch a flight back to Dulles."

"When you land at Dulles, you need to take precautions."

"Emma, you don't sound good. How badly are you hurt?"

"Shut up and listen to me. Doyle might try to have you killed again. So when you land in D.C., call Mahoney and see if he can get the Capitol Police to protect you until we can sort all this out."

"What about you? Who's protecting you?"

"Don't worry about me. I have to go now. I have other calls to make."

———◆◆◆———

Emma had been wrong about DeMarco not being in danger. She'd underestimated Doyle, thinking that he wouldn't know that DeMarco had gone to Mexico because she'd prevented his guys from following him to the airport. What she didn't know was if the call girl had been killed intentionally or if she'd been collateral damage when Shaw tried to kill DeMarco. Most likely, she'd been killed intentionally—which meant that the other two call girls could be in danger. Doyle could be trying to eliminate everyone who could cause him a problem.

Emma made three phone calls. She was on the phone for forty-five minutes. The little nurse came in at one point and tried to tell her something, but Emma shooed her away. When she finished the phone calls, she pressed the call button next to the bed and the nurse returned.

Emma said, "I'll take those pain meds now." Her leg felt as if it were on fire.

"I'll get them," the nurse said. When she came back to the room, she gave Emma a couple of oxycodone pills and said, "You need to rest."

Then she glanced at one of the machines and said, "Your temperature is elevated. That's not good. I'm going to take a blood sample and get it to the lab to see what your white blood cell count is."

Emma nodded and closed her eyes.

42

Doyle hadn't heard back from either Shaw or Burkhart and wondered why. Whether they'd succeeded or failed to complete their missions, it wasn't like them not to stay in touch. They should have contacted him this morning if not last night.

His phone rang—his personal phone and not the burner he used to communicate with Shaw and Burkhart. It was Mortensen. Mortensen was the man he nominally put in charge of Doyle Logistics when he became the president's national security advisor. Doyle had served with Mortensen in the Army and when Doyle became a general, Mortensen had been a colonel and his deputy, and when Doyle left the Army to start his company, Mortensen came with him. He was competent and not overly ambitious. He was most likely calling regarding some issue having to do with the company that he needed Doyle's advice on or approval for, but whatever it was, it could wait. He let the call go to voicemail. Then decided to listen to the voicemail.

Mortensen's message said: *"Call me ASAP. It's about Shaw and Burkhart and I don't know what the hell is going on."*

He called Mortensen back. "What about Shaw and Burkhart?" he asked.

Mortensen said, "I got a call early this morning from a Mexican cop. Shaw was killed last night in Mexico City. He shot up a hotel bar, a man and a woman were killed, and another man was wounded. Shaw was killed by the bodyguard of one of the people he killed."

Doyle was too stunned to speak.

Mortensen said, "Shaw had his ID on him and that led to them finding out that he worked for us. The cop called to ask what he was doing in Mexico."

"What did you tell him?"

"It was a her, and I told her I'd call her back after I talked to our lawyers."

"That's good, but—"

"I'm not done. I'd barely finished talking to the Mexican cop when I get a call from a detective in Fairfax County. Burkhart was killed trying to break into a woman's home in McLean. The Fairfax cops found his truck parked on the block and he had a company parking pass in the glove compartment. What the hell is going on, Eric?"

Doyle took a breath and said, "I can't tell you what's going on. It's classified. Anyway, you tell the cops that Shaw and Burkhart separated from the company two months ago, that you have the records to prove that, and that you have no idea what they were doing."

"I already did that—told them they no longer worked for us," Mortensen said.

"Good," Doyle said.

At the time Doyle had told Mortensen that he needed Shaw and Burkhart for a special assignment—that assignment being to kill Brandon Cartwright—he'd told Mortensen to make it appear as if they'd separated from the company. Although Doyle hadn't expected them to be killed or arrested, if they were, the company could honestly claim that they hadn't been working for Doyle Logistics, which isolated both the company and Doyle. While working for Doyle on the Cartwright matter and everything that followed, they'd been paid out of a slush fund the company used for bribing people overseas and making any other payments they didn't want traced.

Doyle said, "If the cops ask, you tell them the reason they were terminated was that they'd both been exhibiting erratic behavior. Getting into fights, arguing with their supervisor, that sort of thing. You say they may have been suffering from combat-related PTSD, but whatever the case, you had to let them go."

"Records will show that a company jet went to Mexico City," Mortensen said.

"But the records won't show that Shaw was a passenger."

He wasn't worried about the plane. But he was somewhat worried about the cops looking at Shaw's and Burkhart's cell phones to see who they'd been calling and texting but not too worried because the phones were password protected and calls and text messages were encrypted. And the only phone he'd used to communicate with them was a burner.

When Mortensen didn't respond immediately as if he was thinking things over, Doyle said, "Vic, just do what I'm telling you. Tell the cops you fired Shaw and Burkhart and that you have no idea what they've been up to since then. And if the cops try to subpoena our records, get the lawyers involved."

"All right," Mortensen said.

Doyle could tell Mortensen wasn't happy, but he was loyal, and he'd do what he'd been ordered. Mortensen now made three times as much as he'd made as an Army colonel, and he'd been involved on other occasions when the company had been forced to skirt the law.

Doyle said, "You said a man and woman were killed and one man was wounded in Mexico. Who was the man who was killed?"

"A waiter in the bar. I don't know his name."

"And the one who was wounded?"

"Some guy named Joseph DeMarco from D.C."

Aw, shit, Doyle thought. DeMarco was still alive. And if Burkhart was dead, that probably meant that Emma was alive too.

What the hell was he going to do now? He didn't have another pair like Shaw and Burkhart he could call on immediately, and DeMarco and Emma still posed a threat. A threat he had to eliminate.

43

DeMarco called Mahoney as soon as his plane landed at Dulles. Naturally, he wasn't available. He told Mavis to have Mahoney call him as soon as possible.

DeMarco decided that while waiting to hear back from his boss the smart thing to do would be to stay in the terminal behind the security checkpoint.

An hour later, Mahoney finally called. "Where are you?" Mahoney asked.

"At Dulles. The embassy got me out of Mexico. But I've got a problem and you might have one too. Last night, someone not only tried to kill me, they tried to kill Emma too. She's in the hospital."

"Jesus Christ. How bad is she?"

"I don't know. I don't know anything at this point other than the fact that Doyle tried to kill both of us last night. And he might try again. I need some security. Can you get the Capitol Police to provide me a couple of bodyguards?" Before Mahoney could answer, he added, "And you need to beef up your security too. I don't know if Doyle knows you're involved in this or not, and I don't know if he'd be crazy enough to go after you, but he might."

Mahoney was silent for a minute. "Okay. I'll get you some protection."

DeMarco knew that all Mahoney would have to do was say that a credible threat had been made against DeMarco and the Capitol Police would provide some armed bodies. He didn't know exactly what Mahoney would tell them and it didn't matter. They'd do what Mahoney wanted.

DeMarco said, "Tell them to call me when they get to the airport. I'm going to stay behind the security checkpoint until they get here."

Then he sat there, trying to figure out what to do next when it came to Doyle.

———————◆◆◆———————

Four Capitol cops, two men and two women, all of them dressed in suits, all of them serious as heart attacks, met DeMarco in baggage claim after they arrived.

DeMarco said, "My car is in the parking lot. I need to get it and then I'm going to a hospital in McLean."

The guy apparently in charge, one big enough to play on the line in the NFL, said, "We need to know more about the nature of the threat. All Congressman Mahoney told our boss was that your life is in danger."

"I can't tell you more," DeMarco said. "Not until after I've talked to Mahoney and the person I'm going to see in the hospital. All you need to know is that a man tried to kill me last night. So when we leave the airport, look around to see if anyone is following me. And if anyone tries to kill me again, I'd appreciate it if you'd shoot them."

All four cops escorted him to his car, their heads swiveling as they looked for potential threats. Two of the cops joined him in his car, and then with the other two cops following in their car, he drove to the hospital. At the hospital, he got Emma's room number—he was relieved that she wasn't in intensive care—and the four cops went up the elevator with him, making him feel like a rock star with an entourage.

As they walked down the hallway toward Emma's room, DeMarco saw a man wearing a windbreaker, sitting on a chair outside her room. When the man saw five people walking toward him, he stood up and one of the Capitol cops, one of the women, screamed, "Gun!" There was a pistol DeMarco hadn't initially noticed in a holster on the man's hip, the pistol partially obscured by the windbreaker. All four cops whipped out their pistols and pointed them at the man standing near Emma's doorway. A nurse who'd been walking down the hallway screamed and ran the other way.

The woman said, "U.S. Capitol Police. Raise your hands."

The guy raised his hands slowly and said, "Calm down. I work for Jenkins Security. The woman in the room is our client."

The Capitol cops eventually verified the guy was who he said he was and that he had a license to carry. DeMarco told all the bodyguards—his and Emma's—to wait in the hall while he talked to her.

DeMarco said, "Jesus, you look terrible." Her cheeks were flushed and he wondered if she had a fever. She barely had enough energy to speak. For the first time since he'd known her, Emma looked small and weak. She looked her age. She started to say something, then grimaced in pain.

"What happened to you?" DeMarco asked.

"I was shot in the leg."

"Who shot you?"

"His name was Burkhart. He was the guy who was with Shaw when Shaw was following you."

"So what—"

"I don't have much time. They're taking me back to surgery to look at my leg. I've got an infection and they have to cut me open to see what's going on." She grimaced again and said, "Those other two call girls are in danger. I called Javier and Sergio and told them to watch over them until we can decide what to do next."

Javier and Sergio were two lethal bastards that Emma knew from her time in the DIA. They were from someplace in South America and Emma had worked with them there, but exactly what they'd done together, DeMarco had no idea. Emma had arranged for them to immigrate to the U.S.—saving their lives in the process—and they currently lived in Miami. They would do anything for Emma, and a year ago, when Emma and DeMarco found themselves in the crosshairs of a couple of corrupt FBI agents in Florida, Emma asked Sergio and Javier to lend a hand in case the FBI agents tried to kill them. They came armed to the teeth with machine guns and sidearms and had night vision goggles and comm systems and body armor—everything you'd want in a couple of bodyguards. And what Emma was saying was that she'd sent them to protect the women in Costa Rica and Brazil.

Emma said, "And by the way, one of the detectives who questioned me said that Burkhart had been fired from Doyle Logistics a couple of months ago. That's probably a lie but what that means is that we might not be able to prove they were working for Doyle when Cartwright was killed."

"Or when they tried to kill us," DeMarco said.

"Yes," Emma said. "Anyway, as soon as I'm discharged from this place, you and I and Mahoney need to figure out what to do next."

"Yeah," DeMarco said, but he was wondering how long it would be before she'd be allowed to leave the hospital. She didn't look good at all.

Before he left the hospital, he asked the guy from Jenkins Security, "Are you the only one guarding her?"

"No," the man said. "But I'm the only one that anyone will see."

"Good," DeMarco said. "Make sure she stays safe."

"You don't have to worry about that. My boss will kill me if anything happens to her."

44

DeMarco told his bodyguards he was going to the Capitol. He needed to see Mahoney.

He found him in his office, chatting with a woman on his staff. The woman was a redhead in her twenties who was built like a Victoria's Secret model, which DeMarco imagined was the primary reason Mahoney had hired her. After she sashayed away, with Mahoney's eyes glued to her backside, DeMarco told Mahoney more about what had happened in Mexico and what had happened to Emma.

He concluded with "Emma's in bad shape. She got shot in the leg and they operated on her, but now she's got some kind of infection and they were taking her back into surgery when I left the hospital. She's hired a private security firm to watch over her and she's sent a couple of guys she knows, a couple of killers she used to work with, to protect the other two call girls in case Doyle goes after them."

DeMarco took a breath and said, "We have to stop Doyle. That son of a bitch has had five people killed and—"

"Five?" Mahoney said. Ticking the victims off on his fingers, he said, "There's Cartwright, his assistant, Maxine Barkley, and the call girl. Who's the fifth?"

"A server who was in the bar when I was shot. The poor guy was collateral damage."

"Can't you use the guys who tried to kill you and Emma to get to Doyle? I mean, they worked for his company, so even if they're dead, there has to be a way to tie Doyle to what they did."

DeMarco shook his head. "The cops investigating the one who shot Emma were told that Doyle Logistics fired him a couple of months ago. I imagine that's bullshit, but it probably means that Doyle can prove that they weren't working for him when they tried to kill me and Emma. If we could get the cops to subpoena Doyle's phone records, we might be able to show he'd been communicating with them but—"

Mahoney barked a sound that might have been a laugh. "There's no way in hell they're going to get a subpoena to look at the national security advisor's phone records. And even if they got a subpoena, I doubt Doyle would have used a phone that could be traced to him."

DeMarco said, "Well, we have to do something before Doyle has anyone else killed."

Mahoney asked, "Did the gal in Mexico City admit she screwed the president?"

"I already told you she didn't. But I know she did. Right before she was killed, she was negotiating a payment for going on the record, but I never got her on the record."

"What about the other two women?" Mahoney asked. "Have you talked to them yet?"

"No."

Mahoney said, "You need to get them to admit they fucked the president. Then we'd have one solid fact that we might be able to use."

DeMarco said, "Let's say they're willing to say under oath that they were paid to have sex with a man they were positive was the president. All the president would do is deny it and say, 'Prove it.' How would we prove it?"

Mahoney said, "You need proof in a court of law. You don't need proof when it comes to the media. And if I tell the president that one of those women will be willing to go on prime time and tell what he did, he'll know that the public will most likely believe her and not him. He wouldn't want that kind of scandal if he could avoid it."

"But what good does that do when it comes to getting Doyle?" DeMarco asked.

Mahoney shrugged. "Maybe nothing," he said. "But it will give me one hell of a lot of leverage over the president.

"Do you mean *political* leverage?" DeMarco said. "This isn't about fucking politics. This is about making Doyle and his best buddy pay for killing five people."

Mahoney said, "Just do what I said. Get those women on record admitting they fucked the president."

45

DeMarco got a good night's sleep knowing Capitol cops were outside his house, watching over him. In the morning, he peeled back the bandage and took a look at the wound on his arm. It was an ugly-looking gash about two inches long that would leave a scar that he could hopefully use to impress a woman someday. *Oh, that? I got shot while I was in Mexico, trying to prove that the president slept with a hooker.* Okay, he wouldn't say that, but the good news was his wound, unlike Emma's, didn't look infected.

Before heading off to see the call girls as Mahoney had ordered, he went, accompanied by his bodyguards, to the hospital to see how Emma was doing. The same guy from Jenkins Security was sitting on a chair outside her room. Emma's partner, Christine, was in the room with her, sitting in the chair next to her bed, holding her hand.

Emma wasn't awake. DeMarco didn't know if she was sleeping or in a coma. A ventilator was covering most of her face and all he could see were her closed eyes and her short silver-blond hair, which was matted down. She was connected to machines monitoring her vital signs, and there were two IV stands next to the bed with fluids running from plastic bags into her left arm.

"How is she?" he asked Christine.

Christine didn't look very well herself. Her eyes were red rimmed from weeping, and it looked as if she hadn't slept since learning that Emma had been shot.

She said, "She might die, Joe. The doctors have told me the infection she has is about the worst one you can get, something called pseudo-monas, and all they can do is keep pumping antibiotics into her."

Christine started sobbing, and DeMarco, not knowing what else to do, patted her on the shoulder, saying, "She'll be okay. I know she will." He didn't know that at all.

Christine said, "She's the strongest person I've ever known. I've always thought she was invincible. And now she's being killed by some stupid, invisible little bug."

"She's not going to die," DeMarco said. "When's the last time you ate?"

"I don't know."

"Well, go to the cafeteria and get something to eat. I'll stay with her while you're gone."

DeMarco didn't have much faith in the power of prayer. Nonetheless, he prayed.

───◆◆◆───

DeMarco called Javier first. He was in Rio watching over Elena, the third woman the president had had sex with.

DeMarco said, "I'm planning to come down there and talk to the woman you're guarding, and I wanted to know where to meet you." He imagined that Emma had told Javier and Sergio to contact Neil to get the information they needed regarding where the women lived and worked.

Javier said, "I think you'd be wasting your time coming here."

"Why's that?

"I called Emma to tell her but she's not answering her phone."

"She's not answering because she'd got an infection and is unconscious."

"Will she be okay?" Javier asked.

"I don't know. Anyway, what were you going to tell her?"

"The woman here is dying."

"Dying? What happened to her. Did Doyle's guys get to her?"

"No. She's got cancer. The first time I saw her, I barely recognized her. She doesn't look anything like the photo Emma gave me. She probably weighs less than ninety pounds and doesn't have any hair. I went to her house as soon as I got here, and a woman, who I think might be her mother, wheeled her out the door in a wheelchair and they took a cab to São Carlos Saúde Oncológica. That's a hospital here that treats cancer patients."

"Jesus," DeMarco said.

Javier said, "I bribed a nurse to tell me what's going on with her. She has pancreatic cancer and the nurse said she's terminal and probably won't last more than a couple of weeks."

DeMarco thought about the photo he'd seen of Elena. She was only twenty-eight years old and she'd looked like a goddess in the photo. It was impossible to imagine her being at death's door. DeMarco figured he could still go question her and ask her to admit that she'd had sex with the president, and if he offered her a million, she might do it because she'd be able to leave the money to whoever she cared about. But DeMarco needed a living witness to threaten the president with, one who could appear in a courtroom or on cable talk shows if it came to that. The other thing was that it seemed cruel to intrude on her as she was dying. She deserved to die in peace.

"So are you coming down here to talk to her?" Javier asked.

"No."

"Do you want me to keep watching her?

DeMarco thought about that. If Doyle learned about her condition, he probably wouldn't bother to have her killed, as she'd soon be dead anyway. On the other hand, if he did try to kill her and if Javier could nab whoever Doyle sent, they'd have someone they could use to testify against Doyle.

"Yeah, keep watching her. And if you spot anyone else watching her, call me right away. I'm going to go to Costa Rica and talk to the woman there."

DeMarco flew to San José, Costa Rica, arriving late in the day. He rented a car and drove to the address Sergio had given him over the phone. Sergio was supposed to be waiting outside Camila's apartment building, watching over her, but when DeMarco drove up to the building, he didn't see him. He didn't expect to see him. Ten minutes later, Sergio emerged from a shadow and joined him in the car. He'd probably waited to make sure no one was following DeMarco.

Sergio was only five foot six, about fifty years old, had graying dark hair, a thick mustache, and a wiry build. He didn't look dangerous, but DeMarco knew otherwise.

"How you doing?" DeMarco asked.

Sergio ignored the question.

"Have you seen anyone watching her?"

"No," Sergio said.

"Is she alone now?" DeMarco asked.

"*Sí*," Sergio said. Sergio was not a chatterbox.

It was almost seven. DeMarco didn't know what time Camila went to work, but he figured he'd better talk to her before she did.

"Which apartment is she in?"

"Six nineteen."

DeMarco said, "I need to talk to her, but she probably won't be willing to open her door to a stranger. And I don't speak Spanish. So I want you to convince her that you're a San José cop and make her open the door. Can you do that?"

"*Sí*," Sergio said. Sergio was dressed casually in a short-sleeve shirt and jeans, but he looked as if he could be a cop. He had that kind of face— one that was hard and unforgiving—and eyes that radiated suspicion.

He and Sergio left the car and entered the apartment complex. It appeared to be a place that catered to young, well-paid professionals, which Camila was. The apartments all faced a small courtyard where there was a swimming pool. Some of the apartments had balconies with a view of the lights of San José, Costa Rica's capital. Camila's apartment was on the top floor.

DeMarco stood to one side and Sergio rapped hard on her door. A moment later the peephole in the door darkened and a woman said something in Spanish, most likely: *Who are you* or *what do you want?*

Sergio rattled off a stream of words in Spanish that DeMarco didn't understand except for the word *policía.* Camila said something back and Sergio spoke again, and although DeMarco didn't know what he was saying, he sounded pissed off and impatient, and whatever he said must have been convincing. Camila opened the door and Sergio pushed his way into her apartment, followed by DeMarco.

Camila was wearing a red silk dressing gown that reached mid-thigh. Her feet were bare, the toenails painted bright red. Her shoulder-length dark hair was uncombed, and she didn't have any makeup on, but even without makeup she was stunning.

Seeing DeMarco, Camila said something else in Spanish to Sergio, but DeMarco and Sergio ignored her. In English, DeMarco said to Sergio, "I'll take it from here. Wait downstairs and keep your eyes peeled."

Sergio left and Camila, now speaking English and looking scared, said, "What's going on?"

"Relax," DeMarco said. "You're not in any trouble and I'm not going to harm you. But I need to talk to you."

"Why?"

"Because your life is in danger."

"Who are you?"

"Please, sit down so we can talk."

She sat down on a couch and DeMarco in an armchair facing her. He had to force himself not to stare at her legs.

"Who are you?" she asked again.

DeMarco ignored the question. He said, "In July of last year you flew to Washington, D.C., and had sex with a man there."

Camila's mouth froze open. She was too stunned to speak. Finally, she said, "I don't know what you're talking about."

"Yes you do, and I wouldn't be here if I didn't know what you did." DeMarco took out his phone and showed Camila the photo Neil had photoshopped, the one with the president wearing a black mask. He said, "This is the man you had sex with."

He said this as if he was certain. It wasn't a question. And he *was* certain.

DeMarco said, "But you didn't do anything wrong. And you didn't do anything illegal. But now, like I said, your life is in danger."

"Why? I said I'd never talk about that night, and I haven't."

She'd just admitted that she'd had sex with the president.

"The man who arranged your, uh, meeting with the man in the photo tried to blackmail him, and because of that he was killed. And another woman, one in the same profession as you, who also had sex with him, has been killed too. He's getting rid of people who can expose what he did."

"He doesn't have anything to fear from me. I won't talk."

"I believe you, but what I believe doesn't matter. You pose a threat to the man, and you'll be killed if you don't do something to protect yourself."

"Who are you? Why do you care what happens to me?"

"My name doesn't matter. But I work for a powerful man who doesn't want to see you harmed."

"But what can I do? Hide for the rest of my life?"

"No. At this point the best thing for you to do is meet with someone in the media, a big-name journalist, like someone on CNN, and admit you had sex with the man. Once you do that, what you did will be out in the open and he'll be afraid to do anything to you. And there will be no reason to do anything to you because the secret he's been trying to keep will no longer be a secret. And you'll be paid very well if you meet with the media. The person I represent is willing to pay you a million dollars and the media will probably pay you too."

DeMarco had decided—and no matter what Mahoney wanted—that the best thing to do at this point was what he'd told Camila: get her to tell her story to the media so it would be out in the open, and if she did, the president or Doyle would be afraid to kill her and would no longer have a reason to kill her. And the media, with a little help from DeMarco, would be able to start asking questions about Cartwright's death and the men who'd tried to kill him and Emma. And that might force the FBI to get involved, which was all DeMarco had ever wanted.

DeMarco said, "What I need you to do now is admit, on video, that you had sex with him. And I need you to confirm some details that will prove you're telling the truth."

What he meant was, he needed her to say where she met with the president, which he suspected was Cartwright's mansion. And he wanted to know if she'd met Cartwright or Maxine Barkley. Or Doyle.

He said, "If you do that, then I can get the ball rolling and set up an interview. And in the meantime, the man who was with me will be watching over you to protect you."

Camila sat back and studied his face. Without makeup on, she didn't look like the exotic woman in the photo on the escort agency's website. She looked like a pretty young girl, younger than her actual age. She looked innocent.

She wasn't. She said, "And then what happens to me? I become a media sensation for a while and the man is embarrassed and his enemies try to take advantage of the situation, but what happens to me in the end? After a couple of months, I'll be old news and people won't keep paying to hear my story. And a million dollars is nothing. I'm twenty-seven years old. Do you think with a million dollars I'd be set for life?"

Before DeMarco could say anything, she kept going.

"I'm not a stupid woman. I've always known that I can't do what I'm doing forever. I'll get old and over time men will pay less and less to be with me. I'm not going to end up as some pathetic fifty-year-old whore giving ten-dollar blow jobs. That's not going to be my life.

"There's a man, a very wealthy man who lives in Panama, and he wants to marry me. He's so in love with me, he flies here two or three times a month to be with me. He's a good man, a kind man. He's twenty years older than me, and he's wise, and he doesn't care about my past. I'm going to marry him and give him children. But he might not marry me if I do what you're asking—not if my face is on every television set in the world. I'm going to call and tell him what I've done and ask if he still wants to marry me, and I know he'll say yes. And he'll protect me until this problem goes away, which it will eventually. So, no, I'm not going to do it."

DeMarco couldn't help but like her. And like she said, she wasn't stupid. In fact, he got the impression she was quite bright.

"I think you're making a mistake," DeMarco said. "This man you're talking about marrying can't protect you, not from this man."

What he really meant was that he couldn't protect her from a maniac like Doyle.

"Yes, he can," Camila said. "You don't know this man."

DeMarco could see he wasn't going to be able to get her to change her mind—and, in a way, he didn't want to. She deserved a better life. He said, "Okay. The man who was with me has been watching to make sure you're not harmed, and he'll keep watching you until you make other arrangements. But you should make those other arrangements quickly."

"I'll call my future husband tonight," she said.

46

Doyle sat in his office. He sat in the dark with the lights off. He felt like an animal trapped in its lair. He needed to figure out what to do next. He needed to figure out what he *could* do next.

He'd wanted DeMarco, Emma, and the whores dead to put an end to DeMarco's meddling into Cartwright's death, but Shaw and Burkhart had failed him. And their failure had possibly made the situation worse, giving DeMarco more ammunition to use against him and the president.

The problem he had was that he didn't have the assets he needed to finish the job. Shaw and Burkhart had been the only ones he'd used when someone had to die to protect him, his company, or the country. He'd groomed them. He'd bonded with them. He'd spent a lot of time talking to them before he'd ever asked them to do anything out of the ordinary for him, and he had known, without a doubt, that they would be loyal to him and would be willing to kill for him and even willing to die for him. There were other men at Doyle Logistics, soldiers who had also served under him overseas, who were just as capable as Shaw and Burkhart and that he knew were just as ruthless, but he didn't know them well enough to know how they'd react if he asked them to kill. That wasn't something you asked a man to do without knowing in advance what the answer would be. He needed to find replacements for Shaw and Burkhart.

The only good news was that so far their deaths weren't causing him or his company a problem. The cops, the ones in Fairfax County and the ones in Mexico, appeared to be buying the story that the company had fired them and that they'd suffered from PTSD. And the U.S. media wasn't paying any attention—yet—to people dying in Mexico or what seemed to be a failed burglary attempt in McLean in which a thief was killed. More important, it appeared as if DeMarco hadn't told the cops anything that linked him or the president to Shaw's and Burkhart's activities. For whatever reason, DeMarco was keeping what he knew to himself, like the fact that Cartwright had asked the president for a pardon. Which still bugged the shit out of him: that he didn't know how DeMarco had come by that information.

But DeMarco was still digging. Albright's contact in the TSA had informed her that DeMarco had flown to Costa Rica, but as Doyle didn't have replacements for Shaw and Burkhart on hand, he hadn't been able to do anything about that. He imagined that what DeMarco was doing was trying to get the whore in Costa Rica to confirm that she'd had sex with the president. And she might be willing to do that. But not necessarily. The woman had been warned that if she ever spoke of that night, she would suffer. And even if she did confirm that she'd had sex with the president, there was no way anyone could prove she was telling the truth because the president had a Secret Service alibi that he'd been at the house in Gainesville at the time he'd really been with the whore at Cartwright's house. And, of course, Cartwright and Maxine Barkley weren't around to tell a different story. So the worst thing that could come from DeMarco's trip to Costa Rica was the president having to defend himself against accusations of infidelity coming from a foreign whore who would have no credibility and certainly no proof.

As for DeMarco making any claims that Cartwright, Maxine Barkley, and the hooker in Mexico had been killed to cover up the president's escapades, there was no way in hell the DOJ or the FBI would pursue anything along those lines unless DeMarco was able to present overwhelming, incontrovertible evidence. And as far as he knew, DeMarco had no evidence when it came to murder, and the people who'd committed the murders wouldn't talk because they were dead.

Doyle took a breath, centering himself. There was no reason to panic. He'd stay in touch with his contacts in law enforcement—the police chief in Prince William County and his guy at the FBI—to see if DeMarco met with them again. And he'd stay on top of the investigations in Mexico and Fairfax County. He'd also meet with a couple of men in the company who were possible replacements for Shaw and Burkhart. He'd invite them to have lunch with him today, where he'd discuss—in general terms—how the president's national security advisor sometimes needed good men to deal with extraordinary threats to the country.

47

When DeMarco got back from Costa Rica, he reacquired his Capitol Police bodyguards at the airport, then went to see Emma. Christine was still with her, wearing the same clothes she'd had on the last time DeMarco saw her, and it looked as if she hadn't slept since then. As for Emma, she looked the same. She was still unconscious, still on a ventilator, and the antibiotics were still dripping into her. And her prognosis hadn't changed. It still wasn't certain if she'd live or die.

After seeing her, he drove to Mahoney's apartment at the Watergate. There were two Capitol cops in suits stationed outside his door and DeMarco had seen four more sitting in an SUV parked on the street near the apartment complex. Mahoney was taking seriously the security threat that Doyle posed.

DeMarco didn't know where Mahoney's wife was—she'd most likely gone to bed—but Mahoney was sitting in his living room, dressed in boxer shorts and an old, gray Boston Red Sox T-shirt, watching himself on CNN. The T-shirt Mahoney was wearing was one from the 2004 World Series, the first World Series win for the Sox since 1918. It was wash faded and had a hole in one armpit, and Mahoney, with his big bare feet up on a coffee table and a tumbler of bourbon in his right paw, hardly looked like the most powerful Democrat on Capitol Hill.

That evening, however, he'd appeared on a news show to rant about the president authorizing a Hellfire missile strike on a house in Pakistan in which a terrorist was killed along with two innocent bystanders, one of them being an old woman, the mother of the man who owned the house. Mahoney was demanding to know why the White House hadn't gotten the Pakistanis to arrest the terrorist instead of dropping a bomb.

Mahoney turned off the television and said, "So. What do you got?"

"I got nothing," DeMarco said, and told him about the two call girls, the one who was dying in Rio and the one in Costa Rica who planned to hide out in Panama and refused to talk about her tryst with the president.

DeMarco waited stoically for Mahoney's outburst. He expected him to explode and start screaming at him for failing to get the results he wanted. But Mahoney didn't explode. He sat sipping his bourbon, scratching his armpit through the hole in the T-shirt, saying nothing. Finally he said, "Well, I'm gonna go see the son of a bitch tomorrow."

"Which son of a bitch?" DeMarco asked.

"The president. I'm going to lie my ass off and demand that he fire Doyle."

"And that's it?" DeMarco said. "Doyle and the president get away with murder?"

"Yeah, because you can't prove they had anyone killed. You can't even prove that the president had sex with those women. We're back to where we started, with a note in the archives that doesn't prove anything."

"So this is all on me?" DeMarco said.

Mahoney surprised DeMarco. "Nah, I'm not saying that. I knew we'd never be able to get the president. He's untouchable—not only because of who he is but because I'm almost positive he wasn't directly involved in anything Doyle did. He probably didn't even order Doyle to kill anyone. He just made it clear to Doyle that Cartwright had to go. No, all the president did was screw the hookers and he's not going to go to jail for that. As for Doyle, he got lucky when the guys who did the killings got killed themselves, because now the killings can't be traced back to him. But what I can do is lie to the president about the evidence we have and demand that he fire Doyle. And because the president doesn't want what he did to get broadcast to the whole world, he'll do it. At least that way Doyle won't have his ear and won't have a chance to get us into another war and he won't be protected by the White House if he does anything else."

DeMarco didn't say anything. But he was thinking that Doyle getting fired wasn't good enough. Not for him it wasn't. Emma might die, five people were dead, and the only thing that would happen to Doyle was that he'd lose a government job that he didn't need in the first place. There had to be some way to make him pay for what he did. There had to be.

The president might be untouchable, but Doyle wasn't.

48

Mahoney had been in the Oval Office more times than he could remember—and yet the room still had an impact on him. It wasn't the room itself, which wasn't all that special. It was knowing that the man who sat behind the *Resolute* desk was arguably the most powerful person on the planet. He commanded the best-trained, best-equipped military force the world had ever seen. He presided over the world's largest economy. His intelligence agencies could spy on every nation and every citizen. He could help governments in other countries stay in power or he could help bring them down. He could assist the starving or ignore them and let them starve. And whether the man who sat in the Oval Office was intelligent or not, corrupt or not, capable or not, his power wasn't diminished and the checks and balances that existed to rein in his power were often insufficient. And other than the fact that the current occupant of the office was willing to have people killed to hide his sexual escapades, he wasn't, in Mahoney's opinion, the worst person to have held the job.

Mahoney took a seat in one of the two chairs in front of the president's desk.

The president made a point of ignoring him as he finished reading a document. He placed the document face down on his desk when he finished it, looked at Mahoney, and said, "So, John, you got my attention. You told my chief of staff you needed to see me urgently but refused to say what the subject was. Normally, I would have refused to see you because I don't like meeting with people when I don't know the purpose of the meeting. But, well, considering who you are, I decided to make an exception."

He'd decided to make the exception because Mahoney had told the president's chief of staff that if the president didn't meet with him, he'd learn about the subject matter from the media—and he wouldn't like it.

"So, what's on your mind, John?"

As he said this, the president picked up a pen and unconsciously started doodling on the back of the document he'd been reading—and Mahoney almost said: *You gotta stop fuckin' doin' that.* But didn't.

Mahoney said, "Tomorrow morning I want to hear on the news that Eric Doyle is no longer your national security advisor."

"What?" the president said. "Are you serious?"

"Do I not look serious? And if he's not gone by tomorrow morning, I'm gonna go on Chris Hayes's show tomorrow evening and tell Chris how Doyle, acting on your behalf, had Brandon Cartwright, Maxine Barkley, and a call girl killed to cover up the fact that you had three hookers flown into D.C. to screw you."

"What in the hell are you talking about?" the president said, acting confused even though Mahoney knew damn well he wasn't. If the man hadn't been a politician, he could have been a successful actor.

"Save the denials for the pressroom," Mahoney said. "I have proof that Cartwright tried to blackmail you into giving him a pardon after he was indicted for peddling the ass of a fifteen-year-old."

"What proof?"

"I'm not going to tell you. But I will show the proof to my little buddy Chris. And it was after Cartwright tried to blackmail you and you decided not to give him a pardon that you had Doyle kill the man."

"I never gave any such order. That's absurd."

"Oh, I believe you," Mahoney said. "I mean, I believe that you never gave Doyle a direct order. You're way too smart to do something that stupid. You just told Doyle that Cartwright couldn't be allowed to blab about you and the hookers. And Doyle took things from there."

Before the president could interrupt, Mahoney said, "Doyle had a couple of guys who worked for him kill Cartwright and his assistant, then they later killed Maxine Barkley and—"

"I don't know any Maxine Barkley."

"You're probably telling the truth about that too," Mahoney said. "You probably never met her. But she worked for Cartwright and she's the one who arranged for the hookers to be flown in from Mexico, Brazil, and Costa Rica. And when Doyle learned about Barkley by following a guy who works for me, he had Barkley killed too. And then his guys tried to kill the guy who works for me and a woman working with him, and like I already said, they killed one of the hookers you screwed."

"This is ridiculous," the president said. "I don't know anything about these murders you're talking about."

"I believe you don't know about some of them because Doyle wouldn't have told you what he did because he wouldn't have wanted to make you an accessory. But you knew about Cartwright. You may not have given the order to kill him, but you knew Doyle was the one who had him killed and you know the reason why he was killed. And that's what I'm going to tell my pal Chris."

The president said, "You're insane. No matter who you are, no one is going to believe what you're accusing me of."

"Mr. President, I know the names of the hookers. I have their photos. I have the dates they flew into Dulles to fuck you. And I have the names of the guys Doyle used to kill Cartwright, Barkley, and the Mexican call girl. Doyle is telling people that those men were fired from his company before those people were killed, but no one is going to buy that story."

"You'll never be able to prove a damn thing you're saying," the president said—but he looked as if he was about to throw up.

"I don't have to prove it," Mahoney said. "I just have to tell everything I know—like the fact that Cartwright was blackmailing you and asked for a pardon—and Hayes will stare into the camera and start running his mouth. And since you got a reputation for not being able to keep your dick in your pants, folks are going to believe him. And the media might be able to put enough heat on DOJ to force the FBI to do a real investigation into Cartwright's death. The current investigation is being led by a county police chief and I have a witness who will testify that the chief did everything he could to tank the investigation, and I know Doyle was behind that too."

Mahoney noticed the president had made a couple of notes on the paper in front of him as Mahoney was speaking and again Mahoney almost told him: *Quit taking fucking notes!*

Mahoney said, "Now, I'm smart enough to know that the only thing that will happen when it comes to you is that you'll be skewered by the media for screwing the hookers—and for having them flown in on the taxpayers' dime—but that'll probably be the worst of it, as there aren't enough votes to impeach you. But if the media applies enough heat to DOJ, and the FBI investigates the shit that Doyle pulled, they might be able to get him. But most likely they won't, because he's a smart guy and probably covered himself pretty well. So I'll settle for him being fired. At least that way he won't be able use his position to kill anyone else for you. But if you don't fire him . . . well, there's no point in repeating myself."

Mahoney rose to his feet and turned his back on the president of the United States and walked out of the Oval Office.

49

Doyle steered the boat slowly along the shores of Smith Island and the Martin National Wildlife Refuge. Smith Island was in Chesapeake Bay, about fifteen miles off the Virginia shore, and the refuge was home to thousands of migratory waterfowl and red foxes and terrapins. Peregrine falcons nested there. None of which interested Doyle. It was a cool but clear day, the wind barely blowing, and he was going only five knots. He wasn't in any hurry. He had no destination in mind. He was just content to be out on the water alone where he could think about the future.

Doyle had two condos in the D.C. area. One in Reston within walking distance of Doyle Logistics' headquarters and another in D.C., a short drive from the White House. In addition to those places, he owned a run-down one-room cabin near Reedville, Virginia, that sat on ten acres of marshy land. The cabin had been his father's and Doyle had inherited it when his father passed. Near the cabin was a small marina where his dad had always kept a fishing boat, and when Doyle was a boy, he and his dad would stay at the cabin and use the boat to fish the Chesapeake. Doyle didn't have any use for the cabin, as it lacked most modern conveniences and was heated by an old wood-burning stove; he just hadn't gotten around to selling the place. But he, like his dad, kept a boat at the marina and he stayed on the boat, as it was much nicer than the cabin.

Unlike the boats his father had owned, some of them barely seaworthy, Doyle had a thirty-six-foot Tiara Sovran that had cost over three hundred grand. The boat had a bedroom with a full-sized bed, a wall-mounted television, a head with a shower, and a galley with a two-burner stove and a microwave, and it was a comfortable place to spend the night if he chose to. It also had twin 385-horsepower Cummins inboards that could propel it to almost thirty knots if he wanted to go that fast. And when he wanted to be alone or when he needed time to think or when he just wanted to take a break from work, he'd stay on the boat. He might fish if he was in the mood—he enjoyed fishing—but sometimes he just liked to cruise along the shore and enjoy the scenery. Right now, however, he was having a hard time enjoying anything.

He couldn't believe that the president—a man he'd known for thirty years, a man he'd considered his best friend, a man he'd been willing to do anything to protect—had fired him. He'd called Doyle into the Oval Office and, without any preamble whatsoever, said, "Eric, I need your resignation."

He'd been so shocked, he hadn't been able to speak.

The president said, "John Mahoney came to see me this morning and told some outrageous tale about you having people killed to cover up something I supposedly did. He claimed to have proof to back up his accusations and said he was going to spill everything to the media if I didn't dismiss you."

Doyle said, "Mr. President, I—"

The president held up his hand. "I'm not saying I believe Mahoney. The man's a pathological liar. What I am saying is that I can't afford, politically, to have to defend you against his accusations."

"Mr. President, everything I did—"

"I don't want to know what you did, Eric. And I'm sure whatever you did was well-intentioned. But this administration is doing important things for the American people, and it can't become bogged down in a scandal like the one Mahoney is promising to unleash."

Doyle had always known the president could be a cold-blooded son of a bitch when it came to his career and his legacy, but he'd never expected that he'd act toward him in this way.

The president said, "Now, I appreciate everything you've done for me in the past and I still consider you a friend. A loyal friend."

At that point, Doyle almost said, *Fuck you!* but didn't.

"All the press release will say is that you've decided to resign for personal reasons and that you'll be greatly missed. Which you will be."

He'd walked out of the Oval Office feeling as if he'd been literally stabbed in the back. He could almost feel the cold steel of a bayonet lodged in his spinal cord.

He'd just lost the best job he'd ever had. He'd had an outstanding career in the military and his company had made him a multimillionaire, but those jobs had been nowhere near as satisfying as being the president's national security advisor. As the national security advisor, he'd been privy to everything known to the country's eighteen intelligence agencies, and because of the president's confidence in him he'd been able to steer the administration in the direction he thought it should be going to defend the country against its many enemies. And the NSA job could have a been a launching pad for him one day occupying the Oval Office himself—something he'd thought about but never said out loud.

But now all that was gone.

He wanted to know exactly what Mahoney had told the president, but it had been obvious that the president had no intention of telling him. It was almost as if the president had been recording the conversation and he wanted nothing on the record that would implicate him in any way. About the only silver lining was that if all Mahoney had demanded was for him to be fired, that most likely meant that Mahoney didn't intend to ask DOJ to launch a criminal investigation. Which meant that Mahoney knew enough to unleash a media firestorm and become the president's worst nightmare, but he—or his fixer, DeMarco—didn't have the evidence to prove that crimes had been committed. So he wasn't going to go to jail. The only penalty he'd suffer was becoming an ordinary citizen again. Well, a very rich ordinary citizen.

He wished there were something he could do to avenge himself against Mahoney and DeMarco—and the president—for what they'd done to him. But he knew to do anything at this point would be futile insofar as getting his job back and that there could be unintended, negative repercussions. Like having DeMarco killed. That would be enormously satisfying, but if things went wrong, he could possibly end up being indicted as an accomplice to murder. It just wasn't worth the risk. Or like telling the world what the president had done—how he'd had whores flown in to service him—would also be satisfying, as it would humiliate the son of a bitch, but that was about all it would do. And who knew what the future might bring? Mahoney was an old man; he'd be dead before long, and maybe when he was gone the president would bring him back into the fold. No, the best thing at this point was to simply get on with his life—as unappealing as that seemed at the moment.

50

DeMarco had to force Christine to leave the hospital to go home and shower and change clothes. He promised he wouldn't leave Emma's side until she returned—as if him being there would make any difference. There was a war going on inside of Emma's body—the antibiotics engaged in mortal combat with the infection—and there was nothing his presence would do to turn the tide of the war.

As he sat next to Emma's bed, his mind turned again to his father. His father had been a criminal. He'd been a killer. But as the man at the wedding had told him all those years ago, Gino DeMarco had a code. He had principles. He was more than a gun for hire. And it was his code and his principles that had gotten him killed.

A corrupt cop had killed one of Gino's friends, a man he'd known since childhood, and Gino felt he had no choice but to avenge his friend's death. It was a matter of honor. What he didn't know when he made this decision was that the cop worked for his boss, Carmine Taliaferro, and that Taliaferro decided the cop was more important to his criminal enterprise than Gino. So his boss set Gino up and the cop killed him. DeMarco learned the story of how and why his father died years later, when he was working for Mahoney, and he found a way to make the cop pay for what he did. But he didn't kill the cop. He wasn't his father.

DeMarco took Emma's hand. It felt cold and small in his grasp. He didn't know if she could feel him holding her hand, but if she could, he wanted her to know that she wasn't alone. He also knew if Emma had been his father's friend, his father would have done more than just hold her hand. His father would have done something about the man who had put her in the condition she was in.

But he wasn't his father.

At that moment Sergio and Javier stepped into the room. Javier didn't have a mustache like Sergio, but they looked enough alike that they could have been related: two wiry men in their fifties you'd never guess were killers.

Javier said, "We wanted to see how she was doing. And to see if there was anything we could do."

DeMarco asked Javier, "Did Elena die?"

"Yes, the poor child," Javier said. "And the other one, Sergio made sure she made it safely to Panama. Do you trust the men Emma hired to protect her? If not, Sergio and I will stay."

"I trust them," DeMarco said. "And I don't think the man who's responsible for her being here will try anything else."

DeMarco had no idea if that was true or not.

"But what's to be done about him?" Javier said.

And that's when DeMarco made up his mind. "I'll deal with him," he said. "But I need you to do something for me."

———◆◆◆———

Christine returned an hour later to replace him on what appeared to be a death watch. As he left the hospital, he called Mahoney's office and told Mavis, "Tell him I'm taking some time off."

"He was asking if you'd gone to see Bitty Montrose up in Boston. If you haven't, you should deal with that before you go on vacation."

"Bitty can wait," DeMarco said.

"He's not going to be happy to hear that."

"Mavis, I don't care."

51

DeMarco was parked on a low hill above the marina, watching Doyle through a pair of binoculars. Doyle was sitting on a cushioned seat on the back of a boat, drinking a beer directly from the bottle, doing nothing other than gazing out at Chesapeake Bay. He was wearing jeans and a hooded sweatshirt, as it was a bit chilly out. DeMarco wondered what the bastard was sitting there thinking about. He wondered what schemes he was now hatching.

It had taken DeMarco a day and a half to locate Doyle. After Doyle was fired, he disappeared from Washington and, as best DeMarco could tell, no one knew where he was. He wasn't at his company's headquarters in Reston, nor was he staying at either his condo in Reston or the one he owned in D.C. There was nothing reported online or in the newspapers regarding his whereabouts, which wasn't all that surprising. DeMarco was sure that the media had wanted to ask Doyle about his reasons for resigning and what he planned to do next, but Doyle was notorious for not talking directly to reporters. When he'd been the national security advisor, he let the administration's press secretary deal with media inquiries, and when he ran his private security company, he did the same thing, letting the company's public relations people handle any questions. Doyle was of the opinion—an opinion that DeMarco shared—that rarely did anything good come from talking directly to reporters. Their business was entertainment, not journalism: they wanted sound bites, not facts.

DeMarco found Doyle when he went online and saw a photo of him posing with the Israeli defense minister on a boat. The article accompanying the photo said that Doyle was taking the minister on a private, personal tour of Chesapeake Bay, where they'd do a little fishing while they discussed matters of mutual interest to their two countries. The article said that the boat was Doyle's and the name of it was visible in the photo: *Sea Hawk*. He found a second online article, a profile of Doyle when he first became the national security advisor, and that article mentioned that Doyle, when he had the time, liked to escape the D.C. pressure cooker by fishing Chesapeake Bay. After three hours of research—research that Neil could have done in five minutes had DeMarco wanted to involve Neil—DeMarco learned that Doyle moored his boat at a marina near Reedville, Virginia, which was only a couple hours by car from the Capitol.

After he confirmed that Doyle was on the boat, DeMarco watched him for two days, sleeping at night in his car. He didn't want to check into a motel, where he could later be identified. At this point he wasn't trying to decide what he was going to do—he'd already made up his mind—but exactly how he was going to do it. And he needed to confront Doyle before Doyle got tired of living on his boat.

It appeared as if all Doyle was doing was relaxing, maybe unwinding from the stress of being the national security advisor and having innocent people killed. Both days DeMarco had been watching him, Doyle had gone for an early morning jog. He ran for about an hour, then returned to his boat, presumably had breakfast, and took a shower, then just appeared to putter about like a typical boat owner. The first morning he spent a couple of hours fiddling around with hand tools on what DeMarco thought might be a pump, like a bilge pump. DeMarco didn't know anything about boats other than the fact that the guys who owned them were constantly having to fix the shit that broke. After he fixed whatever he was fixing, he spent a couple hours polishing the chrome deck rails, which didn't appear to need polishing. On the second day, the boat left the marina with Doyle at the helm and headed east into Chesapeake Bay, and DeMarco wondered when—or if—he'd be coming back.

While he'd been watching Doyle, he used a burner phone he'd purchased before leaving D.C. to research Doyle's boat. (His own phone was sitting in his house in Georgetown.) He'd learned that a Tiara Sovran with full tanks had a cruising range of nine hundred nautical miles running at seven knots, which meant that Doyle might be gone for days if he decided to take a long cruise. But he didn't. He returned late that afternoon and had dinner at a small diner within walking distance of the marina. He had dinner at the diner both evenings DeMarco was watching him.

He figured that what Doyle was doing was avoiding the press and licking his wounds and contemplating his future. Or he might be sitting there plotting some way to get back at Mahoney for getting him fired. Or maybe he was trying to decide if he should make an attempt to kill DeMarco and Emma again. It didn't matter. Whatever he was planning, DeMarco had no intention of allowing him to fulfill his plans.

DeMarco checked the weather report on his phone again. It still showed heavy rain for tomorrow—which was good.

Tomorrow he'd do what needed to be done.

52

Despite the rain coming down, the next morning Doyle went for his run. He was a disciplined bastard. Then he disappeared into his boat to do whatever boat owners do on days when it's too nasty to be outside or go for a boat ride.

DeMarco drove to a sporting goods store in Callao, half an hour from the marina, and bought what he needed, paying cash. After that, he sat in his car and watched YouTube videos to learn as much as he could about Doyle's boat. At seven, Doyle left the boat wearing a hooded rain slicker and walked to the diner. DeMarco's dinner consisted of beef jerky he'd bought at the sporting goods store and a bottle of water. He knew he should eat something more substantial because he was going to need the energy later, but he was too nervous to eat.

As soon as Doyle disappeared into the diner, DeMarco parked his car behind an abandoned building where he didn't think it would be noticed if he left it there overnight and walked to the marina. There were only about a dozen boats moored there, Doyle's being the most expensive. All the boats except for Doyle's appeared to be unoccupied—again, not surprising in March. Nor did he see anyone walking around at the marina, which also wasn't surprising, considering the way the rain was coming down, and the marina office was closed. Since he'd been there, he'd never seen anyone in the marina office. One moored boat had an interior light on, but DeMarco hadn't seen anyone on the boat while he'd been watching Doyle, and he figured the owner had most likely forgotten to turn the light off.

Like Doyle, DeMarco was wearing a hooded rain slicker. His was olive green, the only color they had in stock at the place where he'd purchased it. He was also wearing gloves, and in a pocket in his jeans he carried a folding knife with a four-inch blade. He walked with his head down at a normal pace. He knew he was visible to anyone who might be watching, but it was dark out and, with the hood on his head and the rain slashing down, it would be hard for anyone to identify him and for a camera to capture a clear image of him. He'd spent an hour the second day he was watching Doyle trying to spot cameras at the marina and hadn't seen any, but that didn't mean there were none. Being picked up on a camera was just one of the many risks he was taking.

He walked down the pier where Doyle's boat was moored and, without hesitating, stepped on board. On the back of Doyle's boat, on the swim step, was an inflatable dinghy that was about ten feet long and had a twenty-five-horsepower Honda outboard engine attached to the transom. DeMarco figured the dinghy was there in case of an emergency or if Doyle had to anchor offshore. Whatever the reason, the dinghy was the main thing that made DeMarco's plan feasible.

There was a hatch that led to the boat's living quarters and he opened it and descended the steps. The interior of the boat was nicer than some hotel suites he'd seen. He knew the hatch would be unlocked, as he'd noticed that Doyle didn't lock it when he went to dinner. The lights were on in the living area, so DeMarco didn't need to use the light on his phone to see. He figured Doyle had most likely left the lights on intentionally to make people think the boat was occupied.

DeMarco took a seat at the small table in the galley, then just sat there, willing his mind to remain blank, not allowing himself to second-guess or change his mind about what he was about to do.

An hour later, DeMarco felt the boat shift slightly and he knew it was Doyle stepping on board.

The hatch opened and Doyle descended the steps.

He saw DeMarco immediately. He said, "What—"

DeMarco shot him in the chest.

53

Doyle fell backward after he was shot, his upper body resting on the steps he'd just walked down. DeMarco saw he was still alive. His eyes were open and he was looking up at DeMarco, trying to say something, but he was unable to speak.

DeMarco had thought about making a speech before shooting him. Telling him that he was going to kill him because it was the only way justice would ever be done. But he didn't bother with the speech. Doyle would know why he had shot him, and all making a speech would have done was give Doyle the opportunity to try to take the gun away from him.

He looked down at Doyle and waited for him to die. He didn't want to have to shoot him a second time if he didn't have to. He figured a single shot on a rainy night with the wind blowing might not be noticed—another risk he was taking—but he didn't want to fire more than once if he didn't have to. He waited five minutes while looking down at Doyle, thinking: *Die, motherfucker.*

Doyle died with his eyes open, silently begging DeMarco to save him.

DeMarco forced himself to think only about what he needed to do next. He'd think about what he'd done later, but not now. And what he needed to do now was concentrate on the actions he was planning to take to keep from going to prison. And he couldn't allow himself to panic or rush things. From this point forward he needed to move slowly and deliberately. He wondered briefly if his father had done the same thing: force himself to think only about the logistics of killing someone and not the potential legal consequences. Or the moral ones.

DeMarco pulled the body off the steps and down into the living area. The only blood he could see was in the center of Doyle's rain slicker. What he'd asked Javier to do for him that day in Emma's room was to provide him with an untraceable revolver; he didn't want there to be any record of him purchasing a gun. And he'd asked for a revolver because he didn't want to have to worry about ejected shell casings and the possibility of the gun jamming. The gun Javier had given him was a used, short-barreled .38-caliber Smith & Wesson. DeMarco didn't know where Javier had gotten it and he didn't ask. After Javier gave him the gun, DeMarco went online to learn about bullets, to find one that would do the maximum internal damage but wouldn't pass through a human body. It looked as if he'd picked the right bullets. There was no blood on the stairs caused by an exit wound. There might have been microscopic traces of blood splattered about the interior of Doyle's boat, but there was no blood that DeMarco could see that he needed to wipe up.

Then he searched the boat to find the toolbox he'd seen Doyle using when he'd been repairing the pump on the deck the other day. He found it. The box was a large Craftsman toolbox loaded with screwdrivers, wrenches, pliers, and an assortment of other hand tools. He found another box filled with fishing tackle, and inside it was lead fishing weights. He dumped all of the weights into the toolbox. He also found a set of socket wrenches and dumped them into the toolbox along with a short but heavy pipe wrench and a sledgehammer with a six-inch handle. With all the additional items added, he figured the box now weighed about forty pounds. He hoped that was enough.

Next, he went hunting for the two keys to the boat's ignition system. He found them hanging on a hook near the entryway hatch. The keys were attached to pieces of foam about the size of a cigar, intended to keep them from sinking should they fall into the water. He went to the bridge next and sat down in the captain's chair.

DeMarco's main problem with executing his plan was that he didn't know a damn thing about boats. He'd never owned one and had never wanted to. Which was the reason he'd spent all the hours online watching YouTube videos to learn how to drive Doyle's boat. He put the keys in the ignition and turned each one and the two powerful inboard engines came to life. It was as easy as that. It was no harder than starting a car. He hopped off the boat and untied the mooring lines. As he did so, he looked around and still didn't see anyone and thankfully the rain was still coming down hard.

He got back on the boat and returned to the bridge. There was a gearshift for each motor that was marked for forward, reverse, and neutral. He figured he didn't need both motors, so he left one in neutral and put the other in forward and turned the steering wheel the way he'd turn a steering wheel on a car and drove out of the marina. Fortunately, the boat was moored on the side of the pier and facing the direction he wanted to go, so he didn't need to back it out of a slip or do any tricky maneuvers.

He could barely see where he was going, but that was okay. As long as he went east, out toward the bay, he figured he wasn't liable to hit anything and doubted he'd run aground heading out to open sea. If he did, well, then he was fucked. There were no other boats on the water near the marina that he could see. He didn't turn on the boat's running lights because he couldn't figure out how to turn them on, so he left the lights on in the living space, hoping that if some other boat headed in his direction, it would see them and not hit him. And he didn't care if someone saw the boat leave the marina. They'd think it was Doyle leaving.

The boat had an impressive array of instruments mounted in the dashboard—instruments that probably showed things like the engines' oil pressure and temperature—and a couple of screens the size of iPad screens. He figured that one of the screens was for a navigation system that would tell him where he was and where he was going. But since he didn't know how to turn on the nav system or how to use it, he used the compass app on his phone to tell him that he was headed due east. And as he left the marina, he turned and looked back at a cell phone tower that would provide a landmark for him when he returned.

The one instrument he could read was the speedometer, and it told him he was going five knots. He engaged the second motor and pushed the speed up to ten knots. He drove for an hour, still heading due east, according to his phone's compass, then put the motors in neutral and let the boat drift.

He looked around and didn't see the running lights of any other boats. Off in the distance, he could see the lights of a large cargo ship, but that was miles away. He went down into the living area and dragged Doyle's body onto the deck and then went back and got the heavy toolbox. He undid one of the boat's mooring lines, which was about twenty feet long. He tied one end of it to the toolbox, wrapped the other end around Doyle, and tied it to the belt Doyle was wearing, then dumped him overboard. Thanks to a depth chart he'd found online, he knew that where he was, the water was over a hundred feet deep, which was why he'd driven the boat for an hour before disposing of the body. He could imagine the toolbox sitting on the bottom of Chesapeake Bay and Doyle's body floating above it for eternity. All he could do now was hope that the tides and currents weren't strong enough to drag the toolbox—and Doyle—toward the shore. With a little luck, Doyle might end up in the belly of a shark.

He went back into the interior of the boat and hunted around until he found a life jacket; he knew there'd be life jackets on board because boats like Doyle's were required to carry them. He put one on. He then went out to the swim step and untied the ropes holding the dinghy to the swim step, pushed the dinghy into the water, then used one of the ropes to secure it again to the swim step. He got into the dinghy—thankful the water wasn't rough enough to knock him overboard—and lowered the outboard, made sure the gearshift was in neutral, pulled out the choke, and tugged on the starter rope. It took four pulls to start it and he couldn't help but think that if it hadn't started, again he would have been fucked.

He threw the revolver he'd used overboard, then went back to the bridge, pointed the boat east, and nudged the speed up to about four knots. He had no idea where Doyle's boat would go. It might keep going east until it ran out of gas, which would take days. Or it might travel in circles. Or it might run aground. He didn't know. All he cared about was that when the boat was found, he didn't want it found near the body.

He managed to get back into the dinghy without falling overboard, untied it from the swim step, and again using the compass on his phone, headed due west—back to dry land. Two miserable hours later, wet and cold from the rain coming down, he was a hundred yards offshore. His cell phone tower landmark appeared to be about a mile away.

He tossed the cell phone he'd been using into the water. He'd just as soon that phone never be found because the phone's search engine history would pretty much show how he'd planned the murder. He put the outboard in neutral and used a rope to tie the tiller so it would keep the dinghy running straight, then took the folding knife out of his pocket, the one he'd bought when he bought the rain slicker. He jammed the four-inch blade five times in five different places into the dinghy's rubber gunwale and the air started hissing out, and then pulled the drain plug in the center of the boat. He'd learned about the drain plug and where to puncture the gunwale from his friend YouTube. He shifted the outboard to forward and hopped into the water. He was hoping the dinghy would travel a couple hundred yards from shore before it sank. However, he figured if it was found, it wouldn't be a problem because the name of Doyle's boat wasn't on the dinghy. He swam toward the shore, the life jacket keeping him afloat.

It was now one in the morning. He was wet and chilled to the bone. He wondered what the chances were that he'd die of hypothermia. He started jogging in the direction of the cell phone tower, hoping that by running instead of walking he'd warm up faster. He stopped once and tossed the life jacket and the gloves he was wearing into a thicket, first making sure the name of Doyle's boat wasn't on the life jacket, then kept jogging toward the cell phone tower.

As he was running, he finally allowed himself to think about what he had done.

He knew he was changed forever.

He'd become his father.

54

———◆———

A couple of unemployed drunks named Kirk and Potter were fishing off Northern Neck Reef, about six miles off the Virginia coast. They were in Kirk's ten-year-old, twenty-one-foot Trophy fishing boat, a boat that was worth about one tenth of Eric Doyle's boat. It was only eleven in the morning, but they'd already gone through most of a case of beer. Luckily, they still had another full case on board. They hadn't caught any fish worth keeping, but that didn't particularly bother them.

They saw a boat coming directly at them. It was a beautiful boat, one they'd only be able to afford if they won the lottery. It was moving slowly, going only three or four knots, and they figured whoever was driving would see them—see they had fishing lines out—and would change course. But it didn't change course.

When the boat was a hundred yards away and still coming toward them, Kirk said, "What's this son of a bitch doing? Does he think he has the right of way?"

"Aw, he's just fucking with us," Potter said. "He'll turn."

"I don't know," Kirk said.

When the boat was fifty yards from them, Kirk said, "Jesus Christ, I don't see anyone at the helm. He must have it on autopilot. That motherfucker's gonna run right over us."

Kirk started the engine, which coughed a couple of times before it started, almost making Kirk's heart stop. Potter grabbed a can filled with compressed air called an air horn and pulled the trigger. The horn gave out a blast of noise that could be heard a mile away. Kirk moved his boat out of the way just as the other boat passed over the spot where they'd been fishing. Potter was still pulling the trigger on the air horn while screaming, "Hey, you cocksucker, what's wrong with you?"

The beautiful boat went by, still moving slowly.

They could see the name on the stern: *Sea Hawk*.

Kirk said, "Something's not right. Maybe the guy's sick or something. He should have heard the horn."

Kirk turned his boat and headed after the *Sea Hawk* while Potter reeled in the fishing lines. When Kirk's boat was next to the *Sea Hawk*, he matched its speed. Potter hit the air horn again and shouted, "Hey, you in there. Are you all right in there?"

No one answered. No one came out on deck.

Kirk said to Potter, "Toss a line over a rail. We oughta see if whoever's on it is in trouble."

"Yeah, I guess," Potter said.

Potter, although drunk, was young and agile enough to scramble onboard the *Sea Hawk*. He went below and a couple minutes later came back onto the deck and said, "There's no one on this thing." He paused and said, "Ain't there some kinda maritime law that says if you find something at sea you get to keep it?"

"We gotta call the Coast Guard," Kirk said.

Potter pointed at the beer bottles rolling around on the bottom of Kirk's boat and said, "That could be a problem."

"They ain't gonna arrest us for being drunk if we're reporting someone missing at sea. Plus, by the time they get here, we oughta be sorta sober. I'll call the Coasties. Then I'll make a pot of coffee while you throw all the empties overboard."

"What about the full ones?" Potter asked.

"Well, shit, we'll keep those, of course."

No one had reported Eric Doyle missing. Doyle didn't have a wife, he didn't have kids, he didn't have a steady girlfriend, and he didn't have a job to report to. Reporters had called him after he left the White House, but they weren't surprised he didn't return their calls. He never did. Vic Mortensen had called him several times because he wanted to know what Doyle's plans were for him and the company, but Doyle didn't return his calls either. Mortensen was annoyed by this but not alarmed. Doyle was a rude bastard who often ignored phone calls until it suited him.

Albright, his former deputy, also called him because she wanted to know what was going to happen to her and to ask if Doyle would make a recommendation to the new national security advisor to keep her on as his deputy. She was also annoyed that he didn't return her calls. She'd been a faithful, hardworking deputy. But she also wasn't surprised when she didn't hear back from Doyle. She'd always known that he was the type who used people like they were Kleenex and then tossed them aside.

The Coast Guard started a search for the missing owner of the *Sea Hawk*, a search that intensified when they discovered the owner was the former national security advisor, Eric Doyle. Three helicopters, two more than would usually have been assigned, began flying nonstop along the coast and over the bay, trying to spot Doyle floating in the water. The Coast Guard learned almost immediately that the *Sea Hawk* was normally moored at the marina near Reedville, and Virginia state cops were dispatched to the marina to investigate.

The cops learned that Doyle had been at the marina two days ago, two days before his boat had been found adrift, that he'd stayed on his

UNTOUCHABLE

boat for several days before that, ate dinner every night at a local diner, but kept to himself. He didn't have any visitors that anyone saw, and no one had seen anyone on his boat other than him. He apparently left the marina one rainy night, although no one saw him leave. The guy who operated the marina said that Doyle would stay on his boat periodically, maybe a couple of times a year, and he'd often go for short cruises by himself on the bay. The one thing that surprised the Coast Guard and the state police was that no one from the White House called to pressure them when it came to the search-and-rescue mission. They thought for sure that would happen, Doyle having been such a good friend to the president.

A week after the boat was found, and after thousands of dollars had been spent on fuel for the helicopters, the search was called off. It appeared as if Eric Doyle had gone for a boat ride by himself and fallen overboard. Or maybe he had jumped overboard. There was a rumor that he might have been depressed after losing his job as the national security advisor. That rumor came out of the White House.

55

DeMarco called Darcy Adams. She had called him three times after he'd returned the key to Cartwright's mansion to her, but he'd ignored those calls.

She said, "Well, it's about damn time. What was on that flash drive you found in Cartwright's house?"

DeMarco said, "There was no flash drive."

"What?"

"Darcy, Cartwright's murder will never be solved, but the men who killed him are dead and the man who hired them is dead. And that's the truth, but that's all I can tell you."

"Why?"

"Because that's the way it is."

"Hey, that's not fair. And what about Harmon and what he did to me?"

"Darcy, you said you were looking for another law enforcement job close to Woodbridge. Where would you like to work?"

"If I had a choice in the matter, it would be with the Virginia State Police at their field office in Manassas. That's close to my mom's house."

"Have you submitted an application?"

"Yeah."

"You'll get a job there. That's a promise. I gotta go now. But thank you for helping me. And good luck."

———◆◆◆———

Mahoney was on the phone when DeMarco walked into his office, and DeMarco heard him say, "Yeah, well, you can tell the Speaker to go fuck himself." And with that, Mahoney slammed down the phone. Slamming down the handset of a landline phone was much more satisfying and dramatic than disconnecting a call on a cell phone.

DeMarco had gotten lucky. While he'd been dealing with Doyle, Congress had been engaged in a nonstop battle to fund the federal government before it ran out of money, and Mahoney had been too busy fighting with—and blaming—his Republican counterpart to notice DeMarco hadn't been around. The last continuing resolution had kicked the budget issue downstream for as long as it could, but it was about to expire, and if a compromise wasn't reached by midnight, there'd be a government shutdown. Which meant that DeMarco and a couple million other government workers—most of whom, unlike DeMarco, had jobs that actually mattered—wouldn't get paid. And based on what he'd just heard, it appeared as if a compromise wasn't likely. He couldn't have cared less.

DeMarco had spent most of the last week—the week the Coast Guard was searching for Doyle—staining his new fence and playing golf by himself and doing chores around the house, trying to concentrate only on what he was doing while pushing all the other unwanted thoughts out of his head. Most of those unwanted thoughts had to do with wondering what mistakes he'd made and if he'd spend the rest of his life in prison. Some nights he was able to sleep mainly because he drank himself to sleep. But yesterday he'd decided it was time to get back to work and had flown up to Boston. It was time to get on with his life. What was done was done. He didn't regret killing Doyle. His only real regret was that he hadn't been smart enough to find another way to make Doyle pay for his crimes. And whether he regretted it or not, he'd have to live with it.

He dropped an envelope on Mahoney's desk. In it was ten thousand dollars in crisp one-hundred-dollar bills. "Bitty wants her great-grandniece to become a congressional page this summer. She's not happy that her property taxes have gone up by five percent and is under the impression you can do something about that. And she's pissed that you haven't done anything when it comes to gun control."

Mahoney opened his mouth to say something—DeMarco had no idea what—but then he didn't. He sat there studying DeMarco's face. Mahoney was so self-absorbed that he rarely paid attention to the feelings or the moods of the people around him. But now, inexplicably, he seemed to be assessing DeMarco's demeanor. Finally, he said, "You heard about Doyle being missing?"

"Yeah," DeMarco said.

"You know anything about that?"

"No," DeMarco said. "Why would I?"

Before Mahoney could respond, DeMarco said, "I'd like you to do something for that detective in Prince William County who assisted me when I was looking into Cartwright. I want you to help her get a job with the Virginia State Police at their office in Manassas."

Mahoney's eyes were still locked on DeMarco's face. But then, after a long pause, all he said was, "Yeah, okay. What's her name again?"

"Darcy Adams."

Mahoney wrote down the name and DeMarco knew he'd pass it on to his chief of staff, Perry Wallace, and Perry would make a few calls, make a few threats, make a few promises, and the Virginia State Police would have a new employee.

"Anything else?" Mahoney said.

"No," DeMarco said.

As DeMarco turned to leave, Mahoney said, "I hope you were careful."

"I don't know what you're talking about," DeMarco said.

⬥

Mildred Washington went to church every Sunday. The truth was, she didn't have much use for religion, and the only reason she went to church was she liked to listen to the choir and liked to socialize with folks after the service. She didn't believe in heaven or hell. She figured when you passed, that was the end of things. And she certainly didn't believe in a righteous God who rewarded good and punished evil. There wasn't any evidence that such an entity existed.

But she did believe in karma.

She believed that people eventually got what was coming to them. Bad people could go a long time without ever paying for their deeds, but eventually those deeds caught up to them. Not always, but most of the time. And she was certain that Lady Karma had caught up to Eric Doyle. And one of these days, the Lady would get the president.

And she might help Lady Karma along. She'd made a copy of the president's notes on the back of the U.N. speech and snuck the copy out of the National Archives building in her purse. She didn't know what she would do with the copy or if she'd ever do anything with it, but she wanted it in case the original disappeared. And maybe one of these days, after she retired and after the president was no longer the president, she'd mail it to somebody. But all she'd do for a while was sit back and see if

Lady Karma would catch up with the president. She was pretty sure the Lady would.

———◆◆◆———

"Thank God, you're here," Christine said. "She's driving me insane. I'll be back in an hour. Maybe. If she needs anything, you can get it for her. Or you can strangle her for all I care."

DeMarco had called Christine to check on Emma several times before and after he dealt with Doyle. The last time he called, she had informed him that the antibiotics had finally won the war. Emma had come out of the coma and a day later she insisted on leaving the hospital. She was rich enough that she could hire a private nurse to come to her home and tend to her.

She had a long road to recovery ahead of her. She would continue to be treated with the antibiotics for a couple more months and would start physical therapy sessions for her leg. The doctors estimated it would be at least six months before she'd be back to normal. Until then, she was making life miserable for everyone who came into contact with her: nurses, physical therapists, doctors—and Christine.

Emma was lying in her bed, reading a Kindle, an IV stand next to the bed, dripping the antibiotics into her arm. She looked much better than the last time DeMarco had seen her. Not quite her old self yet, but better.

When she saw him standing in the doorway to her bedroom, she opened her mouth and he was expecting she'd fling some sarcastic barb at him as she usually did, but then she didn't. She just looked at him.

"I came by to see how you were doing" DeMarco said.

She still didn't say anything.

She was studying him the way Mahoney had.

Finally, she said, "Is there anything you'd like to talk about?"

"No," DeMarco said. "Like I said, I just wanted to see how you were."

After another long pause, she said, "There's a quote attributed to Theodore Roosevelt that I've never forgotten."

"Oh, yeah?" DeMarco said. *What the hell did Teddy Roosevelt have to do with anything?*

"He said, 'In any moment of decision, the best thing you can do is the right thing, the next best thing is the wrong thing, and the worst thing you can do is nothing.'"

She paused before she said: "You didn't do the worst thing, Joe."

As DeMarco was driving back to his place after seeing Emma, he looked into the rearview mirror. The eyes staring back at him looked the same. *He* looked the same. Or at least he thought he did.

He wondered what it was that Mahoney and Emma had seen.

Well, whatever it was, he wasn't going to dwell on it.

He was thinking that if Mahoney's efforts to avert a government shutdown failed and he was temporarily laid off, he'd head south, to someplace warmer, and play golf. There was also a woman he'd met the last time he and Emma were in Miami, and he wouldn't mind seeing her again. More than anything else, he wanted to get out of the cesspit that was Washington for a while.

When he arrived back at his place in Georgetown, he hit the remote on the sun visor and the garage door rolled up. He pulled into the garage and got out of the car, but before he could lower the garage door, two men in dark suits walked into the garage. They must have been waiting for him and he hadn't noticed them parked near his house.

"Mr. DeMarco," one of them said. "FBI."

The two agents standing there didn't look anything like old Al Burton, the last FBI agent he'd encountered.

DeMarco could tell that these two were the A Team.

"What can I do for you?" DeMarco said.

"We'd like to know what you were doing in Reedville, Virginia, on March eighteenth."

AUTHOR'S NOTE

———◆———

In case anyone doubts the plausibility of an archivist at the National Archives seeing notes made by the president, I wanted to share an excerpt from a news article. I "redacted" the names and the date to protect the guilty.

ABC NEWS

By Katherine Faulders, Mike Levine, and Alexander Mallin
November ████████

"Sources said that in at least one interview with ██████, investigators pressed the former vice president on personal notes he took after meetings with President █████ and others, which investigators obtained from the National Archives."

I also took some liberties with the geography of the Reedville, Virginia area. There is a marina near Reedville, but you can't sail due east to reach Chesapeake Bay as I wrote. I changed the geography to make it easier for DeMarco to navigate Doyle's boat as DeMarco, like myself, is not a boat guy. I also want to thank my friend and golfing buddy, Jim VanAntwerp, who is a true yachtsman, for helping me get the boat stuff right. Any errors made are mine and not Jim's.